Desert Deception

By Sandi Dollar

PublishAmerica
Baltimore

© 2006 by Sandi Dollar.
All rights reserved. No part of this book may be reproduced, stored in a retrieval system or transmitted in any form or by any means without the prior written permission of the publishers, except by a reviewer who may quote brief passages in a review to be printed in a newspaper, magazine or journal.

First printing

At the specific preference of the author, PublishAmerica allowed this work to remain exactly as the author intended, verbatim, without editorial input.

All characters in this work are fictitious. Any resemblance to real persons, living or dead, is purely coincidental.

ISBN: 1-4241-2568-5
PUBLISHED BY PUBLISHAMERICA, LLLP
www.publishamerica.com
Baltimore

Printed in the United States of America

This book is dedicated to my family, including my dad and Jason who passed before its completion. It is to show my daughter Caitlin that dreams are possible with hard work and the help of others.

I would like to thank my husband Jim for always encouraging me to grow and helping me when I need it. My daughter for putting up with the long hours and giving me the space I needed and keeping me positive. My Mom and brothers and sister for never telling why this couldn't happen. My friends Jan and Hilary for being test readers along the way and numerous customers and friends for their encouragement. Thank you all.

CHAPTER 1

Donald Murphy turned his car left onto Route 318 almost without thinking. The drone of the warm tires on the pavement was hypnotizing. Although it was only the beginning of June it was a particularly hot and dry day, even for this never-ending Nevada desert. Today the boredom of this ex Green Beret's airplane parts sales route was really taking a heavy toll.

Who on earth chose to live out in the middle of nowhere? That's where most of Donald's accounts were. Smack dab in the middle of nowhere.

Sweat ran down his temples tracing the square of his jawbone onto his shirt. Weaving it's way through the rough lines on a face created from years in the desert sun and a fast and hard lifestyle.

He mumbled to himself, "Another scorcher ladies and gentlemen, and here I am all alone, in the middle of nowhere, calling on customers no one else would bother to see in person. The least they could do is give me a damn car with air conditioning that works half the time. Where the hell did I go wrong!"

He cranked up the radio and started singing along to the Commodore's hit, "She's a brick house. She's mighty mighty just lettin' it all hang out." His hands were pounding out the beat on the steering wheel as he drove down the highway. He began bobbing his head and swaying his shoulders from side to side.

He reflected on his forty-five years again. Lately this was becoming a major pastime for Donald. Advertising for the new Robin Williams movie "Good Morning Viet Nam" had stirred up old memories for "Donnyboy" as he was known back then.

This was the late eighties and everyone in Donald's generation was supposed to be living the highlife by now. Big house, wife, kids, two cars and a golf club membership.

Donald had tried the nine-to-five office life when he first got out of the Army. He actually had some great offers, mostly from fellow Nam vets. He tried, but being tied down to one place and stuck in a building all day just wasn't for him.

He was sick and tired of the roaming he had done since he returned from Vietnam. He knew he wasn't in bad shape for his age. Sure his brown hair had thinned a little since his younger days, his face showed a little more character and these days he sure paid the next morning for kicking up his heels. But, when he tried he could still impress the ladies. That is, when his lifestyle allowed for them. He did miss the passion you feel in a regular relationship. One night stands left a lot to be desired.

Just a few more miles of sweltering discomfort and he would be cool again sitting inside Wanda's diner. An "oasis" if ever one existed.

Wanda's is one of those great little places you pride yourself on finding. It was a friendly stop that offered surprisingly good food. You might even go so far as to say great food. The way most people only wished their Momma had cooked. Once you were there it was hard to leave.

Seeing the small road sign alerting weary travelers that the next exit offered "EATS," Donald found himself driving faster. He got out this way only about six times a year, but Wanda's always felt like a trip home for the holidays.

Wanda's is the kind of place where anyone can feel welcome. There are six booths with dark green, extra padded leatherette seats,

DESERT DECEPTION

and a counter with ten extra padded leatherette stools. Donald was sure that before the interstate had been completed it was filled regularly with high rollers and truckers alike. Only travelers trying to save a few miles on their drive, or the locals even knew Wanda's existed these days.

Two old fashioned gas stoves still sit off to one side of the kitchen. It's a place that has seen the fifties come and go, yet time has left it unchanged. The smell of fresh brewed coffee and home baked goodies always took Donald's mind back to happier times.

To Donald Wanda was a second mother. He had never told her so, but he had adopted her. His own parents had parished in a traffic accident years back. They had been killed instantly. He was now on his own in the family department, no one to tie you down or pick you up for that matter.

After the accident Donnyboy or DB as he was known back then began living out of a liquor bottle. It cost him Katie O'Maley, the woman he was going to marry. She tried her best to stand by Donald. The two had met through Donald's father. After a year of waiting for him to sober up she finally had to leave the relationship. Just one year later she was married to someone else.

Once Donald finally realized this wasn't the way to honor his folks he straightened himself out. From that point on he used the name his parents had given him, Donald Murphy. The name his father had used his whole life.

Donald had been back from Vietnam a little over two years when the tragedy struck. His parents had just moved back to St. Louis, Missouri from a suburb of Los Angeles.

How ironic Donald thought, then and now, that he had spent two whole years in a hell hole dodging enemy fire and three years after that jumping from one disaster to another, and he was still alive. His parents decide to go grocery shopping one day and it's all over in a matter of seconds.

Life could be anything but fair sometimes. Donald would deeply miss them the rest of his life. Wanda made Donald feel like he still had family here with him.

Wanda could have been anyone's Mother or Grandma. In her sixties, she stood about 5'3" tall, pudgy round the middle, with wisps of grey at her temples made more noticeable against her tan skin and reddish brown hair. She still had a hint of the natural rose color in her cheeks. Her green eyes seemed to smile at you.

She always wore the same blue, small print, full apron that concealed any real shape her body may have. She had lived her whole life out here in the desert and took pride in remembering everyone who ate in her diner. A warm welcome would always await you here.

Donald turned into the little gravel parking lot and felt some of his sour mood already leaving. He was glad to see a few cars in the lot. Wanda probably needed all the business she could get since almost everyone now used the interstate. He couldn't imagine Wanda was getting rich off the diner.

The antique store next to her place was open only on weekends now. It was more of a hobby than a business for the Browns the elderly couple who owned the shop.

A smile snuck across his face and he started to walk faster as he approached the door. The little bell on the front door announced his entrance, and the gust of cold air quickly cooled his damp face and neck.

There were maybe five or six customers when Donald walked in. Wanda, as usual, was behind the counter refilling coffee and telling stories about her life out here. She looked over and gave one of her heart-warming smiles to him. Donald waved at her and took a seat at the counter. Once there he was quickly introduced to the young couple Wanda was waiting on.

"Bud, Mary Jo Miller, this is Donald Murphy. I've been feeding Donald about five years now and he's still coming back for more. Bud and Mary Jo here, are on their honeymoon. It's their first long trip away from home."

The young couple turned to Donald and smiled. The young man rose from his seat and offered Donald his hand.

Bud stood about 5'11" with a stocky build, and light brown, almost blonde hair. His arms were muscular and tanned. He had one of those boyish "get away with murder kind of faces."

"It's a pleasure to meet you. If you'd care to join us we'd be honored." Bud motioned to the seat next to his wife. He shook Donald's hand with a sincerity and firmness seldom given anymore.

Mary Jo was slim with a country fresh look to her. Her brown hair fell just below her shoulders, the front was drawn up in a barrette that matched her blue eyes. Her whole face lit up each time she glanced in Bud's direction.

Donald moved down two seats and joined them. It would be nice to have some company. So much of his time was spent alone on the road, he welcomed the opportunity to visit.

Wanda walked around the counter, gave Donald a hug and asked him how business was. After a brief exchange she went to check on her other customers.

Bud and Mary Jo were on their way to Las Vegas, as Wanda had mentioned,.They had never been far from Indian Wells before, a small town just inside of the Idaho border. The excitement of being on this trip showed in both their faces.

"I bet you've been to Las Vegas a lot of times Donald," Bud was asking. "Got any advise for first timers?" Bud smiled and leaned forward eager for Donald's answer.

Donald's first thought was to say, "Yeah don't go." But seeing their joy and remembering his first trip he stopped himself.

He looked into their wide eyed faces and answered, "You two are going to be amazed at all the lights and glamorous casinos. People don't call it "La La" land for nothing. You have to be careful and not get too carried away with all that. Las Vegas has it's darker side too. Keep your valuables with you and when you see you're starting to lose move on to the next place."

Donald smiled at that advise. If he only followed it himself. "It's real easy to lose everything if your not careful. It's just too easy to get wrapped up in the whole excitement of the place. Keep your eyes and ears open when you walk around."

Mary Jo looked a little surprised and asked, "Should we trust the people who work there?"

Donald didn't want to ruin the excitement of their trip. "I didn't mean to scare you. Sure you can trust most of them. Just use some good common sense is all I mean. Anywhere there's a lot of money involved you also have a lot of jerks. You'll have a great time and who knows, you might leave rich." They all smiled at that!

Bud's face lost the worried look of a moment ago and again showed a wide eyed innocence. "This is going to be our only big trip for awhile and everything about it is special. It would take an awful lot to ruin it for us. We're going to be too busy for any more vacations when we get home." He turned toward Mary Jo and added, "At least for awhile."

Mary Jo leaned over and kissed him on the cheek. "When we get back to Indian Wells, Bud's going to open his own repair shop. That means no trips for at least a couple of years." She was obviously proud of Bud.

Bud blushed a little, "I've been working on anything with a motor in it since I can remember. I spent the last three years working at Mr. Thompson's garage, about thirty miles away, and now I'm ready to open my own garage and be a lot closer to home. What business are you in Donald?"

Donald felt his own face redden a little. "I'm a salesman and delivery boy for an aviation parts company. We specialize in parts for smaller aircraft. I travel out here to help some of the desert cattle ranchers and smaller airstrip owners. Some of these pilots are a hundred miles from nowhere when it comes to getting anything for their planes. I service most of independent aviation operations in Nevada, Utah and parts of California.."

"How exciting! How did you ever get into that business?" Mary Jo was asking. "Do you fly planes too Donald?" Her eyes were as big as saucers. Both she and Bud were eagerly waiting to hear more.

"Yeah, Mary Jo, I'm a pilot also, mostly small planes. I flew a few "Hueys," the helicopters used during the war. I guess I've just always loved planes and flying as much as Bud here loves cars. How I came to this job, I keep asking myself. I guess I was just restless after Nam. I kept drifting from one place to another. I guess I figured I might as well get paid for roaming."

Donald paused a minute to look into their faces. An old habit now whenever he had mentioned the war. When he saw there was no animosity he continued, "I ran into an old war buddy one day who said he knew about a job I might like. Well he was half right I guess. I've been doing this for over five years now. The boredom is starting to get me down some. Being on the road can get pretty lonely. Every time I think I'll quit, I find myself behind the wheel again starting off on another call."

Wanda walked over, her arms loaded with their food, and apologized for the delay. She had given the girl who helps her on the weekends and holidays the month off. It was just like her to take on all the work herself so her helper could take care of other business.

Donald didn't even have to order. Somehow Wanda could read his mind. He was convinced of that. In front of him sat fresh slow baked ham, whipped yams with just a hint of pineapple in them and coleslaw. This and the barbecued chicken special were his favorites.

Wanda hurried off to the register to help the two young men who had been sitting at the other end of the counter. They had been so quiet down there that Donald had barely noticed them. They paid, slapped a dollar down for Wanda and they were gone.

As Wanda passed back by she said, "Awful quiet down here. I hope that means the foods o.k."

Bud was licking his fingers as he spoke. "Oh yes Ma'am, this is some of the best barbeque chicken I've ever had, and I've had a lot of chicken."

Mary Jo agreed and asked if there was a secret ingredient in Wanda's sauce.

"Ain't any secrets around here. I'd be happy to write down the recipe for you Mary Jo."

Wanda loved to have people ask for her recipes. Since she had never married or had any children, Donald thought it probably filled a need in her to have family things carried on.

"I'd love it Ma'am. I need to start collecting some of my own recipes now that were married. I could surprise everyone back home with this. Yes Ma'am, thank you, I would love to have it." Mary Jo was pleased. They finished the rest of their meals in silence. Savoring every bite.

When they were all finished they leaned back in their seats very satisfied. The three of them began visiting again like old friends.

Donald looked up and noticed the time. He had been at Wanda's for almost two hours now. He barely had enough time to make it to his next stop before they would close for the day. He didn't want to have to sleep in his car tonight. Tomorrow was Sunday and he hated showing up on the only day off some of these people had. Most of them were unreachable.

"I hate to leave you, but if I don't get going I could lose a whole day waiting for the repair shop to open on Monday. I've really enjoyed meeting you two. If I'm ever up your way I'll stop by your garage to say hello." He got to his feet laid a few dollars down for Wanda and headed for the register.

Bud and Mary Jo needed to be going too. They were right behind him. They all paid their bills and said goodbye to Wanda. Donald gave her a big hug and promised to stop back by before he headed out again.

She thanked them and handed Mary Jo a copy of her chicken recipe. Wanda wished them good luck in all that they do. She hoped Bud and Mary Jo would have time on their way back home to swing by again.

After the three of them had walked to the parking lot, Bud asked Donald if he still had a minute to check out his pride and joy.

"Sure I've got a few minutes to spare yet." As Donald turned to answer, he caught a glimpse of the most beautiful 1957 Chevy he had ever seen. They all walked over to the Chevy.

"Been working on her, little here little there, for years." Bud said, looking like the proud father of a newborn baby. He had every right to be proud.

"I was given Her in trade, for some repair work I'd done. Of course she didn't look like she does now, but the body was clean and the interior was still in pretty good shape. She'd just been sitting, rotting in a barn for years. The lady who had owned it had been dead a few years and no one had even tried to start the car. When her property had been sold the Chevy came with it. The new owners didn't have any use for it. I think I got the better end of the trade." Bud smiled.

Donald stood speechless for a minute. Here sat a car that looked "better" than off the showroom floor. The chrome sparkled and made a wonderful contrast to the most beautiful paint job Donald had ever seen. It was a creamy mint green that you wanted to touch to see if it was real. The car had whitewall tires and a flawless cream interior. Even the chrome tail pipe was spotless.

"How did I miss this beauty on the way in? Bud this is the most beautiful car I've ever laid eyes on. Did you do all this yourself?" Donald was staring in absolute awe.

Bud put his head down and shifted his feet. He was obviously proud and embarrassed.

When he looked up to answer his face was still beaming, "Yep! I rebuilt every inch. The motor and transmission are like brand new. I even mixed the color of paint myself."

After looking it over for what seemed like an hour, Donald noticed ten more minutes had passed. He had to get back on the road. Good-byes were said again.

Donald walks over to his company car, a six cylinder, dirty white Ford Fairmont. He slid sadly behind the wheel and drove away.

Watching them from his rear view mirror, Donald felt a touch of jealousy. For such a young couple they had it all. Someone to love them. Some goals for their future. They would make it, he was sure of that.

Turning onto the roadway Donald thought back to his own youth. He had been much like Bud himself, medium in frame, with arms that showed he worked out or had played in high school sports. In Bud's case, working on cars had probably built up his arms. Donald too had ideas of opening a place of his own back then.

Along came the war and like for many guys, Donald's life was changed forever. He felt it was his duty to serve his country. Hell, he still did. Donald was in college while most of his high school buddies were drafted. As soon as he graduated he volunteered to go to Viet Nam, thinking he was doing the right thing for his country.

He belonged to a group of men sent into some of the most dangerous missions. He had made it into the Green Berets. With only a little time in between he volunteered to pull three tours. He only could serve two in Nam with his unit as most men only spent one tour of duty there. His own high school sweetheart got tired of waiting for him to settle down and married someone else.

Driving down the road he started wondering again how really different things could have been. What if he would have settled down and raised a family? Just the thought made him laugh aloud. Who would have put up with him long enough to raise a family?

He turned on the radio and settled back in his seat for the forty or so miles he had left to go.

Donald couldn't get Bud and Mary Jo out of his mind. They were so much in love and so happy with their life. Was it too late for him to ever feel that way again? Had he seen too much bad in his life? God, he hoped not. There had to be more life had to offer him than this. He couldn't be washed up at age forty three. What would the rest of his years have to offer if this was it?

Just a few more miles and he would be at his last stop for the day. This had been a long day and it soon would be over.

As Donald pulled into the dirt lot, he noticed only Mr. Hall's old delivery truck parked out front. He hoped Mr. Hall had left his other car home today. Donald got out of his car and walked slowly to the front door. He tried turning the doorknob. No such luck! The sign on the door said be back at 8:00 a.m. He looked down at his watch, 5:15 pm, fifteen stinking minutes.

Donald would be spending another uncomfortable night on the road. He could drive back to Wanda's, but this day had been long enough and he'd rather stay put for the night.

At least it had cooled down some. There was nothing to do but try to get as comfortable as he could for the night.

He moved the car to the side of the shop to be out of the early morning sun, and settled in for the night. He opened an old issue of Sports Illustrated he found in the back seat, fluffed up his jacket for a pillow and began reading in the dim sunlight that was left. He was asleep within the hour; long before the sun gave way to the moon. His dreams were of football, Katie and that Chevy.

CHAPTER 2

    Bud and Mary Jo were cruising south along Route 318 again. They were thinking about Donald and Wanda. They both had been so kind to them. It felt like they had all been friends for a long time.
    Back home you didn't meet that many strangers. If you did run into some, they were always on their way to someplace else and didn't have the time or take the time to visit.
    Mary Jo broke the silence; "Do you think Donald will find someone to settle down with? He's so nice and seems lonely for someone to share his life with. I wish he were going to Las Vegas with us. He seemed to know the ropes there. We would have had a great time together."
    "I do too, Mary Jo. I feel like he's a good friend even though we just met. Maybe some day he'll be going through Indian Wells and stop in at the garage. He said he goes all over the western half of the states. He sure has done a lot of different things in his life." Bud paused, then added, "Why don't you try to get some sleep. Once we hit Route 93 we'll still have about a 100 miles to go."
    Mary Jo leaned back and closed her eyes. After the long days drive

it felt good to rest. Her soft brown hair blew softly across her slender shoulders. How sweet she looked in the late afternoon sun.

Bud turned the radio on low. He was a lucky man to have Mary Jo, but couldn't help thinking how exciting Donald's life had been compared to his own. He envied all the places he had seen and the things he had done. Bud had never experienced being as carefree as Donald's life seemed.

They were a few miles from the Route 93 interchange, when up ahead Bud noticed a car pulled over on the side of the road. As he got closer he saw that the hood was raised. Beside it stood a young couple with a small baby.

Bud slowed down to stop and see if he could help. He always carried tools with him for any minor repairs. He had sent more than one driver happily back on their way.

Mary Jo woke the minute the car had stopped. She thought they were in Las Vegas at first. It took a few seconds to realize she had barely fallen asleep. "Bud why are we stopped here?"

"There's a car broken down behind us. I thought I might be able to help. I'll get my toolbox."

He was out of the car before she could turn around and see the red Volkswagen just behind them.

Seeing the young blonde woman leaning against the side of the car, holding a baby, Mary Jo jumped out of the Chevy and started heading for the Volkswagen.

Bud was already talking with the young man by the time she got there. The two of them were busy leaning over the Volkswagen's engine.

Mary Jo walked over to the woman and introduced herself. "Hi, I'm Mary Jo and that's Bud. What a horrible thing to be broken down out here with such a young baby."

The woman said her name was Cindy. The baby was John. They had been broken down about thirty minutes and had almost given up hope of someone stopping to help. She asked where they were headed and if Mary Jo had any kids of her own.

Cindy was tall with slender legs. She was wearing a pair of tight fitting jeans and a man's shirt tied at the waist. Her hair was cut short and her face looked hardened. Not a mean type of hardened thought Mary Jo. Cindy just looked like her life had been tougher than most.

She was still a very attractive girl. The baby was as cute as he could be.

Mary Jo suggested they go sit in the shade of a huge billboard promoting Senator Hudson's new Crime Task Force bill he was trying to get passed. The nut case came from Mary Jo and Bud's home state. The way he tried to handle some state problems the two of them thought he'd spent a little too much time with his skinhead neighbors.

The two girls and the baby had just sat down on the side of the road when Bud found the problem. He asked John if he carried any extra belts for the car.

The fan belt had broken in a clean snap. They weren't going anywhere in this car.

John's shoulders slumped, as he answered, "no." He would have to come back later to take care of the car. All he wanted was to get his family home. They both walked over to where the girls were sitting.

John Sr. offered to pay them to drive his family home. He said they lived just fifteen miles or so up ahead, just a few miles off Route 93.

"Don't be ridiculous; we have plenty of room and it won't be any problem." Bud began helping John transfer a few bags to the Chevy. The girls followed with the baby.

The five of them had only gone a few miles when Bud noticed a gas station up ahead. "Maybe they'd have a fan belt to fit your car. I'd be happy to put it on for you and save you a trip out here later."

"I appreciate your offering, but I'd just as soon get Cindy's car from home and come back, once the baby and her are comfortable at home again."

From the gas station pay phone, one of the men from the diner had been watching with binoculars. He made a phone call as the Chevy drove by. "They're on their way; should be there in about fifteen minutes."

"Great! We're all set here," came across the receiver.

As they drove, Cindy asked all about Bud and Mary Jo. Their honeymoon plans, life back home, everything. She said she didn't get much chance to visit with people out here.

Mary Jo was more than happy to answer all her questions. She was so proud of their plans for the future, she found herself almost bragging. She stopped herself and asked Cindy about her and John's honeymoon.

They too had gone to Las Vegas. Cindy's face became sad. They hadn't brought enough money with them and had to cut their stay short. They wished they had brought more, because it had been so much fun. Since they had moved to the desert this year, they still hadn't gone back. It would be hard with little John so young.

Mary Jo told her they weren't afraid of that happening to them. They had brought along what they thought was enough for three vacations. Besides, neither one of them were really gamblers.

"Just up ahead you'll see a turn off to the right," John said, pointing from the back seat. "It's going to be a little bumpy the next few miles."

A little bumpy was an understatement! About a mile into the road the pavement stopped and a rutted dirt road began.

Bud slowed to almost a crawl. He was sorry he hadn't tried harder to convince John to fix the car today. He hated doing this to the Chevy. He found himself resenting them both for their breakdown. He must be overtired and hot. This wasn't like him.

Up ahead he spotted a small square wooden house, and prayed it was theirs.

With all the dust flying around and bouncing going on it was no wonder, the baby was crying now. Cindy was rocking him and said she was sorry; it was way past his naptime.

"It's just ahead," John said. "We can't tell you how much this means to us. You two will have to come in for a cold drink and a chance to cool off. We might be in the boonies, but we do have a swamp cooler and cold running water. You can use the phone to let your hotel know you'll be a little late in checking in."

Bud noticed a car and a van out front when they pulled up. "You live here with somebody else?"

"Oh no. That was my parent's van. We just haven't done anything with it yet." John knew exactly why Bud had asked.

All Bud wanted to do was get out of here and back on their way. A cold drink did sound good though. He and Mary Jo would come in for just a minute. They didn't want to seem rude but they were already running late.

Mary Jo asked if there was a bathroom that she could use. The bumpy ride hadn't helped any.

DESERT DECEPTION

When they stopped and got out, Bud looked at the Chevy. Her beautiful minty green paint looked more like a mucky swamp with all the dust on it. Mary Jo saw his face and took his arm. "It'll be o.k. A little water and she'll look like new. Let's get out of all this dust."

They went inside. Cindy laid the baby on the sofa and headed for the kitchen. The two men took a seat at the table across from one another.

Mary Jo asked where she would find the restroom and was happy to find an indoor bathroom. this far out in the desert. Bud went with John into the kitchen and called the hotel to say they'd be arriving late.

Cindy had poured a large glass of ice water for all of them. She sat down next to John.

When she came back in the room, Mary Jo took the seat next to Bud, across the table from where Cindy and John were sitting. The baby was already asleep on the couch. A cold glass of ice water looked so inviting in front of her.

From where they sitting, Bud and Mary Jo never saw the two men who came up behind them. Bud kicked his legs up fighting back and managed to knock over all the waters on the table. Within seconds they were both out cold. The chloroform had taken effect fast.

John told the other men they should be loaded with money and the car had to be worth something. He felt a little uneasiness looking at Bud and Mary Jo slumped in their chairs. He hoped they hadn't given them too much and killed them.

The others were standing over them like vultures, including Cindy who immediately began emptying out their pockets. All that Mary Jo's pockets had to offer was a dumb old chicken recipe. They only found $300.00 in cash on Bud.

"Take these keys and bring in their luggage," the man in charge was shouting. He threw the keys at Lou, one of the men with the chloroform rags. Joe had been sitting back watching everything with a smile on his face. "They probably hid the rest of their money there." He now was standing over Bud and Mary Jo's chairs. He remained inside to blindfold them and tie their hands behind their backs.

The other man from the diner had just pulled up and was running toward the Chevy when he yelled, "Well what's it look like we'll get from those two?"

The three of them couldn't have been older than their twenties. They all had the look of lifetime losers, or maybe, your basic idea of a thug was a better description. The two from the diner looked like they could be related, even though one was a dirty blonde and the other brunette. In fact they were John's older brothers, Lou and Rick.

John had always looked up to Lou and Rick and couldn't believe it when they asked for his help on this one. He and Cindy had fallen on some hard times and needed the money.

The third man was in charge. None of them knew his real name. Everyone just called him Joe. He was a couple years older than the others were. He was rougher looking than the rest and bore a nasty scar on the left side of his face, close to his ear.

Once, Lou and Rick had asked about it and were told to mind their own business. They never asked again. Joe wasn't the type of person you wanted to get mad.

John, Lou and Rick returned with the luggage and started tearing it apart. They were throwing things everywhere around the room.

It wasn't long before they found another $200.00 in the bottom of Mary Jo's overnight bag.

The man called Joe, walked back over to Bud and Mary Jo and looked them over. "These two might bring us even more if we keep them alive. Did they have anyone waiting for them in Las Vegas?" He was holding Mary Jo's face in his hands as he asked.

John told him no and reminded Joe even the hotel knew they were running late. No one had told John they might be killed, and he wanted nothing to do with that. Hard times or not he and his family were not going into the murder business.

"Perfect!" Joe said, "I'll call the "MAN" right now. Too bad we can't stay on this route. This one was real easy." He left the room to make the call.

Joe, Lou and Rick traveled the back routes into all the major gambling towns. They knew most of the travelers were carrying a lot of cash with them. How people loved to talk about how they were going to hit it big. They didn't ever have to look hard for their next targets. They would find their victims on the road in restaurants, gas stations, and convenience stores. Most of the time they found them by staying in one of the out of the way motels. Some gamblers loved a "friendly" little game of poker along the way.

It hadn't made them rich, but every so often, they scored big. They would leave the cars stripped out in the desert. Joe would take the victims away in his van and return to an agreed upon place later. Lou and Rick thought he did this so they wouldn't be able to tell the cops where the bodies could be found if they got caught. It would just be Joe's word against theirs.

The three brothers had gone outside to look over the Chevy. Even covered in dust she was a beauty. Cindy had stayed inside to keep an eye on Bud and Mary Jo.

Mary Jo started to come around and was pretty groggy. At first she thought she couldn't see anything because of the dizziness she was feeling. When she tried to move her hands, and couldn't, she realized she was also blindfolded. She started screaming for Bud. Her hands tugging at the ropes that bound them.

Mary Jo's screaming brought Bud around slowly. Something was very wrong! He couldn't see, or move. He felt like his body weighed a ton. His head was pounding; and his heart was racing.

"Mary Jo! Mary Jo! Are you all right? I can hear you but I'm blindfolded and my hands are tied." The ropes were cutting into his wrists as he struggled to free his hands.

"Oh Bud I'm so scared! What's going on here? I've been blindfolded and my hands are tied too." She was sobbing as she spoke.

Bud tried to talk to her calmly, "Mary Jo I'm right here next to you. My hands are tied tight but I'm right here."

He started yelling for someone to explain what was happening. What did they plan on doing to them? He could hear someone chuckling in the room with them.

The yelling brought John back in the room just as Cindy was answering Bud. "What's happening here, is you two goody goodies are being robbed. If you play your cards right and don't try anything stupid you won't get hurt. Oh, by the way, thanks for the ride home." With that she laughed aloud.

John didn't like what he was seeing. Cindy was enjoying this whole thing too much. John was worried about her lately. The more his brothers were around, the more cold-hearted she became.

Mary Jo asked Cindy, "How could you do this to us after all the help we've been? How could you involve an innocent baby in something like this?"

Just then, Joe, Lou and Rick entered the room. Cindy had gotten to her feet and was walking over to Mary Jo.

Joe spoke before Cindy could answer; "You two are in luck. You're about to go on a little trip. Yeah, the "MAN" was real interested in you two!"

He told them to relax and no one would be hurt. There would just be a slight change in any plans they had made. With that he let out the most sinister laugh as he walked outside.

"Let's get those bags back in the trunk." He was speaking to Lou and Rick now. "We'll split up the take and you two take care of their car. You ought to get a good price for those parts. Help me get these two in the van, I want to get out of here quickly." Joe knew the owners of this house were away, but he didn't know for how long. They didn't need any problems popping up for them. Make sure you wipe down everything and leave this place just like we found it. Everyone jumped into action.

Lou took hold of Mary Jo's arm and told her to get moving. She jumped at his touching her. It sent chills down her spine and made her sick in her stomach. Bud was told not to try anything on the way to the van. If he did, his wife's life was at stake.

Bud thought he recognized one of the men's voices. It wasn't John's voice but he knew he had heard it somewhere. Was it from Wanda's diner earlier? He just wasn't sure and needed him to talk more. Bud asked, "You're not going to take our car too are you?"

Lou answered, "You're darn right we're taking your car! It's worth a lot of money to us."

With that Bud was sure it was the same man from the diner. Everything started to make sense now. They'd been set up hours ago. The two men, sitting at the other end of the counter must have been listening to their conversation with Donald and Wanda.

Rick had taken Bud out to the van now. They were put in the back of what Bud felt was a cargo van. Bare metal floors and a tinny sound when the door was closed. He heard the click of a door being locked.

"Mary Jo I think were alone in the van now. Are you alright?" He was trying to talk lower now.

She was still sobbing and could barely speak. "Oh Bud, its all my fault, all of this. If I hadn't told them about all the money we had none of this would be happening. I'm so sorry."

Bud was talking loud now, "No, listen to me, it's not your fault. I recognize one of the other guy's voices from the diner this afternoon. It was one of the guys sitting at the counter. They must have planned this whole thing from there. They knew we'd stop for a family with a broken down car. They learned a lot of things from listening to our conversation with Donald. Boy, he was right, where money's concerned you can't trust some people."

"Bud, do you think they found the money we hid in the Chevy?" Her voice was low and calmer now.

"We have to watch everything we say from now on Mary Jo. I don't think they found it. We have to have a sign between us, a signal. If the opportunity comes up that we can escape, we both will have to be ready. I know. How about a sneeze?"

"A sneeze it is then! Bud I'm so scared. At least we're together. I couldn't stand it if we were apart. What do you think they're going to do to us? I'll try to be stronger." She added softly, "Bud, I love you."

Bud's mind was racing. "I don't know Mary Jo. Just try to keep your ears open for a chance at escaping. I love you so much!"

Back inside everyone was cleaning up. The owners of the house were away on a trip and Rick had stumbled across it a week ago. They couldn't have planned this one better.

The baby woke up from his nap wet and crying. John noticed this was annoying the others. He told Cindy to take the baby and their things to their car. Everyone was tense enough without hearing a baby cry.

Cindy picked up little John and headed for the door where she paused. "Make sure we get our full share. After all, we got the suckers to come here."

"I will! I will! Just take him to the car so we can think in here." As rotten as John had been in all of this, he still cared about his family. He didn't trust the others not to hurt little John if he got on their nerves too much.

Joe told the others he had to get going. He had to call the "MAN" back from a pay phone and work out the details of where to deliver these two and pick up the money.

"You two boys get that car out of here. Get the tires and rims and whatever else you can sell off of it before you dump it in the desert. Don't forget to wipe down any place you touch, but leave some of their prints for the cops to find. We want it to look like they got lost out here and someone just stripped their car. I'll meet you back at the motel we stayed at a few nights ago. I should be there in 4 or 5 days."

Rick said not to worry, they'd be waiting. Joe turned and left for the van.

Rick and Lou started arguing over who would get to drive the Chevy and who would drive the Volkswagen back. They decided to flip a coin. Lou called heads and won.

John asked if they needed him anymore. He wanted to get his family back home. They told him no and Lou handed him an envelope with his share in it. "Go ahead little brother. Hope this helps with those bills. You did alright on this one. Thanks for your help."

John grabbed the envelope and headed for the door. He had looked up to his older brothers all his life. He was proud when they had asked his help. After being in on this job with them and seeing that Joe guy, he wasn't sure what he thought. He felt sorry for Rick and Lou for the first time in his life.

John thought about how much Cindy had enjoyed the whole thing and just wanted out of here.

When he got to their car that had been hidden out of sight, he handed Cindy the envelope with the money. She looked inside and smiled. "That was too easy. I think we did great!" cindy was beaming as she spoke. Within a few minutes they were gone.

Bud heard the car pull away and got a shiver wondering what was in store for them. He had tried to free his hands, but it was no use.

When the van door had opened and someone got in, Bud had asked who was there and was told to keep still. It was the voice of the man in charge.

As the van rolled down the bumpy dirt road, Bud couldn't help but think about the Chevy. He felt a tear run down his cheek. His heart sunk as if he was saying goodbye to a lifelong friend. Bud felt he had let both his girls down and he wanted to get even. He settled back to dream of his revenge.

Rick and Lou made one last sweep of the house. There wasn't a sign that anyone had been there. Lou got into the Chevy and started down the dirt road slowly.

He couldn't wait to reach the pavement. He had wanted to drive this baby since he first laid eyes on her in Wanda's parking lot. God he felt powerful behind the wheel.

DESERT DECEPTION

Lou stopped for a minute once he hit the pavement and stepped on the gas, she purred like a kitten. When he gave her a little more gas she roared down the street. The two brothers had grins from ear to ear riding in this car.

Rick and Lou both were thinking this car was worth too much to just strip her and leave her in the desert to rot.

Rick was the first to speak, "I know we're supposed to make it look like those kids got lost out here, but we could drive this over to Bernie's Car Lot and get a lot of dough for it. Besides Lou, this car is just too primo to tear her up in pieces. What do you say Lou?"

Lou agreed. "I wish we could keep her ourselves, but I know that's too dumb. We can't ever let Joe find out what we did, if we sell her like she is. Sometimes he even gives me the creeps. He can never know, Rick. Never!"

The sun was setting as they reached the Volkswagen on the side of the highway. Lou walked over to the Volkswagen and opened the passenger door. Under the front seat he found the fan belt he had hidden earlier. It only took Lou a few minutes to replace the damaged part. Rick hopped in and started it up. They both headed back to the motel room they had rented last night.

The van was traveling fast along Route 93. It was so much nicer to not be bouncing around on that rough gutted road.

Bud was trying to figure out how many miles they had gone and in what direction? He heard Mary Jo let out a little sigh and knew she had been sobbing again. He slowly slid over until he was touching her side. "It's me," he whispered, "I'm right here." He felt her relax a little.

The van began to slow down. They felt it leave the pavement and now it had come to a complete stop.

Joe turned to them and said, "Don't get any ideas, You're still in the middle of nowhere. I'll be right back. I'll be keeping an eye on the van the whole time."

He had parked a good way from the gas station pay phone. Joe jumped out and started heading across the dirt field. No sense taking any unnecessary chances now. He told the operator he wanted to make a collect call. It was now ringing on the other end.

The familiar husky voice came on the line, "Yes operator, I'll accept the charges." They both waited and heard her go off the line. "Are you calling from a pay phone?"

Joe answered "Yes, an out-of-the-way one at that."

"Very well then ," the husky voice said. "If these two are as good as you said earlier, we will have no problem. That's one thousand dollars each and I don't want them damaged. Go to the Oasis motel out on Highway 6. My man will be in Room #111. Be sure you park away from the motel. He will look them over and give you the money. Have you got all that?"

Joe repeated, "Highway 6, Oasis motel, Room 111."

"Very good. We will do business again I'm sure. Goodbye for now." With that the phone went dead.

Joe stood still for a minute after hanging up the phone. He had never seen the "MAN." He knew there was little chance of that. His voice sounded like he was in his fifties, maybe sixties. He knew he had money and lots of it, because Joe had never had to wait to be paid. Joe wondered what he did with these people once he bought them. Joe never asked because he knew it was better that way. To each his own, he figured. He started back toward the van.

Bud had turned his back to Mary Jo hoping they would be able to work each other's hands free. The cord was just too tight. He heard someone coming and quickly turned back around. Joe jumped in and started the motor. He turned to check on them before driving away.

"You'll be happy to know I'll be leaving you soon. I'll be handing you over to someone who'll probably treat you a whole lot nicer than I would. I'd just as soon kill you as look at you. Just keep on being a good little boy and girl and that won't happen." Mary Jo answered him with a, "Yes, Sir." He let out a laugh and the van started pulling away.

If only Bud's hands were free. He'd show him who was a little boy. This guy sure is tough when he has people tied up! Bud knew he could throw a pretty good right punch when he had to. It took every ounce of control he had not to tell this guy so. Bud decided not to say anything at all. He'd wait for the right second to break free. That's when he'd show them all just who they were messing with. That thought brought a smile to his face.

They had been on the road for over an hour when the van stopped again. The vibration in the back must have put them both to sleep. Bud fought to clear his mind. He still had a slight headache from the chloroform. He didn't want to miss any opportunity for escape.

Joe had no trouble finding the Oasis motel. He checked on his cargo and headed for Room #111.

A man in his late twenties, early thirties answered the door. Joe had seen him before.

He reminded Joe of a kid from one of those private military schools. The type of kid Joe had enjoyed beating to a pulp when he was younger. His blonde hair was cut very short and shaved around the ears. His khaki pants and shirt were starched and pressed, including razor sharp creases in the front of his pants. You could see yourself in his shined black shoes. Joe didn't like this guy at all. To him this guy was nothing but a punk, plain and simple. How this guy ever got tied up with the "MAN" was beyond Joe.

Joe told him he had a delivery to check out. They both walked back to the van. Joe couldn't help noticing the guy even walked like a punk.

Joe opened the van's front passenger door. "Well what do you think? Are they what you're looking for?"

The blonde man turned toward Bud and Mary Jo. "They'll do just fine. You two will be leaving with me soon. You'll have nothing to worry about once we get out of here."

Bud asked the man where he was taking them and was told, "PARADISE, absolute PARADISE."

They heard the door close and lock again. Bud told Mary Jo not to give up. He would still get them out of this somehow.

"Follow me back to the room Joe and I'll give you your money in private. I'll need your help transferring them to my van. I'll pull up along side and we can use the side doors."

"Yeah, Yeah sure," Joe was saying. He wanted out of here fast. "Let's get going then. I have to meet up with some people and I have a long way to go." Joe had other business to finish before meeting up with Lou and Rick.

The transfer of funds and people went without a hitch. Again Mary Jo was moved first to assure Bud's co-operation.

Joe pulled away first, glad to be rid of them. He still couldn't help wondering what these people were up to though. What was this PARADISE this guy always told people they were going to? What should he care? He got his money and that's all that really mattered.

"My name is Toby," this new man was saying. "We'll be there in a little over an hour. Please sit back and relax, you don't know how lucky you two are yet."

Bud started wishing he had used the bathroom back at the house. He asked again where they were being taken and again was told to "PARADISE." This new guy was obviously not all there. Bud didn't know whether this made him feel better or worse. He slid next to Mary Jo and again settled back to wait for an opportunity for escape.

Back at their motel, Rick and Lou had been celebrating their haul. After about four beers each, they decided to clean up the Chevy. They went outside and found a hose in front of the manager's office. They hooked it up to a faucet on the side of the building.

They were running around laughing and squirting each other with the hose. Somehow they also managed to clean the Chevy in all their fun.

It had been a long time since either one of them had washed a car. There was something about this car that made you want to take care of her. They were actually enjoying themselves. When they had finished, they returned the hose and turned in for the night.

Tomorrow they would sell the Chevy and head for Los Angeles to meet up with Joe. Tonight they could party. Everything else could wait a day.

Tonight the Chevy belonged to them and they could go anywhere they wanted in her. They both fell asleep with a smile on their face.

Chapter 3

Donald awoke with one on the worst stiff necks he had ever had. He had slept for twelve hours. The sound of a car pulling in to the lot got him moving out of his car.

Mr. Hall was walking toward the door and had his back to Donald when he called out to him. "Sorry I missed you yesterday. I got hung up on the road and must have just missed you by only a few minutes."

"Donald! Good to see you. Come on in." He was holding the door open. "You didn't stay out here all night, did you? Let me start this coffee maker for us."

Donald said he had and asked for a few aspirin for his neck. He washed them down with a hot cup of coffee. He forgot how rotten aspirin tasted with coffee and wished he had asked for water.

Mr. Hall was busy unlocking doors and removing the closed sign from the window.

"Let me get a few things opened up and we'll get right down to business. I'm sure you're more than ready to get out of here. I can't believe you stayed all night just to bring me a few parts.

I appreciate it a lot, Donald. Aren't too many people would have waited around. I just happened to have a few people who needed to pick up some things this morning, otherwise you'd have had yourself a long wait. There now, all ready for business." He poured himself a cup of coffee and sat down.

Donald headed to his car and opened the trunk. He grabbed the last few remaining parts from it. Mr. Hall's whole order came to less than $60.00.

Donald carried the box in and placed it on the table.

The two of them went over the invoice together. Everything was in order and Mr. Hall wrote out a check for $58.37. The two men sat and finished their coffees.

Donald excused himself so he could wash up. It felt good to get some of the dirt off. He used the facilities and brushed his teeth. He felt human again, even his stiff neck was better. Time for him to start heading back.

The two men said their good-byes and Donald was headed out of the driveway, back toward the Route 93 turnoff. He thought about turning left and heading for Las Vegas himself. Maybe he could catch up with Bud and Mary Jo. He knew they were staying at the Stardust on the strip.

He thought better of it and turned right. What did two young people on their honeymoon need with an old fool like him tagging along? Beside that, he didn't have enough cash for a stop in Vegas. He could just see calling his boss and saying he decided to stay in Vegas awhile. Just imagining his face made Donald laugh aloud.

Lou and Rick were awake early the next morning also. Even after drinking late into the night. They were like young children who still believed in Santa Claus on Christmas morning. Both of them were out of their beds, looking out the window before they even spoke.

"Lou, you got to let me drive it before we sell it to Bernie. Please Lou. You got to." Rick was pleading.

Out in the morning sun, all clean from their night's work, the Chevy sat like a trophy from some great battle. The sun played on the creamy mint paint job and chrome. She looked powerful.

"We're both going to get to drive around in her today. If we had of stripped her, like we were supposed to, it would've taken all day. We can't show up too early in L.A. or Joe might get suspicious. We can cruise to that little bar you like so much, up the road. Your girlfriend might even be there." He gave Rick a little shove.

"Lou, stop kidding me like that. I only said I thought she was cute. 'Sides that, I think she was with somebody." Rick was blushing now.

They cleaned up, dressed, and were out the door in ten minutes. Lou handed Rick the keys and they both jumped in the Chevy. Off they went down Route 93, heading straight for the "High and Dry" bar. It was Rick's turn to feel powerful behind the wheel.

The "High and Dry" was one of those dingy little bars you think twice about entering, that is, unless your packing a weapon or doing a drug deal. The two larger front windows had been darkened so much you couldn't tell if there was life on the other side or not. That suited the clientele inside just fine. When you entered the place, you were greeted with the smell of stale air, stale booze, and cigarettes all at once. It was open from 8:00 a.m. to 2:00 a.m. daily.

When Rick and Lou walked in, there was only one other customer inside. It wasn't "Her." There was a younger man cleaning up and the bartender. They sat at the bar and ordered a couple of beers.

Donald had decided to stay on Route 93 and not turn off for Wanda's. He had already lost enough time on this trip and didn't want to lose anymore. He felt guilty about his decision. He'd make it up to her by bringing a present along next time. He'd stop later and give her a call so she wouldn't worry that something had happened to him.

He noticed his gas gauge was reading low and pulled in to a station to fill up.

"Get your windows for you fella?" the attendant was asking.

"Yeah, sure, and if you got time you might as well check the oil too. I'm sure it's at least a quart low by now. It's been awhile since I've even checked it."

Donald topped off the tank, while the attendant added two quarts of oil. He handed him his company credit card and headed for the bathroom. Might as well make sure he didn't have to stop again for awhile. He ran in and used the facilities.

Donald was walking toward the attendant when he thought he saw Bud's car in a parking lot across the street. No way, it had to be one that just resembled Bud's car. His eyes were playing tricks on him.

"That Chevy over there belong to someone in town?"

The man turned and looked in the direction Donald had pointed.

"No, I've never seen it around before. I'd remember a car like that. She's a beaut. No one round here owns a car like that. Must have just pulled in 'cause I didn't notice it there earlier. Friends of yours maybe?" He handed Donald his receipt.

"Might be. I don't think there could be two cars like that." As he got in his car, Donald was sure there wasn't another like it. After all, hadn't Bud said he mixed the paint color himself?

What were Bud and Mary Jo doing in a dive like that anyway? What happened to their plan for going to Las Vegas? He decided to find out what was going on. He left the station and drove into the "High and Dry" parking lot, deciding to go ask them what happened.

When Donald walked in, he felt every eye in the place was fixed on him. He took a seat at one of the tables and waited for his eyes to adjust to the darkness."I'll take a draft bartender,"he said as he sat down.

The bartender brought over a beer. Once he could see again he noticed Bud and Mary Jo were nowhere in the room.

As Donald looked around, he noticed the two men seated at the bar looked nervous. They asked the bartender for their tab and quickly paid it.

They were almost to the front door by the time Donald recognized them from Wanda's the day before. He slapped down a couple of dollars on the bar and decided to follow them. Just as Donald had thought the two men headed straight for the Chevy.

Donald stood in the doorway until the Chevy pulled out. He ran to his car and followed them from a safe distance. What was going on here? Where were Bud and Mary Jo? How did these two lowlifes get their car?

Donald's head was swimming. He couldn't go to the police. What would he say, "This young couple I met yesterday had a car just like that. I know those two men stole it from them, because they ate at the same diner." The police would get a big laugh out of that one! He had to get more information; he had to have proof.

These guys were definitely guilty of something. The way they left the bar, and now they were driving like they were on fire. He'd just hang back and watch where they were headed for now.

"Lou do you think that guy recognized us in there?" Rick's body was trembling as he spoke.

DESERT DECEPTION

"I don't think so, or he would have asked about the car. That was too close a call. What was he doing in there anyway? We got to dump this thing off at Bernie's right away. Don't mention any of this to Bernie or he'll try to give us peanuts for her. We got to be real cool in front of Bernie, he's no dummy."

Rick kept shifting in the seat and glancing into the side mirror. "Any sign of that guy behind us?" Rick's voice was a bit calmer now.

"No, all I see is some old family car and it's pretty far back there. Maybe the guy was just thirsty for a beer." Lou laughed, "Dumb sucker probably has no idea how much he scared us." They both were laughing now.

Lou slowed the car down a little. No sense getting pulled over for speeding if that guy wasn't even after them. They turned left onto Route 6, just a few miles more and they would be rid of her. All the joy of driving this car was definitely gone.

Donald had slowed also; he had just made the turn onto Route 6 when he caught sight of them up ahead. He worried that he'd lose them on some of these upgrades, and stepped on the gas pedal. He cussed each time he lost sight of the Chevy over the top of the hills.

He saw them pulling off to the right up ahead. His adrenaline was pumping. Donald hadn't felt this alive in a long, long time. He was nearing the place they had turned off and saw it was a used car lot. "Bernie's Reliable Used Car Lot," to be exact. He would watch and wait.

Lou and Rick didn't stop out in front. Instead they drove straight to the rear of the car lot. This obviously wasn't their first visit to Bernie's.

Seeing the Chevy pull in from his office window, Bernie was out back looking it over in a matter of seconds. "She's a beauty all right. Too much of a beauty to sell 'round here. I'll have to take it out of the area, and that means a lower price for you two. I could give you, say, $300.00 for it."

Lou and Rick looked at each other in disbelief. They turned their attention to Bernie.

"$300.00! You know it's worth ten times that!" Lou was shouting, "We won't sell it for only $300.00. What kind of assholes do you think you're dealing with?"

Bernie was looking directly into Lou's eyes as he spoke, "Sure it's worth a lot more, if you came by it legally. But without a pink slip, or bill of sell, I have to wait for just the right buyer. I'll give you $500.00 and not a penny more."

Lou kicked at the ground. "It's a raw deal, but we'll take it if you'll throw in a ride back to our motel."

"Done! I'll get the cash right now. I need to let the lot man know I'll be leaving. Go ahead and get in my car. It's the blue Camaro over there." Bernie turned and headed for the office grinning from ear to ear.

Lou and Rick took one last look at the Chevy. They both were glad to be rid of it. If that guy hadn't shown up like he did, they would've held out for more. Five Bills was better than going to jail any day. They got in the car and waited for Bernie. He was back in a minute with the cash in hand.

Donald had parked beside a small market across from the car lot. He kept tapping his fingers nervously on the dash. He wondered what was taking so long when he saw a car driving away from the rear of the lot. In the front passenger seat he saw one of the men from the bar. The other must be who was seated in back.

He didn't know whether to stay with the Chevy or the two men. He'd leave the Chevy where it was. The two men were the only link to Bud and Mary Jo. He would return for the Chevy later. His gut feeling kept telling him something was very wrong here.

The Camaro was backtracking the way they came. Donald stayed back even farther this time, not wanting to take any chances. They were headed south on Route 93 again. After about twenty minutes the Camaro pulled off into the motel parking lot.

Donald pulled off to the side of the road and just sat and waited.

This time the wait wasn't long. The Camaro dropped the two men off and pulled away. The two men went into a room at the front of the motel.

Donald didn't know whether to wait for the two men to leave or make his move now, inside the motel room. Donald decided to go into action. After a few minutes wondering what was happening. He got out of his car and crept up to the room the two men had entered. Crouching by the window he could hear them speaking inside.

"Get everything together fast Rick, I won't feel safe until we cross the L.A. county line tomorrow. This whole thing still gives me the creeps. I wish we had listened to Joe and dumped that car like he told us."

That was all Donald needed to hear. He took a chance and looked through the window. Neither man had noticed him. Donald waited until the two men were standing together with their backs to the door. He burst into the room catching them both off gaurd. A snap kick to Lou's head sent him flying to the floor. Lou had already hit the ground, by the time Rick turned around. Rick only had time to see the fist coming. He tried to duck, but it was too late. He fell to the ground with a loud thud.

Donald dragged their limp bodies over to the table, which was situated near the door to the room. He quickly removed their belts and used them to bind Rick and Lou to the chairs.

After checking to make sure they were securely bound, he headed into the bathroom. Donald filled the complimentary guest cups with water and returned to the men in the other room. He threw water on Lou's face and brought him back around. Donald's heart was pounding and his fist was throbbing.

"What the hell did you two do with Bud and Mary Jo? How did you get that Chevy?"

Donald was shaking him so hard Lou could barely talk. "We didn't do anything. We don't even know what you're talking about. Who's this Bud and Mary Jo? We don't know anything about any Chevy, dude."

Rick had come around in time to see Donald backhand Lou's face again. Lou's head went limp. Donald turned his attention to Rick.

Rick's face showed absolute fear as he spoke. "Don't hurt us buddy. We'll tell you what you want to know. Just don't hurt us no more." Looking over at his brother, Rick began to sob.

"That's a little more like it. What happened to the kids in the Chevy? What have you two done with them?" Donald was staring directly into Rick's eyes.

"They're with the MAN. We didn't lay a hand on 'em mister. I swear we didn't hurt 'em. All we did was take their car and their money. Joe took 'em, to sell 'em to the MAN. They were fine when he left." Rick would not look at Donald's face.

"Who's this MAN you keep talking about, and where can I find Joe?"

Lou came around just in time to hear Donald's last question. "What did you go and do, Rick? This guy had nothin on us. Joe will kill us for sure now!"

Rick didn't care about Joe right now. This guy was the immediate threat to him. Looking at Lou's bleeding face, he answered Donald. "We ain't never seen the MAN, we only heard about him from Joe. He buys some of the people we hold up sometimes. Joe says he's a rich nut case. Thinks he was raised in some cult or something. I don't even think Joe's ever met the guy face-to-face. He said once, he thought the guy just kept 'em around for fun. He was supposed to call the guy from a pay phone and make the trade somewhere not too far away."

"What's this Joe guys last name and where can I find him?"

Lou sat up straight and answered this time. "We don't know Joe's last name. Hell, we don't even know his real first name. We just called him Joe. We don't know where to find him. He just calls us from time to time with a job. No telling when he'll be calling again."

Regardless of how Rick felt, Lou still feared Joe a lot more than this guy asking questions. No way was he telling him where they were supposed to meet up with Joe. The thought of crossing Joe scared the crap out of Lou.

Donald looked over at Rick, who just sat there silently. "You two better be telling the truth. If you think this Joe guy can play rough, you have no idea how rough I can play." He grabbed them both by their shirt collars and added, "So far I've been real nice to you two. You don't want to see me get mad, do you?" Rick and Lou both shook their heads no.

Donald went to the phone and called the police. He hung up and sat on the bed to think. Donald's hands were bleeding and ached. He wrapped them in a wet towel and waited for the police.

The police were at the motel in ten minutes. The two brothers immediately started hollering they wanted to press assault charges against Donald. They denied knowing anything about a Chevy and didn't have a clue about any Bud or Mary Jo.

The police took all three of them down to the station while they sent a car to Bernie's to look for the Chevy. It didn't take long to locate the car, and Bernie was more than happy to co-operate to avoid any charges against him. He just thought he was buying a car from a couple of brothers down on their luck.

Donald told them everything he knew, and that they could reach him at Wanda's diner if anything new came up.

They took Lou and Rick away in handcuffs. Lou left screaming he knew his rights, they couldn't prove anything. Rick went along quietly fighting back sobs.

Donald was exhausted by the time the police had finished with him. They drove him back to his car. He started it up and headed for Wanda's. He was hungry and tired from the day's events. This whole thing was too bizarre for Donald to understand. He had no idea how to explain it to Wanda.

The police would do all they could, but so far all they had were a stolen car and two missing persons. Their hands would be tied. At least Lou and Rick were safely out of the way. God he hoped they wouldn't be out on bail in a few hours.

The only hope of finding Bud and Mary Jo alive was if the people holding them didn't think anyone was looking. Donald knew he stood a better chance of finding them himself.

He didn't have to play by the rules. His hands weren't tied like the police. Donald was going to need some help and thought of just the right person for the job.

Donald pushed hard on the gas pedal. Suddenly he was filled with hope. With all that had happened, he was actually smiling now.

The minute he got back to Wanda's, Donald would call Fort Erwin, in California. He had heard Bill Halloway, an old buddy from Nam who had stayed in the service, was stationed there. If he wanted anyone's help in this it would be good old Halloway. It would be just like old times, covering each other's ass.

The look on Donald's face as he came through the door made Wanda feel uneasy. She had never seen Donald like this and was afraid to ask him what was wrong.

Donald walked over and put his arm around her. She could feel his pulse strongly in his arms. He asked if they could go in back and talk in private. Wanda walked to the back with him and sat down on the sofa. Donald explained everything to her. She was crying softly by the time he had finished. She was glad Donald was all right but feared for Bud and Mary Jo.

Wanda had seen her fair share of strange things in this desert. People hiding from someone or something. People trying to forget their past. But this one caught her completely by surprise.

If someone other than Donald were telling her this, she would have written it off to too much cactus juice.

Wanda told him he could stay in the spare room she had set up at the diner. She stayed here sometimes rather than drive home. Wanda suddenly looked pale. "They're such sweet kids Donald. Do you really think you can find them?"

Donald had been so busy thinking about Bud and Mary Jo, he hadn't taken the time to think about or notice the effect this was having on Wanda.

Wanda was shaking her head. "All this happened to them because they ate here. I could kill those two animals myself for what they've done."

Donald put his arm around her shoulder "It'll be o.k. We'll find them and everything will be alright." He wiped the tears from her eyes and asked to use the phone. He wanted to try and get some help.

Wanda left the room so he could make his call in private. He called information for the listing. God, he hoped Halloway still was based there.

Donald told the woman in personnel he was an old family friend and had an urgent message to deliver. No, there was no time for Halloway to call him back. The woman put him on hold while she tried a few places on base. Donald was anxious as he held the line.

Halloway was one of the biggest men Donald had ever known. He was black, stood about 6'3" and weighed over 300 lbs. His size scared the crap out of most people he met. What they didn't know was his heart was as big as the rest of him. It amazed Donald that he had stayed in the Military, yet he was one of the best soldiers Donald had served with.

"Colonel Halloway here. What can I do for you?" That old familiar deep voice of his answered.

Donald couldn't believe his ears. "Jesus, it's good to here your voice. Got any idea who this is?"

"What's this all about?" Halloway sounded frustrated. "The operator said there was an emergency. Who are you?"

"It's Donnyboy, you dumb ass, and it is an emergency. I could sure use your help if you can get out of that place for awhile."

Halloway was almost yelling, "Donnyboy, is that really you? How the hell you been buddy? Better yet, where you been? Where are you now?"

"I'm up in Nevada just northwest of Las Vegas. We've got a problem up here I could use your help. I sure wish I were just calling to visit. It's good to hear your voice again, I wish I had called over the years. How are you doing buddy? Got someone else saving your ass now?" Donald was laughing and talking at the same time. How did they ever lose touch, how had so many years passed?

Halloway was sitting at his desk smiling looking at his calendar. "Just so happens I got a few days leave coming. I've got nothing urgent in the pipeline until a few weeks from now. I can be there by late tomorrow. I just need to tidy up a couple of things."

He grabbed apiece of paper and a pencil then said, "Give me directions and a phone number in case I can't make it. Don't know any reason I shouldn't be able to, though."

Donald gave him directions to Wanda's and the number from the phone dial. They said their good-byes and hung up.

Donald stood there for a few seconds wondering where the hell the years had gone and why it took this to bring the two of them back together. He hadn't realized till now just how much he missed his old friend.

Donald went out front to tell Wanda the good news. His face was completely changed when he re-entered the room. He looked filled with hope. In fact he looked happier than Wanda had seen him in a long time.

He could always count on Halloway, no matter what. A better friend a man couldn't ask for.

Wanda smiled and gave Donald a big hug. "I guess from your face it was good news. I can put you and your friends up here as long as you need. There's even an old cot in the storage we can bring in here." Wanda turned to get started with the preparations and asked, "How many people will be staying Donald?"

"Just one other Wanda, only one more." They both left for the backroom together.

After setting up the cot, Donald was more than ready for food. He realized he hadn't eaten all day and was starving by now. Wanda brought him in some of her barbecued chicken. He dug right into it.

When he tried to pay for the meal, he practically got his head bit off. While he stayed here it was "on the house." If he had a problem with it he could always stay in his car.

He felt the least he could do was help clean up after closing. He convinced Wanda he needed something to kill time. Boy, he thought, she could be one tough cookie when she wanted. Living alone out here all these years she had to be.

Donald needed to call his boss. He had to let him know an emergency had come up and he needed some time to take care of it. Someone else would need to finish this weeks and probably next weeks deliveries. When he called, his boss wasn't happy but this was the first time Donald had taken time off since starting this job.

He hung up the phone and the two of them went about wiping down the tables and chairs and cleaning every dirty dish in the place. When they finished Wanda gave Donald a kiss goodnight on the cheek and drove home for the night.

As Donald was lying in bed he was thinking about something Rick had said earlier, "He likes to just keep them around for fun." Who was "he" and what MAN did he take them to? That thought bothered him. What kind of nut were they dealing with?

Donald turned out the light. If anyone could find where Bud and Mary Jo were being kept, he and Halloway could. Tomorrow would be a big day. Donald closed his eyes and after a few minutes fell into a fitful sleep.

Chapter 4

It was dark by the time Bud, Mary Jo and Toby arrived in Paradise. From the sound the tires had made and the constant vibrating of their bodies, Bud and Mary Jo knew they had been traveling on a dirt road for some time. Bud felt like his bladder was going to burst.

Throughout the drive Toby had asked how the two of them were doing. What did this man mean, "How are they doing?" How would anyone be doing after being robbed, kidnapped and tied up? He also had been saying it wouldn't be much longer for what seemed like an hour.

Toby was acting as though they were old friends enjoying a camping trip together. This man was so different from the first driver.

All he kept saying was be quiet and don't try anything if they wanted to live long enough to see each other's face again.

The van came to a stop. Bud heard what sounded like a large metal gate being opened. The van began moving slowly again. They came to a complete stop a minute later. This time Toby turned the engine off.

SANDI DOLLAR

The sound of footsteps approaching from outside made both Mary Jo and Bud tense. The side doors opened and someone got into the back of the van.

"You can take those blindfolds off of them now." Toby was saying. "I'm sure it's been awhile since either one of them has eaten. Tell the cook we'll need two special plates made up. Let's get them out of there and let them start to get used to their new home."

Bud and Mary Jo were helped out of the van. Not pushed and pulled as before. The two men that had entered the van and helped them get out also removed their blindfolds. It took a minute for their eyes to be able to focus on everything around them. They both were unsteady on their feet. The men standing next to them didn't say a word they only smiled.

Seeing each other's face again brought a tear to both Mary Jo and Bud's eyes. They were smiling and crying at the same time. Both of them began looking in every direction. Toby had walked to where they were standing. When he approached the others moved out of the way.

"Let's get you and your lovely wife inside." He was standing in front of Bud now. "I'm sure you would like to be rid of ropes on your hands also. Come along now and we'll see to it you're made comfortable." Toby had turned and was heading in the direction of one of the larger buildings Bud could see.

Finally a face to match with a voice. Toby looked so different from what either of them had imagined. His sun tanned boy-like face, and perfectly cut and styled blonde hair were a surprise. He stood about 5'11" tall with a slim frame. Clad in a khaki colored shirt and pants, pressed with a crease down them that reminded Mary Jo of the youths who followed Hitler in the old World War II movies. Her mouth fell open when Toby had turned away from them. He even turned and walked like the Nazi youth. The two men who had met them at the van led Bud and Mary Jo in the same direction Toby had headed. Neither of the men had said a word since taking them out of the van.

Both Bud and Mary Jo were taking as many mental notes as they could. Where the doors they passed led, how far to the front entrance. It had been hours since they had seen anything, including each other. They wanted to remember everything they were seeing now.

When the large door to the building swung open Bud and Mary Jo were shocked at what they were seeing. The room was set up like a recreation room you might find in an expensive country club.

Near the entrance were couches with matching loveseats and tables with lamps and magazines on them. These weren't the types of furnishings you found in a doctor or dentist's office. These were out of a fancy home decorating magazine. The kind Mary Jo loved to look through and could only dream of owning furnishings like this someday.

Past the entrance the room widened. Off to one side was a television viewing area complete with VCRs. There were two long shelves filled with videocassettes. Three people were watching "Gone with the Wind" as the four of them past by. The three people only glanced up at Bud and Mary Jo, then returned to watching the movie.

Off in the other end of the room sat an antique pool table. Behind it on the wall was a case full of cue sticks. On the opposite wall a ping pong game table was set up.

The rear area Mary Jo and Bud were being lead to had a few card tables and chairs in it. Toby was already seated at one of the tables.

When they approached the table the two men stopped. Toby raised his right hand to the men leading Bud and Mary Jo. They reached for the knives in their pockets and cut free the cords around Bud and Mary Jo's hands. For the first time in hours their arms hung free.

Toby motioned for Bud and Mary Jo to take a seat at the table with him. They each pulled out a chair and sat down. The two men who had escorted them remained back from the table.

Toby began to speak, "I apologize for any discomfort you've had. I can tell by your expressions you are confused by the surroundings. We've sent for some food for you both. I'm sure you are famished by now." He leaned toward them a little and said, "After you've had something to eat I'll explain everything to you. For now just try to relax." He was talking to them with such calmness, like they were here because they wanted to be.

Bud really needed to use the bathroom but didn't want to leave Mary Jo alone. "We both need to use the bathroom," Bud said looking over at Mary Jo. She knew exactly what he was doing and smiled at him.

"How stupid of me. Of course you do after such a long time. My men will take you to them right now." Toby was standing and waving his arm toward the restrooms just to the side of where they were standing. "Please don't complicate things by trying to climb through the window to escape. You'll only harm yourselves from the fall to the ground. As I'm sure you noticed this whole place is surrounded with barbed wire fencing. Any attempt to escape would be useless. Go now and refresh yourselves."

Bud and Mary Jo held hands walking to the bathroom. As she was opening the door, Bud leaned forward and kissed her on the cheek. "It'll be okay. I'll be right here waiting for you when you come out."

"I know you will Bud. I love you." Mary Jo smiled, pushed open the door and entered the bathroom. Bud waited for the click of the lock before he entered the men's restroom.

Mary Jo glanced into the mirror inside. Her usually beautiful long soft brown hair looked more like a dirty mop. She began running her fingers through her matted dirty hair over and over. She stared into the mirror almost in a trance reliving the nightmare she and Bud were in.

Without thinking she turned on the bathroom faucet. The cold water from the sink felt good running over her wrists where the binding had been. She splashed the cold water onto her face, hoping to take away some of the puffiness from all the crying she had done. From the other side of the wall Mary Jo became aware of water running also, then the sound of the door closing. She dried her hands and face and walked out of the room.

Bud was standing in front of the door just as he had promised. A smile came to both of them. With their arms about each other, they walked back to the table and Toby. Two plates with ham sandwiches and sliced apples were sitting on the table.

"Sit down and enjoy," Toby was saying. "The cook was kind enough to bring these while you were in the restrooms. I know you have many questions you want answered. Everything will be explained in good time. First you must eat."

Bud and Mary Jo sat down. The two men from the van were still standing about six feet behind them. Bud was looking down, staring at the food. Besides being mad as Hell he was hungry and tired too. The thought crossed his mind that these people might have put something in the food. Bud grabbed Mary Jo's arm just as she was about to take a bite of her sandwich. She jumped and dropped it onto her plate. She stared at it remembering how they had gotten here.

"I see you don't trust us, and why should you? Think back, I haven't lied to you yet. We are not the barbarians you make us out to be." Toby reached across the table and grabbed each of their sandwiches. He tore a piece from each one then returned them to Bud and Mary Jo's plates. "Here now, I'll prove to you these are only sandwiches. Nothing to fear from eating them." Toby ate both pieces.

Bud and Mary Jo sat and stared at him. Nothing was happening. Toby only sat there with a grin on his face. They waited a few minutes more, all staring at each other in silence.

Bud picked up his sandwich, smelled it, and took a bite. Bud started laughing with the food still in his mouth. He kept laughing harder and harder until they all were laughing. All his pent-up emotions were coming out in the form of laughter. The three of them just kept laughing.

Not only did the sandwich not poison him it was good! Mary Jo began eating her sandwich once she could stop laughing. They both felt drained by the time they had finished. So much of the tension Bud and Mary Jo had felt all day seemed to have left. All that remained was sheer exhaustion.

Toby took a look at each of their faces and decided to hold off on his introduction to Paradise for tonight. He would put them into an intermediate holding room for the night and get them set up tomorrow.

This same room was used occasionally to house "guests" that were causing problems inside the camp.

"I think you two have had enough excitement for one day. After a good night's sleep you'll appreciate all that's being offered to you. Ken and Mike will take you to your room for the night. I'll check to see you're comfortable in a few minutes."

Toby turned to the two men who were still standing in the room, "Ken, is room one set up for company?"

The taller of the two answered, "Yes, there are fresh sheets on the beds and clean towels in the bathroom."

"Very good. Please show Bud and Mary Jo to their temporary quarters then. I'll be there shortly to check on things." Toby turned now to Bud and Mary Jo. "I hope you'll forgive my not explaining things tonight. It would take about an hour to do so. Your faces tell me we do not have an hour before you two will be sound asleep. My men will show you the way." Toby stood and began walking over to where Ken and Mike were standing.

Bud and Mary Jo rose to their feet. All the laughter from before was gone. The reality of their situation was back. Bud took a quick glance around hoping to find a way to escape. Nothing, not a door or window in sight. Both Mary Jo and Bud followed without putting up a fight.

They left the large recreation room the same way they had entered, only this time when they past the T.V. area it was empty. The room now had an eerie silence to it. Both Bud and Mary Jo were glad when they reached the outdoors again.

They were all walking in the direction of one of the smaller buildings to the right of the recreation hall. Behind them the recreation room went dark except for the dim glow of a single small bulb at the top of the stairs leading into it. Against the dark night sky you could barely make out the buildings large size.

Ken and Mike stopped at the entrance of the next building. Toby had continued beyond it and was now out of sight. Ken, the taller man, turned to Bud and Mary Jo, "If you'll enter here we can get you set for the night. I'll have all the lights on in just a second."

Mary Jo and Bud stepped inside the doorway and froze in their tracks. They were looking down a dark hallway with only an occasional night-light marking the way. At the end, off to the left was a room with a brighter glow coming from it. Their hearts sank. Bud turned to look at Mike. The fence was far out beyond him, and Bud decided he was just too tired to fight.

The lights came on and gave the building a whole new look. It appeared to be some kind of storage building. There were a series of smaller rooms off the main hall. Some of these had chicken wire fronts to them, they were laden with cardboard boxes.

Mike took the lead and headed for the other end of the hallway. Ken followed directly behind Bud and Mary Jo, who continued to look closely at everything they were passing.

When the four of them reached the room at the end of the hall, Mike reached into his pocket and produced a key. He opened the metal door and motioned for Bud and Mary Jo to enter.

As they walked in they noticed two twin beds, a small table placed between, and a bathroom off to the side. The front of the room consisted of walls that were chicken wire glass on the top half and steel lower halves. All the other walls appeared to be made of steel. A small single blade fan was turning on the ceiling. The small louver window at the top of the glass section was only six inches wide.

"I trust you'll be comfortable here for tonight. You'll even find fresh toothbrushes and combs in the bathroom. Toby will be by soon to check on you. Goodnight, and welcome to Paradise." This was the first time Mike had said a word to them. He was outside locking the door by the time he had finished.

Bud tried fiercely to turn the doorknob. It wouldn't budge. He turned around in anger only to find Mary Jo's eyes staring into his.

"Bud, were alive and together, let's just try and get some sleep for now. We've been through so much for one day there's no fight left in me. As they say tomorrow's another day!" She lovingly stroked his shoulder and arm then turned and went into the bathroom. Mike's comment about a toothbrush and comb hadn't escaped her.

Bud was exhausted and sat slumped over on the bed. He was angry with himself for not getting them out of this jam. He heard Toby's voice on the other side of the glass. "I'm sorry for all the security measures you'll have to endure tonight. We just can't take any chances. Tomorrow morning we'll move you to more comfortable quarters. Goodnight."

Toby turned away and was out of sight before Bud had a chance to speak. Only the sound of the soles of his shoes could be heard leaving the building. Bud heard the opening of outer door. The hall lights went down, leaving only scattered shadows in the hallway. Bud dropped his face in his hands and wept in angry silence.

Mary Jo returned with a new toothbrush in her hand for Bud. "Honey please clean up a little. You won't believe how much better you'll feel. If we're going to fight these people we both need to get some rest."

Bud took the toothbrush from her and entered the small bathroom. Mary Jo was right, it did feel good to get some of the road grime off.

When Bud came out of the bathroom, Mary Jo was sitting on the edge of the bed combing her fingers through her hair. Bud thought,

God after all they had been through she still looks beautiful.

He sat down gently beside her and started running his fingers through her hair. When she turned her face near his their lips met. A raw passion fueled by their anger and frustration came over them.

Bud fumbled to switch off the room light. He jumped back onto the bed, they wrapped themselves around each other and held one another tight. Bud was slipping off Mary Jo's blouse as she gently unfastened his jeans. They're bodies felt alive with an electricity neither one could control. They traced every curve and line on each other's bodies. They made passionate love to one another, forgetting temporarily everything except the love between them. When they're bodies could take no more they got under the covers and continued to hold each other tight. They were sound asleep not too long after their heads hit the pillows.

Chapter 5

The bright morning sun pouring through the curtain-less window woke Donald up early. He had forgotten to lower the blinds before turning in. He rolled over and looked at a clock on the table in the corner. It read 6:30 A.M. time to get hustling. Wanda would be arriving soon to prepare for any early morning customers. She opened at 7:30 every day.

Donald pulled on his pants and headed into the bathroom. He looked in the mirror and noticed he needed a shave badly.

Donald headed straight for his car. In all the excitement yesterday he forgot to bring in his luggage. Donald's luggage consisted of three shirts, two pair of pants, and three pair of underwear, three pair of socks, a toothbrush and shaving kit. Nothing but first class for Donald. He had been on the road a week now. He checked all three shirts to see which was the cleanest. He wanted to look the best he could when Halloway arrived later. With his shaving kit and clean shirt in hand, he went back into the diner.

Donald washed himself off, dressed and shaved. As he walked out from the bathroom, feeling like a new man, Wanda walked through the front door.

"You're up I see. I half expected to find you still asleep after the long day you had. I'll put some coffee on and switch on the air conditioning. I didn't sleep very well last night and could use a cup myself." Wanda turned and added, "I'm real glad you're here, Donald."

Donald smiled at her. "Is there anything I can do to help?"

"If you really want to help you could bring some of those bags of ice cubes from the back freezer out front and dump them into that cooler." She was pointing to the old ice chest that reminded Donald of the old lift top soda pop containers in the grocery stores. Wanda added, "That's one of the few things I'd just as soon not have to do myself anymore."

"Wanda you want me to bring out one or two for now? I'll be here all day, so let me know which will be easier for you. Today I'm your hired hand so you don't have to worry about a thing. Just don't ask me to cook. I'm a horrible cook." They both got a laugh out of that.

"Two will be fine for now. I'll have us some coffee in just a minute, hired hand." She turned her attention to the drip coffee maker.

Donald had no trouble finding the large bags of ice cubes. Wanda served so little frozen foods in her diner that the ice was about the only thing in there. The bags of ice, some ice cream, french fries, cut up chickens and some packages of breakfast sausage and hamburger. He threw the bag over his shoulder and headed straight for the front cooler. Donald emptied the bag and took a seat at the counter.

Wanda took two cups off the cupboard above the coffee station and poured them each one. She set Donald's in front of him and took the seat at the counter next to him. Donald realized he had never seen Wanda sitting at her own counter before. He smiled. They finished their coffee over small talk.

Wanda got up and refilled Donald's cup then started in her routine preparing for the day. Donald watched her move from one thing to another effortlessly. Heat the griddle, chop the vegetables, start some great smelling soup. His mind wandered from time to time back to Bud and Mary Jo.

The front door opened and in walked the first three customers of the day. A single long-hauler, and two women who looked ready for a break from driving. Wanda took their orders and started preparing their food. Donald took his cup over to the sink and rinsed it out. He

DESERT DECEPTION

went to the back room to try and come up with a plan to work with Halloway. He began by writing down everything he could remember from the day before.

A few hours had passed when Wanda walked in and asked Donald if he wanted some breakfast or lunch. He had worked everything over and over in his mind until he couldn't even form a rational thought anymore. It would only be a few more hours before Halloway would be there. Maybe a break was just what he needed. Donald asked for a sandwich and a glass of coke. Wanda left as quietly as she had entered.

When Wanda returned with his food she said there was a phone call for him. He had heard the phone ringing but paid it no attention. Donald felt a lump in his throat as he walked to the phone. The only person he had given Wanda's phone number to was Halloway, and he wasn't going to call unless he couldn't make it.

Donald picked up the phone hesitatingly. "This is Donald. Who's calling please?" Wanda was waiting to see if it was more bad news.

"This is the police impound department. We were told to call and let you know when we had that Chevy in here. Sorry about the delay, we got backed up today and this is the first chance I've had to call."

Donald was so relieved it wasn't Halloway he stood speechless. He had forgotten about giving Wanda's phone number to the police.

"Hello! Hello! You still there?" The officer was hollering.

"Yes, I'm here officer. Sorry for the delay, that's wonderful. Thank you for calling." Donald put down the receiver and looked over at Wanda. She was wondering what that was all about.

"Did they find Bud and Mary Jo? Are they all right? Donald don't stand there and keep me in suspense. Tell me what the police had to say."

"I'm sorry Wanda they haven't found Bud and Mary Jo yet. They were calling to say the Chevy was safe and sound at the police impound yard. I forgot I had asked them to call when they found it. I was relieved it wasn't my friend Halloway calling to say he couldn't come." Donald put his arms around her and gave her a reassuring hug.

Wanda left the room and Donald returned to his notes. There had to be a clue he was missing somewhere. Donald pushed aside his notes and ate his lunch. He laid back his head to think some and dozed off.

Wanda was shaking his shoulders gently trying to wake him. "Donald, there's someone out front asking for you. He's a big black man with very short hair. He asked for you by name."

Donald opened his eyes and looked at Wanda. "What did you say about someone asking for me?" Donald had no idea he had been sleeping for two hours. He glanced over at the clock and shot out of bed.

"Where is he, Wanda? Why didn't you wake me? What's this person look like?" Donald's mind was going a mile a minute. He knew the person had to be his old buddy and he was nervous.

"Don't jump all over me. All I did was leave you alone in here. Do you always wake up like this?" She was sorry she had come in and awakened him at all.

"I'm sorry for jumping at you. I'm just mad that I fell asleep, that's all. Let's go see who this person is." Donald followed her into the diner.

Standing at the end of the counter was his good friend Halloway. Donald would have recognized him anywhere. Even after all these years. He walked up to him and they gave each other a big hug. There was no hesitation from Donald or Halloway.

"Halloway, I can't believe it's you. You look the same. A little heavier in the middle, but who isn't." Donald pushed Halloway to arm's length. There was just a hint of gray at his temples now. "God, I can't believe how good it is to see you again." Donald just couldn't believe his eyes.

"Donnyboy, I know what you mean. Stand back for a minute so I can take a good look. I have to make sure my eyes aren't playing tricks on me. You know they got older just like everything else." For a minute they just stared at each other shaking their heads in silence.

Wanda and the few customers that were in the diner were staring. After a minute Wanda asked if they would like to go in back to catch up on old times in private. She would bring them coffee. They walked to the backroom with their arms around each other, chatting away like there would be no tomorrow.

Wanda brought in their coffee and Donald formally introduced them both. "Halloway, this is Wanda, the best adopted Mom a guy could ask for. Wanda, this is Bill Halloway the best friend a man could ever have."

DESERT DECEPTION

Both Halloway and Wanda were embarrassed standing looking at each other.

"That was some introduction. I'm very happy you could come. You're welcome to stay as long as you like. I only wish we could be meeting under better circumstances. Glad to meet you, Bill." Wanda offered him her hand. After Halloway thanked her, Wanda returned to her customers outside.

"I think it's time you explain a little about what's going on. You mentioned an emergency on the phone and with Wanda's last comment I guess it's serious." Halloway took a seat at the table.

Donald sat down across from him. "This is going to sound like something right out of a made for T.V. movie more than a true story. I'm still having a hard time believing everything that's been happening myself."

Donald paused a minute to get his thoughts straight. "It involves two young married kids I only met day before yesterday, right here in this very diner. They were on their honeymoon heading for Las Vegas. We talked for a long time and actually became friends." Donald checked the hallway door to make sure their conversation was private.

Donald continued his story for the next half-hour. He stopped occasionally to answer a question Halloway had, or to drink a sip of the coffee Wanda had brought them. When Donald had finished the whole story, they both sat for a moment in silence.

"I know it's a lot, asking you to help with this. I don't even know how much help you could be yet." Donald got up out of his chair and walked to the door.

He turned to Halloway with a surprised look on his face. "I haven't even thought about the fact you might not be able to get time off. It isn't like you can call in sick and stay home a few days. You live at work. I haven't even asked what you're doing now or what rank you hold. I'm sorry Halloway I took an awful lot for granted. I'll understand if you can't help me on this. It's been great just to see you again, even if you have to say no."

Halloway rose to his feet. "Back up a minute there, Donnyboy. I haven't answered NO yet. Just so happens I'm in a position that I can disappear for a few days at a time without anyone becoming suspicious about what I'm up to. As far as my rank goes I made Bird

Colonel going on two years ago. I guess every time someone didn't know what to do with me, they'd promote me." Halloway paused loving the look on Donny's face. He began a slow pace on his side of the room.

He smiled and continued, "I would have to take care of some loose ends on base first. That crazy damn Senator Hudson has driven me half-crazy. I'm sure on your route you've seen his billboards asking everyone to call or write their Senator to pass his Crime Task Force Bill. He wants me to train some of his task force members in desert commando operations even before the damn thing is passed. I guess he's pretty sure he'll get it through this month. With all the major drug busts involving the Mexican border lately, he knows parents are fed up. That doesn't happen for a few weeks though. I'll need to make a call to the base and check on a few things. Besides, I have an idea that might help us out."

"I'll be damned. A Bird Colonel! Congratulations. I always knew you'd be a success." Donald was truly impressed. "With all that's on your plate right now, are you sure you can just disappear for a couple days? What if the Senator needs you right away?"

"Let me make that call, then I'll explain everything. I had no idea you needed me for something like this. I could have made some plans before I left."

Donald showed him the phone and left the room to give him some privacy.

Donald hurried to Wanda to give her the good news. The Colonel and the United States Army was on their team.

Halloway was standing in the doorway motioning for Donald to come back in the room. He was smiling. When Donald was inside Halloway closed the door. Both men took a seat at the table.

"Donald what I'm about to say to you has to stay in this room. Even Wanda can't know of this conversation. I'm sure you'll understand by the time I'm finished." Halloway pushed back in his chair. "I told you I can disappear from base without arousing suspicion. That's because it's assumed it involves army business. Prior to this it always has."

"Earlier you asked what I was doing and I didn't give you an answer. This is where I need you to keep silent. What I'm about to say is top secret. Hell I could be court martialed for telling you."

Halloway stood up, then paced some more as he continued, "I train a very elite group of men. A group that chooses to remain anonymous even on base. My men are not listed in any Army files, or civilian for that matter. To most of the world we don't exist." Colonel Halloway was talking low.

He looked out scanning the inside of the diner and continued, "I am the only one you'll find listed anywhere. That's only to get access to Army bases and information. My men are known as the Desert Delta Force. I know you're aware of their existence and the caliber of men who form it."

"My phone call was to one of my best men. I asked him to contact two others on the team to help us with this. God help all of us if we're found involving ourselves in a civilian situation. I need to get back to base to explain the whole scenario to all three of my men and let them know the risks involved. I'll be returning day after tomorrow. I hope I won't be alone."

Donald's mouth hung open for a second. "I had no idea you were involved in something of this nature. You can count on my complete silence. I won't even ask all the questions running through my head. I'm surprised, and not surprised, at the same time. You always were the best. You saved my ass a few times in Nam. I want to repeat what I said about understanding if you couldn't help buddy. It goes double for your men too."

"Enough of this 'not helping' talk. I'm starving. Let's go see what kind of food this little joint has to offer."

Halloway put his arm around Donald's shoulder and they headed out front.

Donald smiled at Wanda, "We need two barbecue chicken specials, please. My friend's hungry and he has a long drive ahead of him." Donald felt so good right now he could explode. They took the two seats at the end of the counter.

Wanda appeared with two plates piled high with chicken, mashed potatoes and her famous homemade biscuits. She barely had put down their plates when they dove into them.

Smacking his lips and turning his head, Halloway was in chicken heaven. "Wanda you're one of the best kept secrets out here in the Nevada desert. The men back on base would kill for a taste of this chicken. If I thought you'd be interested I ask you to marry me right now."

Wanda was grinning from ear to ear. "Better watch what you say, Colonel Bill. I might just accept. I'll go get you big flirts some coke to wash that down with." She turned and floated off for the sodas.

"You made her day. I think you just made a friend for life, Bill Halloway. I've never seen her blush like that. She looked like a schoolgirl."

"I was half serious. I'm afraid to taste any more of her cooking. My bachelor days might come to an abrupt end." They looked at each other and both started laughing.

When they had finished the food their conversation returned to the task that lie ahead of them.

Halloway stood and rubbed his protruding belly. "I have to be leaving if we're going to get anything accomplished in the short time I can offer you. Three days goes by awful fast." He turned looking where Wanda was standing in the kitchen. "I can't remember the last time I enjoyed a meal so much. I must be on my way and just wanted to thank you for all the hospitality you've shown. See you in a day or so." Both he and Donald walked to the door with Wanda waving goodbye.

As they walked to the car, Halloway gave Donald last minute instructions. "I won't be returning until day after tomorrow, hopefully with my men. In the mean time start checking around for anything irregular in the areas around here. You mentioned those guys thought they were taken someplace nearby. I'll talk to my men first thing when I get back. That will give us a day to set up a cover story for the rest of the squad."

Donald stood outside the door and waved goodbye. "Don't worry about this end. I'll put Wanda to work the minute I get inside. If anyone knows this area it's her. I'll do some scouting myself. See you in a couple days and thanks again buddy."

Halloway jumped in his van, started the engine and pulled away. Donald watched him drive out of the lot, then walked back inside.

The diner sat empty except for Wanda busy cleaning up at the sink. Donald had been so rapt in conversation he hadn't even noticed the other customers as they had left. All the better he thought.

He and Wanda needed the privacy to make some plans. Donald told Wanda what he needed her to do and she was more than happy to help. She went immediately to the phone and started calling her friends.

Donald was impressed with the way she handled these people. She was perfect at getting information without causing alarm. Donald left her to help out with cleaning up the diner. Tomorrow he'd spend the day driving out to the neighboring areas to have a look for himself.

Suddenly it hit him. He knew he was forgetting something important. Donald called the police to let them know he had heard Rick and Lou talking about meeting some guy named Joe in L.A. From the way they were talking about him he got the impression this guy was "in charge."

They would look into it. So far the two of them were playing deaf and dumb since being arrested. For these two playing dumb wasn't a stretch.

The police had reminded Donald he could be facing possible assault charges and it would be in everyone's best interest if Donald stuck around. That's all Donald needed was the police around after enlisting the help of the U.S. Army.

Chapter 6

Mary Jo was first to wake up the next morning. When she opened her eyes she shot straight out of bed. She turned to Bud and began shaking his shoulder.

"Bud wake up. Please Bud wake up. I thought this whole thing might have been a nightmare. It's real Bud, we've got to be ready for them." She was trying to keep her voice low in case someone was nearby guarding them.

Bud could barely peel his eyes open. He slept miserably all night. He finally focused on Mary Jo's panic stricken face. "What are you doing? What's wrong with you?"

Bud shook the sleep from his head and looked around the room. Like a ton of bricks everything came crashing back to him at once. He jumped out of bed and again tried the door. Still locked. He cursed the door and pounded his fists on the glass wall.

Mary Jo walked over and threw her arms around him. "Bud, I had a terrible thought last night. I know it can't be true, but I want to tell you anyway. The question crossed my mind and has been bothering me ever since."

"Go on honey, tell me what's bugging you." He pushed her out in front of him and was staring into her face.

"I'm trying to, Bud. I just feel bad for even thinking something like this." She took a deep breath and continued. "Last night while I was sleeping I kept dreaming about all that's happened to us. How come these people picked us? How they knew we'd stop to help a family with car trouble? What I'm trying to say is, do you think Donald's involved in this? I just kept thinking how he warned us about money and people who would do anything to get it. I feel terrible even thinking it, but we were pretty naive about everyone else."

Bud's face became angry and he began to pace. He had to give this question some thought. They had only met the man. Bud became angry with himself for even thinking Donald had anything to do with this. He might have misjudged John and Cindy but not Donald.

"Mary Jo, I think we're both jumping to the wrong conclusion. If Donald wanted to rob us why didn't he just go with us when we invited him along? If he were involved that means Wanda would have been involved too. We've got enough people to blame already without bringing more into this."

Bud walked over and put his arms around her. "We'll get through this baby, I promise. We just have to stick together."

At the sound of footsteps in the hallway, Bud said, "Shh, I hear someone coming!" Bud pushed her behind him and stood ready and waiting.

Along the hallway you could hear the distinct sound of Toby's shoe soles approaching.

"Good morning. Glad you are both awake. I trust you were able to get some sleep?" Toby was trying to read their faces before attempting to unlock the door. He just stood there smiling waiting for one of them to respond.

"We got a little sleep, as if it really matters to you. We demand to know what's going on here. What kind of people are you to keep anyone hostage like this?" Bud just stared into Toby's eyes as he spoke, "We want to see the person in charge of this place. If it's more money they want we can get it. I own my own auto shop back home, and I can get you money. Just tell us what it is you people want from us?"

61

"I can see you are still very angry. We don't want any money from you. We don't want to take anything from you at all. We're here to give to you. We're offering you one of the greatest gifts of your life."

Just then Ken and Mike appeared next to Toby. "Remember Ken and Mike from last night?" They both nodded to Bud and Mary Jo.

"If you'll back away from the door I'll open it. We'll be taking you out of this holding room and introducing you to your new home. I promised you last night that things would be explained to you and they will." Toby opened the door.

Bud stepped back pulling Mary Jo with him. His eyes never left Toby's face. He was searching for any emotion other than this programmed Zombie robot he saw. He didn't know whether to try rushing all three of them or wait and take the chance later hoping for better odds. He didn't have to think long. Mary Jo was gripping his arms so tight holding him back he wouldn't have stood a chance.

"Please follow me," Toby was saying. The five of them headed down the hall approaching the large door. Bud and Mary Jo followed Toby while Ken and Mike brought up the rear.

When the door to the outside swung open, both Bud and Mary Jo hesitated. In the bright morning sun they could see their surroundings much better than last night. The camp was much larger than they first thought. The whole place was enclosed by chain link fencing topped with rolled barbed wire. Bud looked directly in front of them and saw a guard tower along the fencing. There was someone up there but he couldn't make out a face.

They were headed back to the recreation building they had seen last night. Neither Mary Jo nor Bud had noticed the mesquite trees covering some of the buildings in the darkness. They made a strange contrast to the desert surrounding the entire place. The only other trees for miles were the occasional Joshua trees.

As they cleared the side of the storage building they saw a group of smaller dark beige buildings in two rows across from each other.

Between the larger and smaller buildings there appeared to be the start of a large vegetable garden. Bud and Mary Jo were paying so much attention to everything else they walked right into Toby who had stopped outside the recreation room steps.

"You'll have plenty of time to look around later. Please take a seat in the viewing room and we can get started." He pointed to the area they had seen the others watching the movie in last night. Bud and his wife sat in the first row of chairs.

"I believe we're ready now." Toby asked Ken to turn out the lights." He took the seat next to Mary Jo.

When the room was darkened, a video began playing on the screen. The opening shot was of the camp outside. It showed people walking around smiling and laughing among themselves. There were children running and playing ball. Everyone in the film was smiling the same pitiful smile. Everyone was enjoying themselves, even the people working around the place. The title flashed boldly across the screen. "A Typical Day in Paradise." Bud and Mary Jo both held back laughing at the quality of the movie.

The movie went on to tell of a perfect society, created without crime, hunger, drugs, or poverty. Where children could grow to be productive respected adults, free from all the vices of the modern day world.

This was all being given to a chosen few. They would be the children of the new America, a better America. It would be a totally self-sufficient community, with their help.

Their new leader and provider, known to them only as the "Man," was giving this wonderful gift to them. The gravelly, husky voice of a man welcomed them into this lifetime opportunity. He only asked their support in making his dream a reality.

The children born into Paradise would have none of the outer world's bad influences. They would epitomize what the United States stood for. Strong, self sufficient, good moral values none of the filth that existed outside preying on decent people's kindness. They would be the lucky chosen few. In return all their needs would be taken care of. The closing shots had the same people smiling and waving hello this time. Amazing! There wasn't a Hispanic or Black among the chosen crowd. In fact these people sure resembled the racists causing trouble lately on the evening news.

Toby interjected, "Eventually our community will grow and spread it's morality, and send its purified individuals beyond this colony. We are fortunate to be the first of many generations of superior people."

When the lights came on Bud looked at Toby's face and realized this was no joke. Toby was almost moved to tears believing this crap.

This was more serious than Bud and Mary Jo thought. They were dealing with a bunch of crazies. No amount of money in the world would buy these people off.

"There, do you see what I've been trying to tell you? We aren't your enemies at all. We offer only a life free from the stress and worries of the world you left behind. Here everyone is truly equal. Here we're all one big family." Toby was still staring at the blank screen as he spoke. When he turned toward them his face revealed a true believer, and that really scared Bud.

Bud looked over at his wife and knew she was thinking the same thing.

"Toby, that's really nice of you people to offer us all this, but we can't accept. We can't leave our families and good friends behind. We hate to have to turn you down after rescuing us from those bandits, but we need to be on our way home soon. I just opened my own auto repair shop and I have people counting on me. We promise not to tell anyone about this wonderful place." Bud tried to sound as sincere as he could.

Toby turned and looked straight into Bud's eyes. His tone had changed. He was deadly serious when he said in an almost shout, "What kind of fool do you take me for? You are never permitted to leave here."

Toby's voice was loud and harsh compared to his conversation earlier. "You don't care about Paradise. You can't even see what's right in front of you. In time you will appreciate all that's being given freely to you. As far as your family and friends go, you have a new family now. The family of Paradise. As far as your repair shop I can use your talents here."

He stood and turned to Ken and Mike. "Take them to their quarters and see to it they get breakfast with the others in the dining room. I don't have time for anymore insults." Toby turned and left the room without even looking back at the two of them.

Temporarily defeated, Mary Jo and Bud followed the others from the room.

When they reached the bottom of the recreation room steps they turned headed to the group of smaller buildings they had noticed earlier. Not a word was spoken between them.

DESERT DECEPTION

As they approached the buildings Bud and Mary Jo saw that indeed there was the start of a vegetable garden, a quite large one with a few people tending to it.

The others stood and stared as Bud and Mary Jo passed. No one needed to say a word. Their expressions said it all. These were not the smiling faces in the film. These were other kidnapped victims.

Ken and Mike stopped in front of the second small building on the right. Ken opened the unlocked door and held it open for Bud and Mary Jo.

"This is your new home. You'll find everything you need. You'll be given clean sheets once a week. There are extra towels in the linen closet over here." He moved across the sparsely furnished room to a recessed area. "The bathroom is here behind these louvered doors."

Mike pointed in the direction of the bedroom area and said "You will find new clothes in the dresser and closet for each of you. We had to guess at the sizes. Let us know if they are incorrect and we will replace them."

Both men headed for the front door. Ken said ovrer his shoulder, "Meals are served in the building to the right of the recreation room. You'll hear a bell to let you know when they're ready to serve."

As Mike turned the doorknob it was his turn to give instructions. "As I'm sure you noticed, there are no locks on the door. You are free to come and go as you wish within the camp. We'll leave you now to freshen up. Do you have any questions before we leave?"

Bud and Mary Jo both shook their heads NO. Ken and Mike were gone and they were alone. Bud sat in one of the two chairs by the small front window. Mary Jo took the other and they both stared around the room. On the table between them sat a kerosene lamp and a few wildlife magazines.

The interior of the room was L shaped because of the built in dressers and bathroom along one wall. It gave the effect of a small apartment more than one big room. Across from where they sat was an earth-tone loveseat with another table next to it. On that table sat a small clock radio. It was only 7:30 A.M. and it already seemed this day would never end. Across from the bathroom was the bedroom area. There was a double bed, complete with matching sheets and bedspread. Next to the bed was a nightstand with another lamp on it.

Mary Jo decided to go check out what was in the drawers. She looked in the linen area first. An extra blanket and pillow, three bath towels and a few washcloths were folded neatly on the shelf.

She pushed open the doors to the bathroom and couldn't believe her eyes. It was all color coordinated. There were rust colored bath towels over oak towel rods. Matching oak rings with washcloths in them hung over the small sink. Above those was an oak medicine chest stocked with shampoos, toothpaste, mouthwash and extra bars of soap. Toothbrushes and cups, still in their wrappers, hung from the holder mounted on the door. The shower stall was directly across from the toilet. In front of the sink was a rust and cream colored rug.

"Bud, you've got to see this! Come in here and take a look." She hadn't noticed before but even the toilet paper was cream with rust colored flowers on it.

Bud pulled himself from the chair and walked over to where she was standing. All that looking around the room did for him, was confirm that these people were truly sick.

"Mary Jo, don't get excited about any of this. We don't intend on staying. These people aren't only crazy, they're clever. That combination scares me. Getting out of here is going to take a lot of planning. Don't go and start enjoying this place! We're not here 'cause we want to be'."

"I know that Bud. I'm not falling in love with this place. Do you think I'm one of those people in their propaganda film? I only wanted to show you this. I can't be bought for a matching bathroom!" Mary Jo was angry and pushed past him out of the room.

Bud went after her and grabbed her arm. "Baby, I'm sorry. I know you're not stupid. I'm just upset and confused. Please let's not fight. All we have is each other now, and they can't take that from us." He brushed back her brown hair and held her face gently in his hands. They kissed and stood for a few minutes embracing each other.

Bud went back to his chair to think some more. He had to admit that it did look nice in there.

Mary Jo walked over and opened the closet door. Inside hanging on one side of the rod were four men's shirts, three pair of slacks and one lightweight jacket. On the other side hung three sundresses, one long sleeved dress and a lightweight woman's coat. On the floor sat a pair of tennis shoes and boots for each of them.

DESERT DECEPTION

When she checked the sizes they were perfect. She felt a shiver run down her spine and put the shoes down. She pulled out the blue sundress and put it on. It was a perfect fit.

She next opened the dresser drawers. Underwear, still in its packaging, was neatly placed in the top drawer. She took out a pair for herself. The next drawer contained socks and T-shirts all in Bud's sizes. The third drawer contained three pair of women's socks, two pair of women's slacks, one pair of Levi's. The last drawer contained a couple tank style tops and two sweaters for each of them.

Mary Jo took off the sundress and carried it and the clean underwear into the bathroom with her. There was no law against enjoying a shower she thought and hopped right in.

Bud was only half-conscious of the water running when he heard bells ringing outside. He turned to see groups of people heading for the dining room Ken had pointed to earlier. If they avoided breakfast it might make Toby keep a closer eye on them. He thought the best way to deal with Toby and his men would be to pretend to go along with their crazy idea. He yelled for Mary Jo to get dressed and come quick.

She was trying to quickly dry her hair as she walked over to Bud. "What's the matter? I barely got wet in there."

She noticed Bud was staring at the blue sundress she had on. "This was in the closet. There are clothes in there for you too. It's spooky Bud, they guessed the right size about everything even down to our shoes."

Bud quickly explained his thoughts to Mary Jo and she agreed. Within minutes they were on their way to breakfast with everyone else.

When they reached the door to the dining room Ken was standing just inside. "Glad to see you two for breakfast. Follow me and I'll show you how we do things."

Ken, Bud and Mary Jo each took a tray just like in school cafeterias. There was a woman on the other side of the table asking what they wanted to be served. She looked up and saw they were newcomers and welcomed them. The woman said her name was Alice and she would be happy to fix up whatever they wanted.

Already prepared in metal holding pans were scrambled eggs, sausages, and strips of bacon and rolls. If they preferred pancakes or cereal, they too were available. Eggs could be prepared anyway they wanted.

Bud and Mary Jo thanked Alice and each selected scrambled eggs and sausages. Farther along another woman offered milk, orange or grapefruit juice and coffee or tea. Bud grabbed a coffee while Mary Jo took some orange juice.

Ken was waiting at the end of the table for them. "You pick up your utensils here. After you're through eating you hand in your plates and silverware over there." He pointed across the large room.

The dining room had five long tables with chairs in the center. Outside of them were six smaller tables that sat four people. Along the back wall, where the dirty dishes were turned in, was a raised area that had a glassed in room. A man was positioned behind the glass. He glanced at Ken, Bud and Mary Jo then gave a nod to Ken. Ken waved back at the man, and then he excused himself to find a seat.

As Bud and Mary Jo stood there, holding their trays of food, they noticed everyone was staring at them. They walked over to one of the empty smaller tables and sat down. The people in the room returned to their breakfast. One muscular man stared for a little longer at Mary Jo until Bud glanced in his direction.

Bud noticed one man seated with a woman continued to watch them. The man was now approaching their table. He was a stocky blonde who they both thought couldn't have been more than twenty-five years old.

"Hi there." He said extending his hand to Bud. "I'm Roy and the lady over there is my wife, C.C."

Mary Jo turned to look where Roy was pointing. Bud introduced Mary Jo and himself. When she looked over at the blonde woman expecting her to join them, the woman wasn't even looking their way.

"I know how hard your first day here can be and just wanted to offer my help with anything you might not understand. I'll leave you alone to finish your food. Nice meeting you both." As Roy turned to leave Bud stopped him.

"I do have one question Roy. What's with that glass room and the man watching us?" Bud pointed to the opposite wall.

"That's to make sure you hand in your silverware. They don't trust giving us knives. They're afraid all us happy people might do something naughty with them. Like revolt! Just make sure you let him see you put your silverware into the dishpan. You can't see it from here but he is armed. Well better get back to CC now. See you around." Roy smiled up at the guard in the window as he walked away. The guard just returned a cold stare.

As Roy and C.C. left the room the guard followed their every step until they were out of sight.

"Bud did you notice his wife didn't even look over here once while he was here? She just kept staring at her plate. That "guard thing" was a little strange too. What do you think is going on? Think we're being tested Bud?" Mary Jo was talking very low without moving her eyes from her husband's face.

"Could be a test of some kind Babe. We have to be very careful about everything. I didn't like that look the guard gave him at all." Bud leaned closer to her. "I don't think that part was fake. Just keep your eyes and ears open for anything. Ready to go back to our room?"

Both of them stood and headed in the direction of the glass wall. Mary Jo looked up and smiled at the man on the other side. He smiled back as they left their dirty dishes and silverware behind.

Outside they walked by a few other people who said hello in passing. The same man who was staring at her inside the dining hall smiled and said hello to them also. Bud nodded and returned the greeting.

There was open desert between the bungalows and the fence behind them. It was probably for future expansions. As they approached their bungalow they saw Roy standing out front of the bungalow next door. He and C.C. must be their neighbors.

Mary Jo and Bud decided to walk over to him. There wasn't anything to do inside their own place but look through magazines and they didn't feel comfortable enough to explore the grounds yet.

"I see we're neighbors," Bud was saying as they walked up to Roy. "What's a guy do around here to keep from going crazy?"

"That's a funny question in this place. If you join in, you are crazy, and if you don't, you'll go crazy from the boredom." Roy stood a minute, laughing, amused with his answer.

Bud and Mary Jo only looked at him. They still didn't know if this guy was part of Toby's team or really was a prisoner like they were.

"I'm sorry for laughing. It is a funny question though. As far as recreation goes you've got games and limited TV in the rec room. The others tell me that you were brought in here last night. That room stays open until 10:00 every night."

Roy gestured across the way, "If you're into gardening there's that big patch of ground over there. Then there's a small children's area at the end of these rows with swings, a merry-go-round and a slide. There are books in the rec room you can check out and read in your bungalow. Some of the guys run or jog around the place to keep in shape. Every so often there's a fight to watch, or participate in because we're all frustrated. A regular Mecca of entertainment don't you agree?" Roy was looking at them both a little cynically.

"See that guy at the end of the row? He's been in a couple of fights already and might get kicked out soon." He was pointing at Josh, the person who couldn't keep his eyes off Mary Jo.

"I guess it beats sitting in those little rooms all day. It's not exactly what I want to do for the rest of my life. I'd much rather be working on cars." Bud held back what he wanted to say.

"Where's your wife, CC? I would like to introduce myself if that's alright." Mary Jo leaned to look inside. She could see her sitting by the front window still staring off into space.

Roy's face became serious. There was none of the smart alec tone in his voice as before. "CC doesn't visit much. It's not that she's unfriendly or anything like that. She's just got a lot on her mind these days." Roy motioned for the couple to follow him away from the door.

"You'll hear about it sooner or later so I might as well get it out in the open right now." Roy looked down at the ground and kicked away a small stone. "When CC and I were brought to this damn place she was carrying our first child. She was five months along. I guess all the stress of what was happening was just too much for her and our son. He didn't stand a chance. CC cries from time to time for him."

Roy was fighting back tears of his own. "Our second night here she went into hard labor. With the baby so premature there were all kinds of complications. Toby was away getting supplies or something. The other jerks around this place didn't know what to do. Thank God for Trish. Trish heard about what was happening and came to our bungalow to help. Trish told everyone what to do. She said she had been a nurse for a few years."

He turned facing Bud. "She saved CC's life that night. The baby was stillborn. Ever since that night CC hasn't been the same. She seems to be getting worse with time. Sometimes she talks about the baby like we never lost it. I think that's her way of coping with everything."

Mary Jo put her arm on Roy's shoulder. "I'm so sorry for both of you. Is there anything that I can do to help?"

"I don't want you guys to think she's crazy or anything like that. She's just got a lot of things to still work out in her mind. CC is one of the most loving and thoughtful people you'll ever know. Just give her a little time is the best you can do for her. Thanks for asking if you could help. I think you and CC would get along great." He wiped a tear from the corner of his eye.

"Would it be alright if I did introduce myself? I won't stay long if she doesn't want me to." Mary Jo was almost pleading.

"Sure you can talk to her. She might even enjoy it. I just didn't want you to think she was dangerous or anything like that." They all walked inside with Roy bringing up the rear.

Mary Jo went over and kneeled in front of CC's chair. She spoke softly, "Hi CC, I'm your new neighbor. My name is Mary Jo and this is my husband Bud." Bud nodded his head.

Mary Jo looked at Bud then back at CC, "I was hoping we could become friends. I would love another female to visit with. I hope we can do that real soon. We'll be leaving now so just let me know when you want to visit." Mary Jo stood and both she and Bud started for the door.

"Mary Jo,. Mary Jo." CC was looking over at them as she spoke.

"Yes CC, Mary Jo is my name. I would love to talk with you if you aren't too tired." Mary Jo motioned for Roy and Bud to leave them alone.

Bud invited Roy back to his place to give the girls some privacy. Roy hesitated for a minute than agreed to leave.

When Bud got to the door he looked back at Roy. "They'll be fine Roy. Mary Jo is real good with people. She'll come get you if CC needs you. Probably do them both some good to talk." Bud walked out and started for his and Mary Jo's new home. Roy walked slowly after him, glancing back at his own bungalow.

Bud tried to imagine what Roy must be feeling. "I'd offer you a cold beer but I don't have any. I know we both could use one right now." That brought a smile to Roy's face and made Bud feel more at ease.

"So you're a mechanic huh? They're installing a lot of machinery here. Maybe you'll get to do something other than be board stiff like the rest of us." Roy was more relaxed about leaving CC.

The four of them visited through lunch and much of the day. Mary Jo with CC and Bud with Roy. The girls came back to Bud and Mary Jo's bungalow when Mary Jo saw CC was getting more nervous being away from her husband.

When the girls came in Roy knew CC needed a nap. She looked tired. He didn't want to her push it. CC hadn't been alone with anyone other than Roy for any length of time since her breakdown.

Bud couldn't wait to continue his conversation with Roy. He kept himself busy looking for listening devises in the bungalow, but couldn't find any.

Following her nap, Roy and CC showed up at bud and Mary Jo's door just before the dinner bell sounded.

They entered the dining hall and grabbed a small table away from the guard behind the glass wall. Another boring trip through the food lines. Another round of small talk. The four of them finished as soon as they could so they could drop off the ever-dangerous silverware. Once again they were outside where they could talk more freely.

They stopped first at Bud and Mary Jo's, but CC wanted to go home. Mary Jo also excused herself and went next-door to visit with her new neighbor. Mary Jo still didn't talk much to CC, but she knew Bud felt freer to talk with Roy without anyone else around.

"Tell me a little about Paradise Roy. It sounds like you've been here awhile and probably know all there is about this place." Bud wanted to learn all he could about the layout of Paradise and still needed to make sure Roy was on the level. He felt he could trust Roy, yet the last few days had been filled with too many surprises. Both he and Mary Jo didn't need any more things going wrong.

Roy's face took on a saddened expression. He sat back in his chair and looked directly into Bud's eyes. Bud for a moment felt he was being looked over for his sincerity also. Instead of feeling threatened, it actually made him feel better. Bud's ideas about people and the world in general had suffered a severe blow in the last few days. The only thing he felt good about, and was thankful for, was he and Mary Jo still had each other and had been kept together.

Roy began speaking without looking away from Bud's face, "CC and I have been here a little over nine weeks. It seems more like a year. We were on our way to Reno for one last trip before the baby would take up all of our time. One last selfish fling I had to talk CC into!" Roy turned his face away hiding the pain and hurt he was felling.

The events of the last few months had taken a toll on Roy. He couldn't remember ever crying since he was a young boy before he landed here. He had to fight the urge more now that Bud was around. Bud had to see he was strong enough to fight these bastards when the time came.

Roy felt in his bones the two of them were thinking along the same lines. This was definitely a temporary situation, regardless of how many stupid videos they had to sit through.

Bud didn't say a word as he saw Roy struggling to keep himself together. His own sense of pride knew just how Roy was feeling. He wondered how long it would be before he started to break down. Bud just sat there as if nothing was going on and waited for Roy to continue. Just another thought to keep his anger at these people alive.

After a few seconds Roy felt able to speak, "Along the way we stopped at an out of the way motel. You know so we would have more money to gamble with once we got to Reno. We met some guys in the lounge that night that really seemed to know a lot about gambling. They asked us back to their room to give us some pointers."

Roy paused. "Like damn greedy fools we accepted. Next thing we know we wind up here without so much as a penny. I still can't believe anyone would slip a mickey to an obviously pregnant woman like that. I don't think taking us alive was their first thought."

Roy stared off as if he was re-living that night wishing he hadn't been so damn greedy and selfish.

"Most of the people here got pretty much the same story. Some were loaded with cash, others had only a few bucks. We all were using less traveled roads instead of the interstates and we were all a lot more trusting than we are now. The one thing we all have in common is we're all of childbearing age. The people running this show really believe in that bullshit film they show everyone. You and your wife did see the wonderful plan they have for us didn't you?"

Bud shook his head. "Yes, first thing this morning. On an empty stomach to boot." They both got a big laugh out of that. "Go on though Roy, tell me more about this place and the others being kept here."

Roy continued, "We're smack in the middle of nowhere. After CC and I had been here a week, two of the other men and myself decided to break out of here and get some help.

CC wasn't getting any better and I figured the only chance for her to recover was away from this place." Roy glanced over at his own bungalow wondering how CC was doing. This was the longest they had been apart since his escape attempt.

He regained his thoughts and continued, "We planned everything so well. We dug under the back fence a little bit each day. Back by the children's play area at the end of the housing. One of the guys has a little girl, so we would all pretend to just be playing with her. Two of us would be pushing her in the swing while the other one 'rested' near the fence.

He looked off and continued, "We spent two days digging the hole and covered it with some old tires they had for the kids to play in. We all got out OK. That part was really easy. We slowly circled around to the road leading in and out of this place. About a half a mile down the road we ran into a problem we hadn't counted on. The road branched into five different directions. We figured it might split somewhere but in five directions was insane. That explains why everyone here arrives blindfolded."

There was frustration in Roy's voice now, "That's where our plan fell apart. We all took a different route and promised the first one out would search for the others after he had found help. We wished each other luck and headed off in three different directions. The road I took went around in a big circle. I knew I was walking in a curve but had no idea how much of one. After a couple of hours out there I wound up back here, less than a half mile from the entrance. They were waiting for me by the gates and drove to pick me up."

Roy paused for a few seconds. "While I was out there one of the guards had decided to check on CC. He didn't believe her when she said I had just gone visiting some of the other people in the compound. That's when all hell broke loose. They searched the whole place and found out all three of us were missing. What a time for the guards to develop a conscious."

"I guess they didn't think anyone would be so stupid as to go out in the hot desert on foot. The last few days here have been a little milder but it gets pretty unbearable outside on some days. The trees help, but it's still a desert."

Roy turned his attention to the desert, "I know the others didn't make it out either. At first I really wanted to believe they did but we were hotheaded and foolish. They would have been here with help by now. Toby sent out a van to look for them, but they came back empty. If they are still alive, they're so lost by now they probably are wishing they weren't. As punishment they locked me up for a week in the holding cell you two stayed in last night. They wouldn't tell me how CC was doing or anything."

Roy wiped a tear from his cheek that had finally managed to fall. "I think we should continue this tomorrow Bud. I don't feel good about leaving CC for this long." Roy was already headed out the door. Bud knew it hurt Roy thinking about the others. He knew Roy was feeling guilty in some unjustified way for surviving. Hell, he'd feel the same way if it were him.

Bud followed him to the door. "I'm sorry for making you think about all that's happened Roy."

As Roy started to leave Bud touched his shoulder and said,"I do want to hear more tomorrow though, if that's all right with you. What you guys tried took a lot of guts. I hope all my questions haven't upset you too much."

Roy shook his head slowly. "Don't worry. It's not your fault I'm getting emotional. It's just frustrating to get that far and fail. You would have really liked those guys. They were stand up men. I'll never forgive the people running this place for what's happened. Never!"

Roy was pacing in a small circle outside of his bungalow. "The guard from the cafeteria was the worst at taunting me while I was apart from CC. He was the guard stationed down by the children's area while we dug our escape hole. Since then they moved the guard tower closer to the playground."

Roy was getting his courage back. "I'd love to be alone with him outside of here for a few minutes." They both entered the bungalow in silence.

Mary Jo was a little relieved to see them come through the door. C.C. was very nice, but it had been mostly a one-sided conversation. Mary Jo was selective about her words and had run out of small talk. She was ready to go back to the cottage and relax.

"Well CC I guess I have to be going. Our husbands have returned. I enjoyed the visit. Hope we can talk again soon." Mary Jo could tell by Roy's face that it was time to leave.

CC turned to where Mary Jo and Bud were standing. "I enjoyed the visit also. I don't have many friends and talking with another girl has been nice. I'm sure if Roy and your husband are working together we'll see each other again."

"Working together?," Roy and Bud said at the same time looking at Mary Jo. She just shook her head no. It just seemed easier to tell CC that at the time, besides they were sort of working together.

Roy was so happy to see his wife talking to someone it didn't really matter what she made up about how they met. He turned to Mary Jo and thanked her. He had taken her hand and was shaking it up and down so fast and hard as he spoke her head was bouncing. Once he realized what was happening he let go and they all laughed.

Mary Jo and Bud left on that happy note. Roy's face once again took on a happy glow as it had when he was being cynical earlier.

It was dark within minutes after Bud and Mary Jo reached their place. The day had seemed long and they undressed for bed. The soft glow from the kerosene lamp next to the bed made the perfect setting for cuddling. As they lay in each other's arms they exchanged the information they had learned from Roy and CC.

They both agreed Roy and CC were only prisoners like they were. Eventually they were going to have to trust someone beside themselves a little. It felt good not to be alone in this nightmare. Mary Jo was happy to have CC to talk with, even though she mind wondered off to happier times while they talked. Perhaps CC would come out of this better than the rest of them.

Mary Jo started to think of home for the first time since they had arrived at Paradise. Visiting with CC had allowed her to let down her guard enough to enjoy a small part of today.

They lay quietly, staring at the ceiling. Finally Mary Jo turned to face Bud. "What do you think our families know about us disappearing? I don't think my Mama could handle news like that very well. She was so happy when we left I couldn't stand to see her hurting now. I know she's probably wondering why we didn't call to say we arrived in Las Vegas safely. Now I know why parents always ask for a call when you're going someplace away."

"Mary Jo don't start getting upset about things we don't know for sure. We don't even know if they know we're missing yet. If you remember we told everyone we know not to even think about bugging us on our honeymoon. I just hope right now that they don't suspect a thing."

Bud slowly stoked Mary Jo's face. "It's just one more thing to worry about and I think we got enough on our minds already. Your Mom might think we're having so much fun that we have forgotten all about home for now. I hope we can work something out quickly to be free from this place and these people, and then be able to tell everyone about this whole weird story in person."

Bud put his arm around Mary Jo and she snuggled against his side."It's nice to know if things don't work out we've got people who will come looking for us. You know country folk when they get riled up." His voice changed to a ridiculous country bumpkin accent. "Why lordy, little lady, they're likely to do anything! They ain't got no learnin' or morals." They both laughed out loud at his big city folk description of how all folks who live outside city limits live.

They lay in each others arms enjoying the good thoughts they had just remembered.

After Mary Jo had fallen asleep in his arms Bud turned out the lamp. He thought about their families and their life outside of here. He thought of the Chevy. A chill ran down his spine just thinking his pride-and-joy was in the hands of those creeps, the ones that started the whole mess they were in. They were going to pay for what was happening to them. This was a promise Bud made to himself, every single one of them!

He stared for a time at his wife's peaceful face and drew some calm from it. He fell asleep thinking he knew exactly what Roy had meant about feeling like a failure. They were supposed to protect their wives. Perhaps together they could change this situation. Working together they might just succeed.

CHAPTER 7

A noise from inside the diner had Donald out of bed in two seconds. His head and body felt like they weighed a ton.

The last thing he needed was to have to confront someone who had broken into Wanda's, especially in his boxer shorts.

Donald flew through the backroom door with only a broom in his hand for a weapon. He almost got the person too, until he realized it was Wanda laughing her head off at the sight of him.

"My, my, Donald. I've heard about people who hate to get up but this isn't at all how I pictured them acting." Wanda turned her head, half out of courtesy and half so she could continue her laughter.

Embarrassed, Donald slid into the backroom before he spoke. "What are you doing here so early Wanda? I thought there was a prowler out there."

There was slight pause while he put his pants on. He was still waiting for an answer.

Wanda took a deep breath, "Donald it's almost time to open. I was trying to get the coffee started quietly." She paused to stifle another laugh, "I'm sorry for surprising you like that. I'm delighted to see the interest you've taken in this place though."

As Donald re-entered the room he said, "You're lucky I didn't have a gun. And by the way, you can stop laughing now."

Donald put his hands on his hips in mock anger, " I was tossing and turning most of the night. So needless to say I feel bad enough this morning without feeling like a total jerk."

That did it, they both broke into laughter. All the frustrations of the last few days had finally mounted up until they couldn't keep them in any longer. They were laughing hysterically. After a few minutes they were able to control themselves.

Donald left the room to finish dressing. When he returned they both had their composure back. At least he hoped they both had!

The coffee was ready so he sat down to drink the cup Wanda had sat on the counter for him.

Donald slowly blew on the coffee, then took a short sip. "I'm going to be gone most of the day. I need to get started looking for some clues to where they have taken Bud and Mary Jo. Right now they could be anywhere."

With the cup in his hands, Donald put his elbows on the counter, held the cup up to his nose and slowly sniffed the contents.

He turned his head toward Wanda, "Have you heard anything from your friends?"

All the laughter was gone from Wanda's face. "I haven't heard about anything out of the ordinary from anyone I've called yet. I'll make some more calls today during the slow times."

Wanda turned and started arranging things on the counter. "All we can do Donald is continue to pray for their safe return."

She walked from behind the counter to finish setting the table. "I've got a few more things I have to do around here. Help yourself to more coffee while I get ready for customers."

Wanda began refilling the napkin holders and ketchup bottles that sat on the counters."

Donald sat staring into his cup. So much doubt had crept into his mind last night.

Yesterday seeing Halloway again made Donald feel like he could do anything. He had felt twenty years old again. This morning the euphoria of yesterday was gone. He felt so helpless and old.

Last night he dreamed that Bud and Mary Jo were being held far away from here. That Lou and Rick weren't as dumb as they had seemed. They were only buying time for the rest of the kidnappers. Donald didn't dare tell Wanda about his dream.

He slammed his fist against the counter lightly and went to get the ice for the soda cooler and get somw extra water glasses. Today he would bring three bags of ice out. He had no idea when he'd be returning this evening.

When he finished stocking the ice, he went back to the counter to finish his coffee. "Wanda I'll be leaving now. I'll call you later to see if there's any word from your friends." He leaned and kissed her cheek.

Wanda walked to the end of the counter and pulled a bag out from under it for him.

"I packed a lunch for you to take. There's some soda and water in there too so you won't die of thirst."

Wand's face softened slightly, "Please be careful Donald. Those people sound like they'd stop at nothing to get what they want. Promise me you won't try to be a hero. I couldn't bear it if you got hurt." They gave each other a loving hug.

"I promise Wanda. No Lone Ranger heroics. The way I felt this morning I couldn't have taken on a gnat and won. Today is just for looking. I promise!"

Donald grabbed the lunch bag and headed out to his car feeling a little more hopeful than he had when he first woke up. Wanda had a calming effect on him.

Donald knew the police were investigating things around the motel where Rick and Lou had been staying. If Donald started looking around there they would guess he was more than just an observer. He couldn't risk them knowing he was taking things into his own hands.

So far Donald had escaped being charged with anything and didn't want to push his luck.

He was so absorbed in thought he didn't even realize he had reached his car. He unlocked and opened the door. As he settled into the drivers seat he set the lunchbag on the passengers seat.

Donald had to be sure no one learned of Halloway or his men's involvement in this. Donald had explained to Wanda that Halloway and some of his buddies had some leave coming. They had to remain anonymous while they were here. The government frowned on any involvement with a crime on the outside. Wanda understood and would remain silent.

Once he started the engine, Donald rolled down the window to let some of the heat out. Having no air conditioning was a killer. He decided to head south. He knew that's where all this trouble began. Maybe someone would remember seeing them or at least the Chevy. Donald took a deep breath and guided the car onto the highway.

Wanda watched from the window until he was out of sight. She sensed Donald's feeling of hopelessness and was trying to fight off her own. She turned the sign on the door to OPEN, flipped on the outside neon light, and immediately went to the phone. She had made a list of everyone she could think of to call. Some of these people she hadn't chatted with in months. Some she hadn't talked with in over a year.

She knew one thing for sure, she would be up to date on all the local gossip after today.

As Donald headed south to the Route 93 turnoff, he scoured the roadsides for any clues. He had never really paid much attention to the desert around here before. So much of it looked the same that you just took it for granted.

He made the turn slowly onto Route 93 without paying attention to traffic and was narrowly missed by a semi truck. Donald, shaken a bit, checked his rear view mirror and saw it was now safe to go slow enough to scan the roadside.

Today he was noticing every piece of trash that didn't belong. He wondered how so many beer cans, spray painted rocks and truck tire pieces had escaped his attention before. Once you did notice all the junk, it was scattered everywhere along the side of the road. People were pigs. He kept his eyes on the emergency pull-off hoping to see signs of a scuffle. He only hoped Bud hadn't put up too much of a fight.

Occasionally Donald would pull off the pavement to check out the areas where he could tell that more than one car had left the road. He glanced at his watch after one such stop. He had been at this for a couple of hours now.

He was getting hungry and grabbed the sack lunch Wanda had made him. When he had finished eating the sandwich he slumped down next to his car and began throwing stones at the soda bottles someone had left behind. He stopped when another truck passed and shook the car and him.

Donald dusted himself off and started on his way again. The truck had given him an idea. He knew that there was a gas station up ahead. He prayed they had needed gas. At least it would tell him how far they had gotten. That thought made him forget completely about the roadside trash that he had found so interesting earlier. A few miles up the road might be some answers.

Donald took the turnoff and was heading up the hill leading to the station. Driving into the station he saw the only other customer was the semi that had snapped him back into action.

Donald told the attendant to fill it up and walked over to the driver at the diesel pumps. Two chances that someone might have seen the Chevy was more than he hoped for driving into the station.

"Howdy. I'm looking for some friends that seem to have gotten lost out here. You drive this route regularly?" Donald was trying to sound just a little concerned.

The man removed the nozzle and set it into the pump then turned to face Donald. He just stood there a minute as if he wasn't buying what Donald was saying. "Yeah, I run this route regularly. What do you mean by your friends might'a got lost?" His eyes stared through Donald.

"I was expecting some friends a few days ago. They were driving in a classic green '57 Chevy. When they didn't show up I thought they might have broken down. Like I said it's been a couple of days and I haven't heard anything, so I'm a little worried. You didn't happen to see a Chevy like that broken down did you?"

The driver walked over to Donald instead of shouting his answer. "I'm only along this way every four days. I'd of remembered a classic like that if I had seen one. Used to have one myself years ago. Sorry I can't be anymore help. I can't imagine somebody being lost on this stretch of road for that long. Maybe they had a change of plans. You're probably worried for nothing."

The driver turned to pay the attendant and hopped up in his rig. Before pulling out he turned to speak to Donald again. "I'll keep my eyes open just in case. Hope you hear from them soon. See you around." He started the truck's engine and pulled away.

Donald repeated his story to the gas station attendant. He was working a few days ago but hadn't seen the Chevy or anyone that looked like the people Donald described.

Donald paid for the gas and sadly headed for his car. He noticed a few phone booths off to the side of the station. The same phone booth used by the kidnappers. He walked over to one and called Wanda. She answered after only two rings. "Wanda's Diner, how can I help you?" You could hear the tension in her voice.

"Hello Wanda. It's Donald. I'm out on Route 93 and wanted to see if you had heard anything from your friends?"

Wanda started talking fast and excited, "Not a thing yet Donald. Your friend called to say he and his buddies would be here for sure in three days. They needed the extra day to get everything together. It's been slow here today so I've been able to call almost everyone I know."

She hesitated before asking, "I take it you haven't been able to find out anything new either?" Wanda wanted so badly to have some good news for him when he called. At least his friends would be able to help.

"I stopped to ask around at the Shell station here on 93 south. No one remembers seeing them or the Chevy. That's great news about Halloway though. I'm going to keep poking around for awhile longer. I should see you in a few hours unless I find something. See you later Wanda, goodbye."

Donald walked slowly back to his car and started the engine and headed back for Route 93. He headed south again and returned his focus to the roadside scenery.

After a few miles, Donald felt a wave of total hopelessness sweep over him, just cruising' the highway for clues. He turned and took the next exit and headed back the down the highway the way he had come.

The "High and Dry" bar was the last place the Chevy had been. Donald was going to head back there and see if anyone had information about Rick or Lou. Maybe he'd get lucky and that Joe guy they had mentioned would be there.

Police, or no police, the only lead he had was the stretch of road he had covered following Lou and Rick. He had to retrace all of their steps if he was going to piece anything together. If the cops noticed him he'd just say he was checking to see if they had any new information.

Donald passed the exit to Mr. Hall's plane repair. He had forgotten all about Mr. Hall. He didn't want to just show up asking a lot of questions. He would call from Wanda's as soon as he got back. Maybe he had seen something on the way to work that morning.

Donald decided to drive by the diner and check again with Wanda before heading to the "High and Dry" bar to ask questions. He knew a place like that would be the last place to volunteer any information. It was still worth a try. He just hoped he wasn't headed for an old fashion bar fight. He felt better about going out there with someone knowing where he was headed.

Wanda was busy at the register with her last customer when the phone rang. She ran across the room and answered after only the third ring. "Hello, Wanda here."

She thought it was Donald again. "Wanda, this is Ben Johnson. I don't know if what I have to say will be of any help to you or not. After talking to you last night I gathered you wanted to know about anything even a little strange happening around here."

"Ben, stop apologizing and tell me what you got?" Wanda's heart was pounding.

"Well after we hung up last night I remembered something a friend had told me a few weeks ago. He works in a propane station over in Highland off Route 93. We were visiting on the phone when two men pulled into the station to refill their propane tanks. My friend told me these guys come into town twice a month and fill 10 medium tanks." Wanda's heart started racing.

" My friend thought it was odd they needed so much fuel so he asked a few questions. They told him they live with their wives out here somewhere. We both thought it's a little strange for two families to be going through that much propane, especially this time of year. He told me they always pick up some things for babies at the same time. You know diapers and such. They said they got three kids between them. The more I thought about it the stranger it seemed. Do you think seven people could use that much gas in a month?"

Wanda tried to contain herself. "Ben, I think this is just the type of information I'm looking for. Can you find out when the last time these guys refilled their tanks?"

"Already checked on that this morning. I didn't want to call you in case they weren't around anymore. They were in there yesterday morning. Can you level with me why you're so curious about things out here? I know you too well Sweetie, I don't want you getting hurt!" Ben's voice showed concern.

Wanda wished with all her heart she could confide in Ben, but just one slip-up could cost people their lives.

"Ben, I'm sorry. I hope I can tell you everything soon. For right now I have to insist on this staying between us. I don't want to involve you or anyone I care about in this just yet. Please be patient a little longer. And Ben, thank you so much for calling."

"Wanda you better not be putting yourself in any danger. I'll honor your wishes for now but the first I hear about you getting yourself into trouble I'll back out of this deal. These people might be into drugs. Some new way of growing the stuff using heat or something. Take care, Wanda. For now your secret investigation is safe with me." Ben hung up filled with a thousand unanswered questions. She knew from his voice that he was really worried for her.

Wanda and Ben went back many years. They had gotten into mischief together for years as kids. They had tried dating for awhile, then Ben went off to war. He wrote her regularly and she wrote him back. They drifted apart and when the war was over Ben returned with an English bride. Wanda liked Louise and enjoyed her friendship until her death a few years back.

Wanda had left the desert briefly with a husband of her own. She and Mike didn't really have anything in common and stayed together a little over two years. Wanda wasn't a big city girl and living in Los Angeles with a husband you really didn't care for wasn't for her. After the divorce Wanda returned to the desert and never remarried.

Ben still hoped they could be more than friends, but Wanda liked things just the way they were. She hated not being able to tell him everything and at the same time knew that was impossible for now. Ben had always been her good friend.

She quickly snapped back to the here and now, and couldn't wait to tell Donald she had something to report. She stared at the phone hoping it would ring.

The sound of a customer entering the diner brought her back to reality. She went over and took his order for a cup of black coffee for here, and a soda to go.

Wanda tried her best to make small talk with the gentleman at the counter but her attention kept shifting to the silent wall phone. It already seemed hours since Ben's call. Where was Donald? Why wasn't he calling? She didn't even remember the man leaving with his "to go" order.

Donald felt uneasy pulling into the lot at Wanda's. He had hoped to have some good news by the next time he saw her. His frustration was getting to him now. He felt as helpless as he had at times in "Nam" watching young men die in battles they didn't even understand.

Maybe Wanda had heard something from the police by now. That thought helped pick up his pace returning to the diner. He found himself almost running by the time that he reached Wanda's door.

He was barely inside before Wanda was pulling him into the back room. He could tell by her face something had happened.

"Donald I've just heard from an old friend and he told me about something that might be of some help." Wanda told him about what Ben had said earlier. She was talking so fast it took Donald a minute to digest what she had just told him.

"Wanda that's the best clue we've got. You said they don't know exactly where these people live but at least we know it can't be too far." Donald's mind was racing now.

How could he cover the whole area without getting the police involved? Not that he didn't respect the police. This ex-commando just felt better investigating on his own.

He sat down to think while Wanda went back to the few customers that had arrived before him. His mind suddenly thought of Mr. Hall's small planes. He could cover a lot of territory with one of those before Halloway returned.

He phoned Mr. Hall to let him know he'd be coming by to discuss something very important tomorrow morning.

Donald told Wanda he needed to go back to the "High and Dry." He would be gone for about an hour. It was late afternoon and there would be more people there now. Wanda loaned him the Jeep and told him please be careful.

As he drove to the bar Donald wished he hadn't spent so much time along the roadside. He wanted to be ready for the Colonel and his men when they arrived. As he neared the bar he felt butterflies in the pit of his stomach. The parking lot had six cars and three Harleys in it. This could get ugly fast.

When he walked inside it took a minute for his eyes to adjust to the darkness. The place was full of bikers, ex-bikers, and wanna-be bikers. As he stood there the bar got very quiet.

In the back, the two pool tables had two players each. Off to the side of them sat a single toothless man. He was in his late fifties or early sixties. He still wore a biker bandana and Harley T-shirt. The shirt hung loosely off his skinny body. He had the look of living life hard and fast.

The two front tables had a few couples in leathers seated at them. They already had a table full of empty beer bottles in front of them.

Four guys with their club name across the back of their vests were playing darts. They all turned to look at the stranger as he stood inside the door.

The bar had three more people sitting at it. At the end of the bar stood a very large, very mean looking man. Donald assumed him to be the bouncer.

Donald stepped up to the bar, nodded to the bartender and ordered a beer. When the man brought his beer Donald asked if he knew anything about Rick, Lou, or Joe?

The bartender said he didn't know any Rick, Lou, or Joe. Why was he looking for some people by those names?

All his old training kicked into high gear. The Green Beret turned as he heard someone walking toward him. He kept his back against the solid bar.

Two of the pool players came up to him and asked, "What the Hell you want with Rick and Lou?"

"I just need to talk to them about some mutual friends we have."

"What friends would that be?," they were asking.

"Bud and Mary Jo." Donald barely got the names out before one of the men came at him with a pool stick. Donald used the man's momentum to throw him into the bar and send him crashing to the floor.

The second man was smiling holding his cue stick in both hands pushing at Donald, taunting him with it.

"I forgot how much I love stick fighting. Brings back some memories of fond Nam." Donald was doing his own taunting holding the stick he had grabbed from the first attacker.

The man swung and landed a hit to Donald's left side. As he tried to retrieve the stick Donald pulled him closer to him and knocked him to the ground. He sat on top of the biker and placed the cue stick under the man's throat.

He looked up briefly to see the bouncer's face staring back at him. Much to Donald's surprise the bouncer gave him the go-ahead nod and Donald yanked the pool stick against the man's throat hard enough to knock him out.

Just as he did this the first man he hit was coming at him from the right side. Donald pulled the stick out to the right and hit him hard enough between the eyes to send him flying back to the bar out cold.

As he got up Donald felt pain every where he had been hit. He knew he couldn't show how much pain he was in. The whole bar was dead silent.

He looked at every face in the place as he turned to exit. With every step he glanced from side to side waiting for the next attack. His side where he had been hit hardest hurt with every step.

Donald had almost reached the door when he heard the first hand clap. It caused him to jump a little after the dead silence.

As he took another step the clapping got louder until everyone in the place was clapping. When he turned to look back, the toothless man who had obviously started the clapping hollered "All right man, I've wanted to kick their asses for years. Way to go buddy."

Donald smiled at him and walked out to the Jeep. Once inside the car he couldn't believe what had just happened. He started the engine and drove quickly back to Wanda's.

When he got there he walked straight to the backroom to take care of the cuts and bruises. Wanda rubbed muscle cream on his side to help with the pain and swelling. He was fine just a little roughed up. "You should have seen the other guys Wanda. I still got it in me." Donald felt pretty damn good.

Wanda needed some fresh produce and a few supplies. She would be gone for a few hours and wondered if Donald would mind closing down the diner for her.

She had gotten behind in her routine from making all the phone calls and didn't want to run out of food when their company got there.

DESERT DECEPTION

It would be no problem for Donald to close down the place. In fact it would take his mind off Bud and Mary Jo for awhile.

By the time Wanda returned Donald had everything cleaned up and put away. It took them no time to put the supplies in the storage room and boxes of produce in the cooler.

CHAPTER 8

Bud and Mary Jo spent their first night in their new "home" with a million questions going through their minds. They both slept a little better than they had in the holding cell.

Mary Jo stirred at the sound of what she thought was a rooster. Her eyes opened to find Bud's sleeping face next to hers. She nudged him to wake up.

There it was again. There was a rooster crowing. From the sound it made it couldn't be too far away.

"Bud wake up. I hear a rooster crowing and the sun's already out." She ran to the window to see where the rooster was.

Bud's eyes strained to open. "What's all the racket about?" It was obvious that last night he slept like a log. By the time he had rolled over and rubbed the sleep from his eyes Mary Jo was already up and dressed.

"Get dressed Bud. There's already a few people outside in that garden. It's seven o'clock and breakfast will be soon."

Bud grabbed some clean clothes and stumbled to the bathroom for a quick wake up shower without even answering her. The warm water felt good running off his body. The shower gave him time to think uninterrupted. He couldn't wait to continue his conversation with Roy from last night. It felt good knowing they would not be alone when they escaped from here.

When he turned off the water he heard voices coming from the other room. As he listened closer he could make out Roy's voice. Somehow Roy already made him feel better about their situation. Maybe just knowing they weren't the only fools to be caught up in this helped. Bud threw on his clothes and was towel drying his hair as he walked out.

Roy was sitting in the chair by the front window. "Howdy stranger. Just thought we might go to breakfast together. I was just telling your lovely wife I couldn't thank her enough for whatever she said to CC yesterday." If he smiled any bigger his face would crack Bud thought.

"She was more her old self last night than I've seen her in a long time. Well what do you say? Want to be seen with a low life like me?" Roy continued to smile.

"After seeing the way that guard looked at you yesterday you're probably not too far off in what they think of you." Bud snapped him with the towel and continued, "Yeah walking in with you two ought to piss them off pretty good. Sorry, Babe." Bud knew she didn't like him to talk like that when she was around. He didn't miss the fact she smiled when he said it.

"I'll be right back with CC. Don't want to keep 'em waiting." Roy had barely turned around when the meal bell rang.

The four of them were on their way. Once in the dining room everyone stopped and stared the same as the day before. This time there was no smile from the guard, only a questioning stare.

Roy loved all the attention, while it made Bud a little uneasy. If they were going to be able to break out of here they needed to start keeping a low profile.

Once they were seated he let Roy know his fears. Bud looked directly at the guard behind the glass and nodded hello. Mary Jo did the same.

Roy agreed they needed a low profile. He couldn't resist one last smart ass look at the guard. Few things brought him joy these days. He was going to miss this ritual.

The rest of the meal went without a hitch. Roy didn't even look up when he left his utensils. Bud thought he even caught a smile from the guard again for Mary Jo and CC.

Toby was approaching them and stopped directly in front of Bud. "Sorry to interrupt your meals but as I mentioned to you Bud we could use your help on some of the trucks here. Please stop by my office later and we can go over what I need you to do. Again sorry ladies for the interruption." He turned and marched away.

Back at the bungalow they needed to find out more about their new home. Roy would be more than happy to oblige.

First Bud had better go see what Toby needed before they got started. Didn't want any guards having an excuse to drop in on their conversation.

"I'll be back as soon as I can. Can my wife stay with you guys while I'm gone? I shouldn't be too long." Bud was already half way out the door.

"No problem buddy, hurry back!" Roy closed the door behind his friend..

Mary Jo offered to style CC's long blond hair for her. That would keep them busy while the men talked. She couldn't wait to find out more herself. She hoped her husband wouldn't be long.

As he walked nearing the building that was both Toby's office and home Bud felt the stares of all the guards. The man at the door was waiting for him and led him to Toby's office. The commandant was waiting for him.

"Have a seat, please. As you have seen we have a couple trucks sitting outside. One of them seems to be over-heating shortly after being started. My men can change the oil, and spark plugs, but that pretty much is it. I need you to look it over and see if you can fix the problem. What do you say?"

"Sure I'll look at it for you. Beats being bored. Let's go give it a look." As they walked out to the truck and opened the hood Bud couldn't help but notice the armed guards accompanying them all the way.

Once under the hood it took him two minutes to see the problem. The cooling fan belt was broken. Bud removed it and handed it to Toby. Toby sent one of the guards, with the broken belt, into the rec. hall basement to retrieve the part Bud needed.

They had amassed quite a collection of parts for all the vehicles and generators around this place. This only confirmed Bud's suspicion that a lot of money was behind this place.

Bud needed to remove one part to reach the belt better. Once that was done it was only a matter of minutes to replace the worn out belt.

Dirty and a little tired Bud returned to his bungalow about fifty minutes after he had left. "Honey I was getting worried," His wife said as she wrapped her arms around him.

"I'm fine. Just a little dirty. I'm going to clean up Roy, then we can have that conversation."

Feeling better now Mary Jo went back to her make over on CC.

Although CC still didn't talk much, she seemed to be listening more now. Mary Jo got some round nose scissors from the bathroom and what little bit of makeup she had left in her pockets. CC was enjoying her hair being worked with and seemed to relax for the first time.

She was actually a very pretty girl. She was a little heavy for her frame but that was understandable after being pregnant.

Mary Jo first applied a little blush to her cheeks. Next some mascara to show off those blue eyes. As she started combing her hair CC spoke, "Just a little trim. Roy likes my long hair and would be mad it I got it cut short."

Mary Jo felt like crying. This was the first time CC had started the conversation. "No problem. Bud's the same way. We'll have you so beautiful Roy won't know what to do."

"Oh he'll know what to do all right." Remarked CC.

They both laughed and soon forgot all about the men being there. They were trying out all sorts of hairstyles and decided on pulling the sides and front back to show off CC's made-up face. They hadn't even noticed the guys had gone outside to continue their talk in private.

As Roy was speaking to Bud his posture kept getting straighter and straighter. Bud hadn't noticed before just how muscular Roy was. He definitely had worked out at some time. This could come in handy should something go wrong with Bud's plans for escape.

Bud had not mentioned anything to Roy yet. He had to be safe for Mary Jo's sake. All he knew for now was he liked having Roy around. Things didn't seem totally hopeless.

"So Roy, how about the others here? Don't they care what's happening to them?"

Roy knew how Bud was feeling. "Sure, they care. Most of them don't want to be here anymore than we do. I guess I'm kind of to blame for some of them giving up. You know, the foiled escape plan?"

Roy looked around before he continued. "I'm sure if push came to shove they would help out, at least some of them. They kind of shut down a little to survive the boredom and hopelessness of this place." He was looking over Bud's shoulder when he added the last line.

Bud turned to see a brunette man looking their way. He waved to them but kept his distance. Bud waved back.

When he turned to face Roy again he could see this wasn't one of Roy's favorite people.

"That's Tom. He's no threat physically but watch what you say around him. He's the only one who really likes it here and doesn't want anyone to ruin his comfy little set up."

Roy was trying to talk very low, "He'll tell you how he's never had it so good before and we should all be grateful. He's also a snitch for Toby."

Tom went off about his business and Roy continued. "You're anxious to know all about the camp so I guess I'd better start filling you in.

There's eighteen of us here besides you and Mary Jo. Four couples, two with children, two single females, the wife and small daughter of one of the guys I left with and three single males. You already saw one of them, Tom.

There's Josh. He can be a hot head. He's already been in the holding cell twice. They told him if he doesn't calm down he might have to try his chances out in the desert after all.

The other one keeps to himself. Well, most of the time. I only talked with him once for any length of time. His name is David. He doesn't say much about himself. I can't even tell you where he's from. He's only been here two weeks." He paused, "I can tell by looking at him he hasn't accepted what's happened. I think he might have been coming off of drugs his first couple of days."

Roy glanced around again before going on. Two of the couples were headed straight for the recreation room. Two of the men had started working in the garden down the way.

"I already told you a little about Trish. She's really a dynamite person. I don't know if CC would be alive without her."

Roy glanced back to the bungalow, "She's a little older than the rest of us. You wouldn't know it to look at her. She even served as a nurse or something in Vietnam. Can you imagine being barely out of high school and seeing all that?" Roy paused and shook his head.

"The other girls keep to themselves most of the time. I think they're more scared than any of us are. You know being alone in all of this? I'm sure with as friendly as your wife is you'll know everyone in no time."

Bud's mind was racing now. He couldn't imagine how so many of them couldn't overtake this place.

"What about the guards? How many other people live here? Who is this MAN?"

"Slow down buddy. One question at a time." Roy motioned for them to sit on the front steps.

"Do you see those buildings along the fence?"

Bud looked to where Roy was pointing. "Yes. Are those where the guards live?"

"You guessed it. Five of them live here in beautiful downtown Paradise with us. Only three of them live someplace else. They've been gone a lot lately. Probably getting the final things to shut us off completely from the rest of the world. Two others come in from time to time with supplies or to relieve one of the others when God knows what comes up." Roy paused to say hello to one of the other prisoners.

After they had passed he continued. "The only one that really scares me is that jerk in the cafeteria. He took my attempt at escape personal since he was the one on guard duty when we left. He seems all too happy to be carrying that gun of his. He's all right as long as Toby's around."

"As far as the MAN goes I don't have a clue. He's got to be two things for sure, rich and crazy! Thinks he's the Messiah or something. I can't figure out if Toby's related to this Man or not. I know they go way back. I think he's a friend or something with Toby's father. Toby worships the "MAN." I think Toby grew up with this bullshit and doesn't know anything else. He lived in the woods in northern Idaho. I think his parents must have been "skinheads."

Roy nudged Bud's arm to alert him to watch what they say. He started talking about the garden now. "Yeah it isn't much now but we could really turn it into something with some hard work."

Bud caught on and looked over into the garden. There was Tom working his way closer to try and hear more of their conversation.

What a little weasel, Bud thought. He didn't even know this guy and already didn't like him.

"My wife loves to work in the garden. She'll enjoy having that to keep her busy. Speaking of wives, it's probably time to check on how they're doing." The two men rose to their feet and walked back into Bud's bungalow.

The expression on Roy's face when he walked in the room made the girls giggle.

"Do you like it Roy?" CC was asking. She looked beautiful!

"Like it? I love it! Turn around and let me take a good look." His heart was pounding from seeing his wife happier than she had been in weeks. She looked so much like her old beautiful self, before any of this had happened.

"Mary Jo you missed your calling. You definitely should be in the beauty business."

Mary Jo blushed. "With such a pretty subject I couldn't fail. She was so worried you wouldn't like it. I wish I had a camera to show your expression when you walked in." This made everyone laugh.

"I trust you two had a nice visit? We started to wonder if you would be back to see the new and improved CC." Mary Jo added.

Roy couldn't take his eyes off CC. "We sure did. I think it's time we let you guys have a little time to yourselves. Besides that I want to get C.C. home so I can have this lovely lady all to myself."

As they walked to the door CC turned and thanked Mary Jo. "I hope our husbands will be working together for a long time. I had a lot of fun today. See you later."

So what if she wasn't a hundred percent back yet. CC sure was better than the first time they had talked. Mary Jo smiled and waved goodbye. She turned to face Bud and to her pleasant surprise he had the most loving expression on his face.

"You never cease to amaze me. What you've done in two short days with that lady is something else." Bud walked over and hugged Mary Jo. "God knows how you wound up with me, but with me your going to stay." They kissed and quietly held each other.

Mary Jo was the first to break the silence. "Tell me everything you found out Bud. You guys were gone for over an hour. For awhile there I couldn't keep my mind on what I was doing. I just kept wishing I could be with you guys. Tell me Bud. Tell me!"

"Alright I'll tell you. I think we should sit down over here and talk." He was leading her away from the open window. He didn't want anyone else to hear.

Tom didn't like the fact Roy and this new fella were becoming friends at all. He didn't believe Roy's story about finally liking it here. Tom shook his head slightly. Talking about the garden. Sure they were talking about the garden. Then it suddenly dawned on him, he better let Toby know that these two seemed to be up to something and fast.

Toby was on the phone when Tom arrived. "Yes Sir I'll hold." He looked up and motioned for Tom to wait in the hall.

Tom noticed he wasn't on the regular phone. This one had a funny box attached to it. He excused himself and sat in the hall.

Toby walked over and closed the door. This made Tom slightly upset. Hadn't he proved to Toby yet that he was on their side? Oh, well no big thing. Toby would be glad he came once he told him about Roy and the new guy spending so much time talking alone.

Toby went back and sat behind his desk. When the caller finally came back on the line Toby said, "Yes Sir, I'm on the secure line. I'm sorry to be bothering you but I needed to place an order for some supplies. Everything is going well and the new couple will please you. They're very healthy and seem to be adapting well."

"You didn't get any problem from that Joe guy did you?" The familiar gravelly voice was asking.

"None Sir. He is a strange man for sure but he gave me no trouble. I'd hate to think what would happen to these people if you hadn't taken them in." Toby paused and pulled his notepad closer. "What I called for was more food. Until the whole generator project is complete we just can't seem to keep enough. Soon we can maintain a few months worth at a time, until we are able to grow enough food."

The MAN sounded pleased. "I'll have some money transferred and have the truck rolling tomorrow. Good to hear from you, Son. Keep up the good work. Goodbye."

The phone went dead before he could answer. He got up and opened the office door. "Come on in, Tom. Sorry for the wait but you caught me in the middle of an important call. How can I help you?"

As Tom spoke he couldn't help looking at the box on the phone. "I just thought you should know about something. It has to do with that trouble maker Roy and the new folks."

"Sit down. I'm listening." Toby again closed the door, which made Tom feel as important as that phone call.

Tom went on about his suspicions and how the two of them talked for awhile. The fact that two men had a long conversation wasn't strange in itself. The fact that Roy was a troublemaker made it interesting and something to keep an eye on. They agreed that Tom should keep watching them without arousing suspicion. Tom left the office feeling glad he had decided to tell Toby what he had seen.

Bud filled Mary Jo in on everything he had learned. She sat quietly for a few minutes, still absorbing it all.

Tomorrow they would all start working in the garden. From there they had a better view of the place. It might also prove handy for setting aside some food if the opportunity for escape came up. Tonight after dinner they all would be shown another film discribing the virtues of being in Paradise.

Bud and Mary Jo decided to take a little walk on their own. They headed down in the direction of the children's area, past the two rows of bungalows. They knew they were being checked out as they passed some of the other houses.

Out of the last bungalow on the left came a beautifully tanned brunette lady. She had the shape of someone who worked out regularly. Her teeth were bright white and her smile sincere.

She called out hello to them as they neared where she was standing. "My name is Trish, I don't think I've had the pleasure of an introduction yet." She was extending her hand to them.

"Hi there. I'm Mary Jo and this is my husband Bud. We're new to this place and thought we'd see a little more of our new home." Mary Jo said shaking Trish's hand.

"I'm mighty glad to meet you, Bud and Mary Jo. Won't be the longest walk you ever took but I'm sure for right now it's one of the most interesting."

With that Trish shrugged her shoulders knowing how their curiosity must be killing them right now. "Didn't mean to hold you up. I just wanted to say hi. See you around." She turned and went back inside.

They walked a few feet before talking. "She seems like a real nice person Bud and what you told me about her only confirms it. I think she and I will get along just fine."

Bud had the same gut feeling about Trish. She looked much younger than Roy said. They continued their walk another twenty yards before coming up to the fence. They stopped at least ten feet away and looked up at the guard tower that had been placed there in honor of Roy and his old friends.

The guard smiled and said hello but never took his eyes from them. This felt eerie. Both of them tried to act as natural as possible but Bud felt his wife tremble a little.

They turned left and headed for the buildings off to the side of the storage room where they spent their first night. Bud hadn't noticed the trees next to it that night, somehow they now made it appear less menacing.

Out of the doors walked Ken and Mike. They looked a little startled to see their new charges wandering around.

"Bud, Mary Jo how are you? Can we help you find what you're looking for?" Mike was trying not to show his concern for where they were walking.

"No thanks. We just felt like walking and wound up here. What is this place anyway?" Bud was asking knowing full well he was standing in front of Toby's quarters.

Just then the door opened and out walked Toby. "Well, well, it's good to see you two are up to inspecting your new surroundings. How are you finding our home so far?"

Bud started to answer but got jabbed in the ribs so hard by Mary Jo he couldn't speak.

" They're fine Mr. Toby. I especially will enjoy the garden. I've always tended to plants and think I will enjoy that the most. Everyone we've met has been very kind to us. We weren't thinking the other night when we got here but we want to thank you for saving us from that awful man." Mary Jo was squeezing Bud's hand as she talked.

Bud about threw up with that last comment but had to admit it was a good one. Judging by Toby's face he fell for it entirely.

"Well I'm glad to see you're feeling a bit more comfortable about being here. Please don't call me Mr. Toby though. Everyone here goes by first name only. See you at dinner." He turned and was off with Ken and Mike at his side.

That was weird. Toby hadn't eaten with them since his sandwich the first night. He must have eaten his other meals in his quarters.

They decided they had caused enough excitement on one walk and headed for home to wash up before dinner. The walk had done some good. For two active people, a few days in here could bore you to death.

Again they walked to dinner with Roy and CC. This time CC held her head up high showing off the new look. Along the way she even got a few courteous wolf whistles from the others.

In line the same fat cook from the morning asked who the new lady was. CC loved all the attention. Roy just stood back and gave her the spotlight. It was obvious he loved this lady very much.

The four of them sat at a small table off to the side. Before anyone began to eat, an announcement was made that Toby wished to say a few words.

Most of the others just casually glanced his way. Everyone, except Tom who stopped everything to listen to what Toby had to say. The staff listened too, for that matter.

Tom sat up straight and waited to hear every word. Bud thought it really was a pathetic sight.

Toby began by welcoming everyone. He wanted to thank them all for coming tonight. He hoped they would enjoy the evening as much as he would.

"I've spoken with the MAN today; he sends you all his love and prayers for our continuing success here in Paradise. He only wishes he could join us here but must wait for the perfect time. I want to remind all of you that a film will follow dinner tonight. No one will be excused until the film is over. Now sit back and enjoy your dinner."

The staff, and Tom, applauded. The rest of the room dug into their food.

Mary Jo became aware of a young couple in the opposite corner with a very small baby. They were sitting with Trish.

She leaned over to Roy so as not to be heard by the others. "I haven't noticed that couple before with the baby. Are they new here?"

DESERT DECEPTION

"No they've been here almost as long as CC and I have. Their baby is the first person born here. It was born a couple of weeks early. The mother doesn't get out much. It's only been two weeks since the birth."

"Once again it was Trish to the rescue. I think that's what pushed CC more into her own make believe world. I only hope it doesn't start crying or she'll notice it." They both turned away from the couple before Bud and CC wondered what they were looking at.

The room stayed pretty silent throughout the meal. Everyone was instructed to hand in his or her utensils so the movie could get underway.

The lights dimmed and there were the same smiling idiots from the first film waving hello again. This movie ran more like a documentary. It showed how through hard work and dedication everyone could achieve true Paradise. The garden was huge and had ten or twelve people busy working in it.

In another sequence some of the people were busy tending livestock. Dairy cows and chickens. This made Mary Jo remember the rooster from this morning.

Huge generators produced enough electricity to run a whole small city. Women were busy at sewing machines and large ovens. Children played in the streets.

The background was not the desert surrounding them. It made Bud uneasy to think there might be more than one of these places. God he hoped this film was staged!

The film was ending now. Another shot from land of the zombies. In bold letters it read "Remember others only dream about what is freely given to you."

On came the lights. Everyone in the room was looking at each other. Kind of a subconscious sanity check.

Roy was already to his feet. "Well let's head on home. The main feature is over." He winked at Mary Jo.

"Come on Bud I'm ready to stretch my legs after all this sitting. How about you CC.?"

Bud looked at Mary Jo trying to get even a clue of what she was up to. She shot him her best "don't ask" face.

"Maybe we can visit a little on the way home, Mary Jo." CC was walking to the door by now. "I enjoyed this afternoon so much."

"Sounds good to me too. I'm sure we'll have plenty of time to visit like that." When they were safely away from the dining hall, and that baby, Mary Jo let out a soft sigh. Thank God the baby had slept threw the entire film.

"CC I'm going to start working in the garden tomorrow. How would you like to help? We could spend a large part of the day over there."

CC's face lit up and she answered like an excited child, "I'd like that a lot. I used to be pretty good at growing flowers. I guess vegetables couldn't be too much harder."

They had reached Bud and Mary Jo's steps. CC started toward her bungalow. "See you tomorrow then. Tell Roy I've already gone in. Goodnight friend."

"I will, sweet dreams." Mary Jo smiled at the friend part and walked inside only minutes before Bud.

Bud looked around the room to see if they were alone. "Roy already explained what the rush to get out of the dining room was all about. Can you imagine having to worry about every little thing like that?"

He pounded his fist into the pillow. "These people should pay for all the damage they've done to people's lives. All of them, including the bastards who first grabbed us. Especially them!"

He needed to let some of the frustration out. Mary Jo didn't even mind his language. She knew he was holding so much in for her sake. She was proud of Bud for not having tried to take on the whole camp by now. Her husband was growing up.

It had been another long day and getting some sleep sounded good. They were settled in bed within minutes.

They kissed and ran their hands over each other's bodies. Their excitement grew until they could hold back no longer; again they made deep passionate love. When their bodies were exhausted they lay silently together, except for the pounding of their hearts and heavy breathing.

Bud was just reaching for the lamp when Mary Jo spoke, "Do you really think we can make it out of here? I mean all of us Bud."

Bud's voice had a soothing tone to it, "I'm sure of it. As sure as I am that I love you. Now go to sleep honey."

DESERT DECEPTION

Bud blew out the tiny wick and the room went dark. His wife slid her body into the curves of his legs, against his back as if they were one. She laid her arm around his chest and could feel the pounding of his heart. They laid in silence until both of them drifted off to sleep.

Chapter 9

At Wanda's Diner Donald awoke very early. It was still pitch black outside. In fact he wondered if he had slept at all. He glanced over at the alarm clock. He had a meeting with Mr. Hall in three hours.

He had gone over and over all night in his mind getting Mr. Hall to lend him a plane. The only thing he hadn't thought about was what if he said no.

Donald tried to dismiss that thought completely. Whatever it took he was getting that plane. He had become so rapt up in this nothing else mattered. Nothing!

He slipped into his pants and splashed some cold water onto his face. He was wide-awake now. He'd been so busy the night before he didn't notice that Wanda had washed all his laundry and left it folded on the dresser. She was so amazing he thought.

He wandered into the diner and without thinking was standing directly in front of the drip coffee maker. This should be pretty interesting. It had been a long time since Donald had made anything but instant coffee. To tell the truth he wasn't even good at that. Oh well, he thought. It would certainly be better than no coffee and besides he'd seen Wanda make it lots of times. Here goes nothing, he thought.

Donald slipped the coffee basket into the slot on the grinder and switched on the button. The smell of the fresh ground beans was helping to wake him up already. After everything looked about right he flipped the switch on the coffee maker and went to finish washing up. Looking in the mirror he decided today would be a good day to shave. He looked pretty scruffy to be begging for a favor from anyone.

The smell of something resembling coffee greeted him as he came out of the back. He took a small sip. A little weak but not too bad. He sat down to gather his thoughts.

Donald unfolded the road map he had taken from his glove box last night. There was a lot of area to cover, in the little time he had.

Donald knew that with every day that passed the chances of finding Bud and Mary Jo grew slimmer and slimmer. In a sense they had reached out and saved Donald and now he had to return the favor.

He thought about Bud and Mary Jo's families and how they were going to react. The police had agreed to hold off telling them anything for a few days until they had something solid to report.

"No sense worrying them over nothing," the officer had said. "You know how young folks are. They're probably going to walk in like nothing's wrong and tell everyone about the change of plans they had." Donald had sat in silence shaking his head.

Again he looked at the clock. Only five minutes had passed since the last time he had checked it. At this rate he would be crazy in probably twenty minutes. He needed to keep busy and decided to help get things ready for Wanda.

He went to the walk in cooler and grabbed three bags of ice. No telling what time he'd be returning tonight. The three bags filled the soda box nicely.

Donald filled the napkins and brought the clean silverware out to put under the counters. From the cooler he brought out two flats of eggs, and a tub of butter. These he placed next to the griddle for Wanda.

He had just poured himself another cup of coffee when the front door opened.

Wanda stood silent a minute surveying his work. "Looks like little elves have been busy in here. They must have sneaked in while you slept Donald." She let out a sigh "Yes, must have been the work of elves."

Donald smiled. "Sit down and have a cup of coffee with me. I still need to work on my coffee making a bit, but it's not the worst you'll ever have." He poured her a cup and placed it on the counter next to his.

Wanda sat down after one last look around the place. "You wouldn't be interested in teaming up with a cantankerous old broad after this is all over would you?"

She took a sip of coffee and added, "You're right about needing more practice in the coffee department though. You need a little less water next time."

Donald fought off laughing. "Wanda I'm shocked. You are anything but cantankerous, and as for being an old broad I'd smack anyone who called you that!" They both laughed.

Donald had to excuse himself to finish getting ready for his meeting with Mr. Hall. Wanda got up and started some real coffee.

Not two minutes after he left the room the bell on the front door signaled the first customer of the day. When Wanda turned she was surprised to see it was her dear old friend, Ben Johnson.

Wanda poured his coffee before speaking, "Howdy Ben, I guess I don't need to ask what brought you here?"

Ben knew she would be upset but he didn't care. He had to see that she was all right. He had to take the chance that she would be upset with him for awhile.

Ben tried his best "don't be mad at me" smile on her. She wasn't buying it. He did look cute trying though.

"I got to thinking how long it had been since I made it over here after our phone conversation. I thought, What kind of friend would let so much time pass between visits?"

He shifted knowing she wasn't going to believe any excuse he gave. "Wanda I give up, okay? I was worried; and wouldn't have felt easy until I saw for myself you were not in any trouble."

"Ben, I know you mean well but I told you I'm fine. You've known me long enough to know I can handle myself. I told you nothing's wrong. Do you think I'm too old to handle things myself anymore?"

DESERT DECEPTION

Ben started to answer just as Donald entered the room.

Wanda broke the silence first. "Ben I would like you to meet Donald. He'll be staying here awhile to help out." She knew by the look on Ben's face their previous conversation was not completely over.

Donald offered his hand, "Pleased to meet you Ben, sorry if I interrupted anything."

"Not at all, Sir. You just surprised me, coming from the backroom. I haven't seen Wanda in awhile and got the urge for some of her good cooking."

Donald could tell there was more to this than missing Wanda's cooking, but he didn't have time to play along. He had to be on his way to Mr. Hall's.

"Sorry to have to go but I've got a business meeting that I'm running late for."

Donald turned to Wanda. "I'll be back as soon as I can, Wanda, to help out. Nice to meet you Ben. I'm sure we'll see each other again before I'm on my way." Donald grabbed the roadmap and headed out the door.

Halfway to the car it hit him. Ben Johnson, Wanda's friend who told her about the propane buyers. God he hoped he was only curious and seeing if Wanda was okay. He hoped he was not going to mess things up for them. Wanda was smart; she would handle Ben's curiosity.

As Donald's car left the lot Ben looked straight at Wanda and said, "Are you going to tell me about what's going on, or do I have to become part of the fixtures around here?"

Wanda had to admit she was enjoying some of Ben's concern. He actually seemed a little jealous of Donald's staying here. That thought brought a little smile to her face.

"Ben if we didn't know each other as well as we do I'd think you were concerned about a handsome young man like Donald staying here. For your information I've known that young man for years now. He's like a son to me. He has business in the area and needed a place to stay while he's here."

"I'm enjoying the company and extra help he's given me. About the other information I was asking for, I told you I needed a good friend who would wait until I was ready to tell why I was asking about strange things. I hope your coming here and seeing business as usual has satisfied your curiosity."

Ben looked a bit embarrassed. "Wanda I'm sorry. I didn't mean to pry like some old coot. I just was worried, and have to admit I still am a little, but I see your o.k. I won't stick my nose where it's not wanted.

"Good. What do you want me to fix up for you old buddy?"

Ben smiled, "Ham and eggs with biscuits with some of your famous country gravy."

Donald was just turning into the old repair shop parking area. Mr. Hall came out to greet him with a puzzled look on his face.

"Everything okay with my checks to you? I went over things after you called and I couldn't find a problem."

Donald smiled as they entered and apologized for giving him a scare. He never thought about Mr. Hall wondering what could be so important as to bring him right back after a sales call.

" Mr. Hall I think after all this time you know me well enough to know I'm not crazy. What I'm going to tell you is going to test that theory but I can't help having to tell you anyway. I only hope after I'm through you'll agree to the importance of my being here."

They studied each other briefly before Donald continued his recounting of the last few days.

Donald spoke for close to half an hour only interrupted with a few questions here and there. Of course he could not mention the help of his good buddy and his men. Throughout his conversation he gained more and more confidence watching the expressions on Mr. Hall's face.

On a few hot summer afternoons, over an iced cold beer, they had both bragged about past flying experiences in the wars. Dave in World War II, and Donald in the Viet Nam war. They had a mutual respect for one another that had formed over the few years Donald had been servicing this area.

Once when Donald had brought an engine part out they had to "test fly" it together.

Finally the question needed to be asked. "What I've told you must of course be kept between us. I need your help in finding them. I know it's asking a lot, but I desperately need a plane to cover that much area. I'll be happy to stay on and work off the debt by helping with repairs around here. I'll pay for all fuel I use up front. Well what do you say?"

Mr. Hall shifted in his chair before answering; "First of all, I think you should call me Dave from now on. That sounds a lot better now that we'll be partners for awhile."

Donald was about to explode but let Dave finish.

Dave spoke slowly and, "If even half of what you suspect proves to be true these people need to be stopped. Don't worry about my keeping quiet, if I did tell someone they'd say I'd been out here in the sun too long and lock me up. Are you sure you'll be okay?"

"Dave, I'll be extra careful, I assure you. I'm not as young as I once was and don't have a hero complex, I swear. All I want to do is find them, and make sure they're all right. You know first hand I'm a good pilot. I won't do anything to jeopardize your plane."

Donald had to admit to himself that he would love to get his own hands on this Mr. Big or the "Man" as those two idiots had called him.

Dave walked to a board filled with keys and handed a set to Donald. " Whenever you're ready let me know."

Donald's adrenaline was pumping now. " Let me study this map a little more and I'd love to head out today if that's alright with you?"

" Anytime your ready is fine. Dave pointed to a Cessna sitting out on his small taxiway. That one's already filled up and purrs like a kitten. I've got to get on with other things before people show up for they're parts." With that he went into the backroom.

Donald debated calling Wanda with the news. He decided to wait until after his first flight. Looking at the maps he decided to focus on the areas well enough away from the military areas in the desert. Even a crazy wouldn't hold people on government land. He was losing precious flying time and couldn't stand sitting at this table any longer.

Donald walked into the backroom and didn't even have to speak. Dave was halfway to him the minute he hit the door. "Let's get started Donald. I haven't been able to concentrate on anything else since you got here." They both headed out to the hanger behind the shop. "Good luck son I hope you're successful."

The plane started right up. Donald felt better than he had in a long time. He felt right with the world. Dave flagged him past the old shed and out onto the small dirt runway. Within minutes he was off and running.

The plane's controls were loose and easy to maneuver unlike older Cessnas this one had only the best of care. After trying a few dips and turns Donald felt he knew her capabilities pretty well. He stalled the engine to coast quietly for a few seconds. It restarted without a hitch.

Donald headed East first. He was going to run in large circles starting at about ten mile intervals. His center of these circles would be the propane station. Donald would be over it in about one minute. Again he glanced at his charts although he had them about memorized.

His first ten-mile radius produced nothing. A few cars heading near the station which also served as mini market and mail depot for some people this far off the main roads.

The second pass proved more boring than the first. His spirits were going down. He opened a thermos of coffee he had packed and returned to scanning of the desert below. Occasionally through his binoculars he could actually see a hare running for cover below. Without even thinking he had made his third pass. He had planned on covering a fifty-mile radius today.

Halfway into the fourth pass he saw something and headed in closer for a better look. Not wanting to scare anyone off or get himself in trouble he had to keep some distance from the structure he was seeing below.

The first pass was too far away to see anything well enough. He did a dip and turned away acting like any other pleasure flier might have done. The second pass came from wider out and gave him a better view. Just an abandoned miners shack now taken over by a few holdout hippie types. The man and woman were as interested in his presence as he was in theirs. Donald laughed aloud wondering if they were destroying their stash of drugs right now.

Donald poured another mug of coffee and started the fifth pass. He checked the fuel level and knew he would be okay. A few more hares some abandoned cars and trucks, falling over shacks, nothing to get excited about.

The sun had just started its downward climb when he was approaching the last few miles of round five. Frustrated he turned back, not headed for Mr. Halls but the opposite direction to keep widening his search. He was becoming as obsessed man.

Into his sixth pass about seventy miles west of the propane station he saw something that at first did not seem strange. After turning his binoculars away it hit him. Trees, green trees grouped together in an area where nothing else was green. It was worth a second look. Again the dip and turn just in case. This time he came in from the East still keeping a safe distance. Peering through the binoculars he stalled the engines and coasted in closer.

There were buildings in there; some big ones and more small ones. The whole place was fenced. There was a road leading into the place and small roads off of it. He could see some movement. He couldn't see actual people, but it seemed they were moving headed for one of the larger buildings. He drifted away heading south before restarting the engine. He prayed he hadn't been noticed. Man he wished he could go in closer but that little voice inside said no.

Donald hastily marked the map and headed Southeast for home. He knew in his head and guts this had to be the place he was looking for. He goosed all the power he could out of the Cessna. The trip back went by fast. His mind thought of a million things and the plane practically flew itself. Much like a rental horse headed back to the stables.

Donald landed without a hitch. He was getting out of the cockpit when he saw Mr. Hall running toward him.

Mr. Hall heard the Cessna's engine and was ready and waiting. " I started to get a little worried. Thought you'd be back before now. Judging from your expression you found something. Come on in and tell me, son."

Donald told Mr. Hall about the cluster of buildings, and asked him if he knew of any military functions outside the territory shown on the maps. He'd never heard of any in the twenty years he'd lived here.

Donald had to get back to Wanda's. She was probably ready to call the police by now. He made arrangements to come back after this was over and pay for the fuel.

It was already sunset by the time he'd pulled into the empty parking lot. He could see Wanda had her back to him and was busy washing dishes. She turned as he walked in. A smile covered her face.

"Donald I have half a mind to yell at you for scaring me so much but the look on your face tells me it was all for the good. Sit down. I put some of the pork roast I baked today in the warmer for you." Two minutes later she was back with the food. God, did it smell good too! He had forgotten about food until he smelled this.

As he told her about the strange settlement he'd seen in the middle of nowhere, hidden by Mesquite trees. Wanda listened with the excitement of a young child first hearing about Santa Claus.

He stopped sometimes to take a bite just at a key area just to keep her guessing. He was having fun for the first time in days. This only confirmed his feelings that he had found the kidnapper's hideout. Donald had hope again.

The phone startled both of them as it rang. Wanda answered and it was Halloway. She handed the phone over to Donald

"Hey buddy, sorry for not being there already. A slight change of plans is necessary. We've been doing exercises out at the old mines out past Calico. The place is ideal for my men to train in but some of the brass at the nearby base has been getting nosey lately. I think to avoid any unnecessary snooping or jealous rivalry we are going to come up there in two shifts. My whole unit is on board. That way they won't notice all of us leaving as much. Same old bullshit with the brass except now I'm part of it. What's been happening at your end?"

Donald turned facing the diner before he continued. "I got hold of a Cessna and did some long range snooping. I think I've found what we're looking for. Out in the middle of nowhere, there's a small compound nobody around here seems to know exists. Pretty strange for an area like this where the people depend on each other so much. I need to do some more spying from the ground before I involve you or your men. I'll spend most of tomorrow trying to get a good look from the ground. I hope that doesn't ruin any plans on your end."

"Donald that's perfect. I'll be up there late tomorrow night, or early the next morning. You've got to promise me you'll be careful. Even dealing with radical groups like I do I'm still amazed at their behavior when they're threatened. I really wish I could be with you tomorrow. Don't take anything for granted, nothing." Halloway was genuinely concerned for his buddy.

"Don't worry. Someone told me years ago, that heroes usually die and good soldiers live to tell about them. I definitely want to tell about this one. Halloway I think I understand why you stayed in even with all the bullshit when we first got back. I'll have more information for us by tomorrow night. Thanks buddy." Donald hung up the phone and just stood for a minute before telling Wanda the plan.

They went about cleaning up without talking. Neither dared break the silence until they were done.

Wanda made plans to arrive early tomorrow. She couldn't bear the idea he might be gone by the time she got there.

Donald studied the maps after she left over and over again. He tried to go over a makeshift plan he had thought out. The small hill he had seen to the east was his best approach on land.

He would still need binoculars to see the place but he wouldn't be noticed from there. He would borrow Wanda's Jeep Cherokee to go the distance from the main road to the back of the hill. There was a few Joshua trees scattered between the hill and the compound. One smaller mesquite tree was closer to the one of the larger buildings he had seen, off to the other side. Maybe he would have enough cover for a closer look. This place was large for no one to know it existed. No matter what it was he would have to be very careful.

Hours had passed while he worked out different scenarios and now he needed sleep. Donald tried to shut off the flood of thoughts going through his head. While he was in Nam he did this sort of thing all the time. Back then it took him only a little while to come up with a plan. He realized how mentally out of shape he was also.

The best Donald could do now was to try to think of sleeping. Finally he dropped off into dreamland from sheer exhaustion.

Chapter 10

Mary Jo awoke to the sound of the water running in the shower. She rolled over to look at the clock and could make out 6:30 A.M.

What on earth was Bud in such a hurry about? He was definitely up to something, and sooner or later she would figure it out.

The shower went silent and two minutes later Bud was smiling down at her. "Hey babe, got to get an early start on that garden you know."

Resting on her elbows she just laughed and said she'd join him there in a few minutes.

Bud was out the door and into the garden before she got out of bed. It had been years since he truly worked a garden. As a boy he used to help his Momma with the family garden. He could tell the tomatoes, broccoli, corn, peppers, beans and swiss chard just by the leaves. Some of the herbs stumped him, and the vines could be melons or pumpkins.

He was picking off some damaged leaves when Roy tapped him on the shoulder. He about jumped out of his skin. "You son of a bitch. I can't believe you sneaked up on me that quietly. I don't recommend making a habit of that. You're lucky I didn't come up swinging.

Pleased with himself Roy said, "Good morning to you too. Do you need me to run over and grab a cup of coffee for you from the rec. hall? I see you got an early start or did you just spend the night out here?"

"What's all the commotion about over here? You two are supposed to be hard at work." Mary Jo was there just in time for Roy's last comment. "And Roy if you're going I'll take mine black."

Bud smiled and added, "Great idea, honey, I'll take a cup too, Roy." Roy headed off for the rec. hall looking like he'd been had.

Roy returned with the coffee and for awhile they all just relaxed working on the garden, sipping coffee and swapping stories. Bud and Mary Jo gave Roy a crash course on vegetable identification and culling of plants. Mary Jo almost believed her husband's interest in the garden was genuine, almost.

The time past quickly and the bell was already sounding for breakfast. After a quick stop inside to clean up, they picked up C.C. and all headed in the dining hall's direction.

The guard in the tower and Tom both were curious about their sudden interest in gardening. Tom was going to keep a close eye on them, just as he had promised Toby he would do.

After their meal, the four of them, and Trish headed over to the recreation hall to play some cards. Down at the opposite side of the room you could barely see some little kids playing with toys. Just out of sight you could hear the sound of someone playing ping pong.

This would seem like a nice resort for a week's vacation. No worries, no outside world creeping in. Knowing your life now existed of three buildings and movies from years past didn't have the same relaxing effect. The gun towers watching over you were the icing on the cake.

Trish was glad to see CC enjoying herself. She had only checked on her a few times after the miscarriage and that was to make sure she was physically okay. Aside from those check ups, losing the baby was never mentioned again. Today looking at CC she knew everything would be alright. It was great to see life in her again. Laughing and talking with the others had brought some of the natural beauty back to her face.

It was hotter today than yesterday so most of their time was spent inside between the recreation room and their "homes."

The men had come up with a plan of their own for escape. They would work in the garden for two reasons; it would be easier to watch the coming and going of people from the compound without being noticed, and when they did go for their escape they would need some food and water with them.

CC wanted to go home for awhile so the girls dropped her off on their way to Trish's bungalow at the opposite end near the children's play area and guard tower. Trish was great to talk with because she had experienced so much and seemed to know everything.

Trish offered her new friend some sun tea. The guards had picked up a box of special tea bags for her on one of their supply runs. She had made her table in the sitting area up like a little tea service cart. There was a large jar of tea, four plastic water glasses, two plastic spoons and four packets of sugar.

Trish handed Mary Jo her glass of tea. "I hope you don't like a lot of sugar, that's the hardest thing to get."

She leaned back in her chair and continued, "Mary Jo give the people here a chance at becoming your friends. They are all a little less trusting of strangers now and some are just plain old still in shock. I've been here about four months and I'm still in shock myself. My car broke down and I was hitch-hiking when this van pulled over to help. I don't remember much after that until I woke up here. Most of these folks are just like you and I. They're good people inside."

"Four months! How do you keep from going crazy?" Mary Jo asked.

"Keep busy." Trish answered shrugging her shoulders. "I jog around the buildings in the early evening to keep fit. I draw a lot, you can get paper and pencils at the craft area in the rec. hall. I visit other people during the day. When it gets hot I head over to the recreation area and play a few games or read. It's the only place you can hang out that's always kept cool. I've actually gotten pretty good at praying too.

Their ultimate plans are for us to become self sufficient and raise most of the food ourselves. They've even got some chickens here now on the opposite side of the rec. hall."

Mary Jo interrupted her. "I knew I heard A rooster yesterday. I told Bud I thought I heard one."

Trish continued, "They're building a giant generator here, wind and solar powered I think. It's under the dining area but when I jog I see them working on huge glass panels out by the fence so it must be partially underground.

One of their early morning deliveries I saw some things that looked like propellers unloaded off the truck. I haven't seen them since so they must be working on them somewhere out of sight for now. They're allowing us to just acclimate and vegetate while the generator gets up and running. I don't think they planned on this many people so soon."

While the girls were talking CC was resting. Roy and Bud had headed back to the garden. Tom was busy watering and straightening the mesh used to filter the hot desert sun from some of the plants. Bud was convinced they were sitting on some underground spring, or something to explain the large trees and ample water for a garden this size.

Tom was the first to speak. "I see you two have taken up gardening. I didn't know you cared for this, Roy. I haven't seen you here at all before today."

"Yeah I never had anyone tell me how rewarding it could be. Bud here talked to me about it. It's a great way to kill time. I'll be here a lot more from now on." Roy loved the puzzled look on Tom's face as he spoke.

Tom wasn't quite buying it. "You know everyone needs to help with the running of the camp. The sooner that happens, the better off we'll all be." Tom told the two of them that they needed some more mulch. This was kept in a pile at the opposite end of the row of small houses. Bud remembered seeing it behind them while walking the other night. They grabbed the wheelbarrow and headed off in that direction. They nodded at the girls as they passed Trish's open windows.

The lunch bell sounded as they reached the end of the buildings. The time had passed quickly between meals.

Roy was the first to notice the plane off in the distance.

Bud noticed about two seconds later. They squinted and watched as it made a big circle and dipped its wing. They thought they heard the faint sound of the plane's engine stop and start again.

"Bud, tell me you saw all that." Roy was so excited. "That's the only plane I've seen since being here! Where do you think it's from? What do you think their doing out here?"

The smile on Bud's face matched that on Roy's. "Slow down buddy. I agree that's a good sign, but they were pretty far away. Let's not go getting our hopes up too soon. If they saw anything it probably was a group of trees."

Bud pushed the wheelbarrow closer to the pile of mulch. "Let's get back with this before Tom wonders what happened to us."

They were too late for that, since Tom too had seen the plane. He had gone to the end of the building to get a rake to spread the mulch. Nosey old pilots he thought. They better stay away from here as far as he was concerned. Still maybe Toby needed to here about this new development. Tom headed straight for Toby's office.

When Ken told Toby that Tom wanted in to see him, he had a pretty good idea why. Toby had noticed the small plane circling a few minutes earlier also. He didn't pay much attention until it seemed to slow and circle. From inside his office he couldn't hear the engine stall and start again.

The knock at the door announced the arrival of Tom. Toby motioned for him to have a seat. "That will be all for now, Ken, thank you, we'll be fine.

"Toby I know you must think I'm a pain sometimes, people usually do. I saw something just before the lunch bell that I think you need to know about. As Tom described the sights the commandant had seen for himself Toby just sat back and listened in silence. When he got to the part about the engine stopping, and starting back up, he became very interested. "Tom are you sure you heard the engine stop and start back up?"

The interest on Toby's face made Tom glad he had come to him. "Well yeah, of course you could barely hear the engine anyway. I thought you needed to know. I don't want any of these old desert folks messing things up."

Toby thanked him for coming and sent Ken off with Tom. He asked Ken to see about still getting some food for him, since he had missed the lunch call.

After he was alone again in his office he began pacing back and forth wondering whether to call the "Man" or not. The plane was far

DESERT DECEPTION

enough away and there was no law against flying over the desert. If he calls and it's nothing he might think he's not capable of making decisions on his own. Then again, if he doesn't call and something does go wrong their whole plans for a perfect society will be ruined. The "Man" had been telling him lately, "Son you need to address the task at hand." That's what he'd do.

Toby decided to call in the guard at the tower closest to the plane's area. After talking with him he decided the pilot was probably too concerned about his stalled engine to have noticed anything else. Besides if some nosey neighbor did drive up to the gate he would politely remind them this was private property and ask them to leave. He'd sleep on it tonight and decide whether to call the "Man" in the morning. Tomorrow was laundry day and he'd ask the women to carefully listen for any reference to the plane.

Roy pushed the wheelbarrow up to the garden area and ran in to get CC for lunch. Trish and Mary Jo had walked back with the them and waited outside for Bud to wash up.

"When they entered the dining hall Josh made a wolf whistle sound as the girls walked passed. He was starting to bother Mary Jo with his flirting. She seemed to be running into him every time Bud wasn't around. She hadn't said anything to Bud about him. Now he was flirting in front of her husband.

Bud smiled at Josh, assuming he was trying to make CC feel good about her new look. His wife on the other hand shot Josh a dirty look. Trish caught her and wished she could ask her friend what was going on right now.

All through their meal the guys were exceptionally quiet and kept looking at each other. This was driving Mary Jo crazy because she knew Bud was keeping something from her too.

Even Trish knew something was up. If she was reading them right it was something good. She declined their offer to join them after lunch. She thought Mary Jo would burst if she had to wait any longer to ask Bud what was happening.

Trish offered to stay with CC seeing that the three others needed to be alone. Roy thanked her and hurried back to his neighbors.

Roy entered as Mary Jo was pleading, "Bud I know you too well. Tell me your big secret or I'll scream." They both told her to sit down.

"Now, honey, don't read too much into this when we tell you, and remember you can't say a word to CC. Roy doesn't want to get her hopes up and risk relapse." They explained what they had seen and just hoped the plane wasn't lost. They hoped someone was looking into what this place was right now. If the pilot saw anything they hoped it was the guard towers and barbed wire on the fences. Those would peak anyone's curiosity about this place.

As Roy walked Trish to her bungalow she couldn't keep still any longer. "Roy please be careful. I don't know what's up, but if I noticed you guys were acting different so did the others. I can't afford to lose the few real friends I have here. You guys be extra careful whatever you're up to." Roy told her not to worry they would be fine. He gave her a friendly hug and walked back to his place.

The rest of the day drifted by with everyone thinking about that plane. One little plane had caused so much excitement, and despair, by simply flying too close to the camp.

Mary Jo took a long warm shower before bed. They had closed all the windows to talk and she felt sticky and still dirty from working in the garden. The feel of the water helped clear her mind and eased her tight muscles. She let it run until it almost ran cold. She sure hoped her husband wasn't headed for a big disappointment. It was only a plane off in the distance. She shut off the shower, and towel dried her hair, as Bud brushed his teeth and got ready for bed.

Mary Jo decided to hold off telling her husband about Josh's advances. He was so excited about the plane she didn't want to ruin his good mood. Maybe Josh was just a big harmless flirt. Which ever he was she didn't want to be alone with him.

Bud came out of the bathroom and wrapped his arms around her tightly. "Not quite the honeymoon we had planned, is it Mrs. Miller? I don't know what I would be doing if I didn't have you with me right now. I love you so much sweetie!" For a minute they forgot all about where they were and lost themselves in their kiss.

As they made love all Mary Jo's doubts and fears left her. All she felt was the passion and love they shared.

Chapter 11

Donald was ready to go at the crack of dawn. He just knew in his gut he was on the right track. Wanda had filled him in on the area last night. He only had one day before Halloway would be here. There was a lot of work to get done. To avoid any suspicion Halloway would wait until the next morning to leave. For Donald it was good to have a little more time for research.

Wanda was already busy cooking bacon and eggs when he walked into the diner. "I thought you'd be getting out of here early today. I know you'll probably forget to eat later so I thought I'd better fill you up now. I gassed up the Jeep last night after I left. You should have more than enough."

Donald was pouring himself some of Wanda's real coffee. "You been here all night? You're going to fall asleep on your feet before you close today. I'll make sure you're set up before I go. I'll be on my way in a little while. Thanks, Wanda, for everything." He was already headed off to the freezer before he finished his last statement.

Wanda filled him a thermos of water and set it next to his breakfast.

"What is that wonderful smell coming from the oven?" Donald asked, returning with some ice.

"That's today's special, meatloaf and gravy. You better come home in one piece if you want any." Wanda returned to the stove and basted her masterpiece.

Donald inhaled his breakfast and headed for the door with Wanda's car keys. He turned to throw his own keys back to her. "I got the better end or this trade but if you need to go anywhere it will get you there."

He was in the jeep checking off the supplies he knew he would be needing; Mr. Hall's high powered binoculars, map, water bottle, lightweight jacket, hunting knife. In the jeep Wanda had also left a first aid kit on the seat. He hoped he wouldn't be needing that.

He had dressed in khaki pants and shirt hoping to blend in with the background of the desert. He started the Jeep and headed off in the direction of the encampment.

After adjusting the seat and mirror, he turned on the radio and settled in for the long drive. The Eagles song "Hotel California" was playing. With a grin he cranked up the volume. In the whole world there couldn't be a better song for where he was off to. Donald got a laugh when he thought what perfect timing it was to play this great classic. He still had no idea how well this song fit Paradise.

About twenty miles down the road the sun started to peak over the horizon. According to his map he could stay on route 318 for most of his trip.

From long ago Wanda knew the area that he saw the encampment in. She had forgotten about the big mesquite trees located there. One of the underground springs that snaked its way through this desert ran right under there. She hadn't realized that property had been sold since the old couple who had lived there died about five years ago. She did know about an old abandoned mining road that ran close by. It didn't show on any maps but she remembered it well from her wild and crazy days. They both hoped it was still there and hadn't been blocked off.

He drove on planning his day ahead. He had brought along some paper and pencil to try to map out everything he could see today.

After about an hour Donald was nearing where the turnoff should be. It sure was nice having the Jeep. It rode so much more comfortable

DESERT DECEPTION

than his old Fairmont. Just ahead Donald saw the milepost Wanda told him to look for, milepost 152. Who knew what they were measuring from out here. It definitely wasn't the ocean. Must be the state line.

Up just ahead on the right he saw where the road had once been. He slowed and made the turn into the now rutted sagebrush lined trail. An occasional Joshua tree branch tilted over the edge of the road, looking like they were falling over from their own weight. There were a "no trespassing" and "private use only" signs filled with holes laying on the side of the road. Victims of past target practice rampages.

It would be slow going which was fine with him since he didn't want to stir up much dust anyway. In the distance he saw the series of small hills he had seen from the plane. His whole body felt electrified.

The road came within fifteen yards of the first hill. Donald would park here to get his first look at how close he was to his target. He grabbed the binoculars and headed for the base of the hill.

He was happy to find a few tumbleweeds and a Joshua Tree as he rounded the far side. With his binoculars turned to the highest setting he still could barely see the buildings. He needed to get to the second hill.

His mind flashed back to his time in Nam. Most of his work while there had involved surveillance, staying undetected. He could walk in the opposite direction of the Jeep and stay hidden for awhile behind the second hill.

There were enough trees here to scurry from one to another for cover. He had a lot of sunlight and didn't need to rush things. He grabbed his supplies and headed for the second hill.

As he started, he was fully hidden from view. It didn't take long to lose the benefit of the hill's complete cover. Down on his belly behind some sagebrush he was trying to make it to the base of the second hill. He made his way slow and sure. Donald had seen first hand what happened to people who just rushed in. He could still see some of their faces from time to time.

As he moved from spot to spot he tried to note anything that might help conceal the rest of the men, too. He didn't know if they would have to wait for nightfall for their entry so he was trying to note each tree's location to make the surprise attack come off easier. As he crawled he kept telling himself it didn't hurt where he had been hit with the pool stick.

The approach he was taking was the only direct route. They would have to follow behind each other, which would be time consuming, or go in a little riskier all at once. The sun was high in the sky as he reached the smaller hill's base.

He would go to the eastern side to try to be in the little bit of shade the hill provided. He was glad for whatever provided water to the plants that were giving him cover. Wanda had told him there was a lot of water under the desert in areas throughout Nevada. There was even a place farther north called Thousand Springs.

He reached the hill's eastern side and he built up a good spot to spy from by adding a tumbleweed behind some well placed Joshua trees. He could sit up unnoticed here and take better notes.

When he first looked through the binoculars he noticed he wasn't really alone out there. He was being watched by a jack rabbit from the entrance of an old underground shaft in the distance. When he turned his attention to the camp he was a little shocked to see towers on the outside of a fence topped with razor wire.

This place was scarier than he thought. With the towers on the inside that told Donald that these people wanted to keep something inside, not something out. He could make out one man in each tower. The farthest one he was guessing at because he could only see occasional movement in that one. It sat on the opposite side of the compound. What the hell was this place? It looked like the old Nazi prison camps.

Donald sat for sometime without seeing anything else. Then he made out at least two other people pushing something at the end of one of the rows of the smaller buildings. He noticed while they were there the guard in the tower kept a close eye. He assumed that meant they could be friendlies.

He would love to get up to the third hill but for now needed to play it safe. Once the two people loaded up a cart they headed back the way they came. The man in the tower sat back down once they had left the immediate area.

Donald kept watching the men in the towers. The one he could see well seemed unconcerned with the desert side and only occasionally stood to watch the interior of the camp more closely These were not military trained men, that much he could tell.

Donald could only see shadows down the row the two men with the cart had come from.

Off to the right of the tower, someone caught his eye. It was a man dressed in what looked like a uniform, khaki military jacket. Khaki pants, and even from out here, shiny black boots. He was standing at the fence looking off into the desert. Donald hunched even lower as the man seemed to scan every segment intensely with his own binoculars. As Donald watched another smaller man came running up to the man by the fence. As he approached his arms would fly in the air every so often, as if he was excited about something.

Donald prayed they didn't look out in his direction while talking. That would mean he had been spotted and his mission was blown. He hoped they hadn't found the Jeep. He could not see it from his vantage point.

God, he needed to shake off this doubt and continue with his original plans. He pulled himself back together and watched as both men turned and walked slowly in the direction of one of the larger buildings.

As Donald aimed his binoculars away from them he noticed the man in the closest tower was scouring the desert with his own pair of binoculars. He didn't seem to be focusing on any one area just scanning the horizon.

All Wanda's coffee and water was taking effect and he really needed to relieve himself.

He waited until the tower guard moved his focus away, then slid backwards on his belly to the other side of the hill. From there he could see the front of the Jeep, barely peering out. He relieved himself and felt much better.

While crawling back to his vantage point he heard a faint sound, like a bell. He scurried back and within seconds saw people and shadows mixing in the row in front of the tower. They were heading toward the same large building the two men from the fence had gone to. Donald looked at his watch, 12:30, must be some kind of meal bell.

For the first time, all day, he thought about the food Wanda had packed for him. He reached over and opened the pack to find a thick roast beef sandwich crying out "Eat Me." Orange segments and apples rounded out his lunch. He sipped some more water from his bottle and watched as the guards were relieved and new guards took over.

That made at least six unfriendly and probably at least three more in the large building where the food was being served. A camp this size he would guess took at least twelve to fifteen people minimum to run it.

Donald tried to think what it must be like for people being held here. What common thread did they share? Bud and Mary Jo must be totally in shock if this is where they are. This is the United States of America for God's sake, not some third world country. That's when it hit Donald. This whole setup, this whole mess, it had to have some heavy backing. What the hell was going on? There's no way this ended here.

As he continued to watch the encampment the sun stared to shift and now provided some shadows to possibly make it to the third hill. Just a little more coverage and he would risk it.

The newer guards seemed pretty complacent to watch the row where only an occasional shadow moved now.

Halloway and his men would be arriving soon and he needed more information to pull off any rescue plan they came up with. He still had to make sure this place needed rescued. He needed to go the fifty yards or so to the third hill.

Donald put his pencil and pad in his back pocket, tucked his binoculars inside his shirt. One last look through his backpack to make sure he wouldn't need anything else. He said a little prayer and started off. He wanted to move slow enough to not stir up any dust but fast enough to not be spotted. He rested for a minute behind a Joshua tree that was about twenty yards out.

He felt clumsy and out of shape. Another ten yards, another welcomed rest stop. It seemed like an eternity to make it to the third hill. He had stayed way to the right to better avoid being seen. When he finally made it he was almost afraid to pull out the binoculars. He didn't want to be looking at someone looking back.

When he focused his binoculars it looked as if time had stood still. He swore the guard was sitting in what had to be the exact position as when Donald started.

This was a much better spot. From this vantage point he could make out most of the camp. The row in front of the towers had doors and windows like cabins. He watched a brunette woman come out of an end unit and head down the row into another unit. They must have some freedom inside the camp.

About five minutes later the brunette returned with another female that was the same size and hair color of Mary Jo. They stopped briefly, by what appeared to be a child's swing set and said something to the guard before entering the end unit again. He didn't know that it was in fact Mary Jo and Trish he was watching.

Donald stayed put for another hour just watching an occasional person walk by or the guards stand to stretch. It was time to start heading back with the information he had gathered today. Donald made the decision to turn his back to the camp and crawl out facing forward. This would get him out quicker yet it put him in greater jeopardy of being spotted without knowing it.

As little surveillance as he'd seen on this side of the camp, it was well worth the risk. Donald moved quickly from hill three to hill two, only pausing briefly to check the man in the tower. He gathered the rest of his belongings and made hill one in good time.

The Jeep started on the first try and he began backing slowly down the rutted road. He didn't want to turn around just yet so he could keep the dust to a minimum. When he was well away from the first hill he straightened out and headed for Wanda's.

Once he reached 318 he started to relax a bit. His body ached from head to toe. His arms hurt from holding the binoculars to his eyes most of the day; and the scrapes they got from pulling his body along. He leaned his head back against the headrest to try and relieve his neck.

Donald's mind was racing, trying to commit to memory, everything he had seen. Every tree, everything inside and outside the camp. He knew he had drawn it all out, but still wanted to make sure he hadn't forgotten anything. His foot was heavy on the gas pedal and he was making excellent time back to the diner.

It was a little after 7:00pm when Donald walked through the doors of Wanda's. She was just finishing up the last of the days dishes; when she dropped her towel, and ran to him, throwing her arms around him, so relieved he was okay.

"Donald I have been worried all day, even some of the customers asked if everything was okay because of how distracted I was. To top everything off a couple of the officers who arrested those thugs at the motel came by to talk to you and keep you up to date. They still haven't gotten any information out of them. Evidently they're more afraid of the guy they worked for than prison."

"I told them you had to call on a lot of your accounts to make up for the time you lost trying to help those kids. They said they'll be back by next week or you can call them if anything new comes up. I could barely have eye contact with them knowing what's going on. Tell me everything!" She was off pouring him a cup of steaming coffee as she finished her last statement.

It took him a minute to let everything she had just told him sink in. He took a sip of the coffee and started to tell her what he had learned.

"I know now we're on the right track. I saw so much from the spot you told me about. That place is creepy and they're definitely keeping people against their will. It's not a camp run by pros, or ex G.I's because these people are too sloppy. Don't get me wrong, that's a good thing."

Wanda sat on the stool next to him, anxious for the details. Donald started re-living the day, "I parked close to the first hill and was able to eventually reach the third smaller mound unnoticed. There are armed guards positioned at two sides of the place. I could make out at least two rows of what seemed to be barrack like housing."

Donald turned and placed his hand on her arm, "Wanda, I don't know if I was out in the sun too long, or just really wanted to so badly, but I think I might have seen Mary Jo"

Wanda put her hand on Donald's and a tear ran down her cheek as he continued on. "That place reminds me of a cult compound I saw in the news a few years back. People roamed free inside but weren't allowed to leave."

"I was trying to figure this place out all day and it just clicked when I said it to you. That's exactly what it reminds me of. Some off the wall cult, only with razor wire and gun towers. There were specific times to eat for everyone. It seemed as if the people in there could roam free the rest of the time. There were a few areas that seemed off limits. A couple of times the guards acted concerned and got up to watch more carefully." He was trying to recall everything.

DESERT DECEPTION

"There are some children's swings, and a play area. That really bugs me knowing there might be young kids inside there. I didn't see anyone using it but we need to assume we might run into frightened children. I remember your friend Ben's comment on the large purchases of diapers and baby formula. Wanda this whole thing is so weird no one would ever believe us. As a matter of fact I wouldn't believe someone if they told me a story like this. Thank God Halloway still trusts me. The kind of trust he and I had to have in each other in Nam doesn't ever end."

Wanda noticed Donald's arms were scratched up and red. She got up to get some antibiotic gel to rub on his forearms; and some aloe vera lotion for his sunburned face. By the time she returned he was almost asleep at the counter, finishing up some quick sketches. She gently touched the gel to his arms so she wouldn't startle him.

"Donald it's been a long day for both of us, and tomorrow will be even longer with Halloway and his men arriving. Why don't you go in and lay down so you can get some rest before they arrive. You did very well today. I certainly hope those kids will appreciate everything you're doing for them. Go on now I'll close up and get some sleep soon myself."

Donald picked up the Aloe Vera and went into his room. Two minutes later he was sound asleep.

Wanda locked the front door and sat down at the counter for a minute. She thought about everything that had been happening lately and she began to pray. "God I've never asked for anything I've wanted as badly as this, please keep that boy in there safe. He's a good person and I'm proud to be his friend. He needs all the help you can give him, and his friends. Those kids need your help too. I'm sure you're already involved in this but I'm asking for some extra attention for all of them. Thank you Lord, amen." She got up and finished cleaning. Ten minutes later she was headed home to her own bed. She was getting too damn old for this kind of stuff.

Chapter 12

Toby woke early the next morning. He decided he was just being paranoid about the pilot yesterday.. He would instruct the guards at the perimeters to keep an eye out for anything strange today. Toby was sure if the plane was looking for anyone here that it would return today.

He had to face the fact that someday a lost traveler or nosy old coot would drive right up to the gates. He just hoped for now that happens during a meal so the guards could keep the less appreciative guests inside. He and Alice would greet them as a couple and send them on their merry way. He made himself a cup of coffee and was pleased with his decision to keep this to himself.

The new gardening committee all started bright and early. All four of them. Oh yes, Tom wasn't going to miss any early morning fun.

Roy and Bud dumped the mulch and went for another load. This worked out pretty well because it gave them privacy to talk without him around.

While the two of them were gone Tom and Mary Jo had begun first spreading the mulch thick around some of the more tender plants.

"You seem to know what you're doing." He added, "Must have a garden of your own back home huh?"

Mary Jo just kept working as she answered. "Yeah, got a great garden. It's not as big as this one but it keeps me busy." She could feel him staring at her every move. This guy was creepy. Her gut told her he was bad news.

She was glad when a few of the others asked if they could help out with the gardening today. They started working down a few rows from Tom and Mary Jo.

The boredom here would kill you if you let it. This was a nicer way to spend your time, although she didn't buy it from Bud and Roy. She knew they were up to something else. Her husband loved working with his hands but a garden wasn't what he loved working on.

The two of them returned just in time. Mary Jo didn't know how much time she could spend alone with Tom before going nuts.

"Hey we see you called in some reinforcements while we were gone." They were pointing to the couple spreading mulch on another row.

"Yeah it's hard to throw a party without people crashing it anymore. Did you guys get the food and the booze?" They all couldn't believe themselves, Tom was being funny.

Saved by the bell had new meaning as the call to breakfast sounded. Time to run and wash up. Mary Jo felt like the governor had just pardoned her after being alone with Tom.

When they finished their meal and exited the dining hall they noticed women with carts outside their bungalow. "Don't worry that's just the laundry detail. They're in and out so fast you don't even notice them. Most of the support services here are out of sight." Roy forgot to tell him about them and saw the concern on Bud's face.

When Bud asked her if she wanted to work with them on the rest of the mulch, Mary Jo declined. She would rather go down with Trish and visit. Roy asked CC and she accepted the invitation. She got down on her knees and started right in spreading the mulch. She would stop occasionally to remove a leaf that was damaged.

The laundry staff was still in her bungalow when Mary Jo went in to change her clothes. They exchanged hellos and the staff asked her how she and her husband were getting along? They seemed nice enough but Mary Jo felt they were the enemy and kept her answers short and sweet.

She took her clothes into the bathroom and finished getting ready. She said goodbye and headed for her friend's place. Both the ladies agreed she seemed fine and Toby had nothing to worry about with these two.

Mary Jo smiled at Bud as she passed the garden and went to Trish's. As she passed Josh's bungalow he was standing in the doorway. "Hello beautiful, coming to see me?" Just the way he looked at her gave her the creeps. She looked back down to where Bud was and decided Trish's place was closer.

"Yeah right Josh, you know I'm happily married. Just heading to my friends place. Take care." She continued walking the whole time she answered him. When she got to Trish's she was visibly shaken.

"Come in, sit down girl. What's got you so flustered?" Trish glanced around and didn't see anyone else outside.

"Trish I don't know what to do. Josh has been coming on to me. Just now, he didn't care at all that I told him I was happily married. The guy is really creeping me out. He looks at me like he's undressing me. I can't tell Bud because he'd kick his butt and get thrown in the holding cell and I'd be alone out here with Josh. I really don't know what to do."

Trish sat down next to her friend, "I'll try talking to Josh. He's a little weirder than the rest of us so keep away as best you can. I'll come get you from now on, okay?"

Mary Jo felt a little better and remembered why she had come. She wanted to tell Trish what the boys had seen yesterday. Sharing what she was told made Mary Jo feel closer to her. She had sworn Trish to secrecy and wondered what she thought it all meant.

Trish thought about everything for a minute than replied, " It gives us all hope. Hope is a wonderful thing and we all need to hang on to it. It's something these people can't take away from us, like they did our freedom. Hope is something you have to give up yourself, and we all need to fight to keep it. Just make sure they don't do anything stupid. That plane does bring hope, but it still was just a plane flying over the desert. I pray they won't be let down."

They continued visiting and went for a walk around some of the buildings. The guards all said hellos as they passed, and Mary Jo could tell they all really liked Trish by the way they acted toward her.

Trish showed her where she saw the solar panels and where the chickens and rooster were kept. For a little while they were just two friends out for a walk, a not prisoner in God knows what camp.

Later that day Mary Jo told Bud how creepy she thought Tom was. He warned her not to trust him at all. Tom was definitely a weasel. They knew he went to Toby with everything he heard. She also shared her conversation with Trish. Not the part about Josh after her husband's comment about creepy little Tom. She agreed with Trish's view on yesterday's big event and was glad they let her confide in Trish.

Bud was glad too! He had learned so much about this place through his wife's conversations with Trish. He saw a more secure wife coming back to him; and he needed her strong if they got their chance at freedom soon.

Toby had gone unnoticed as he past them in the garden earlier. He was feeling good about his decision to handle things himself. The towers had nothing to report and some of the people had actually taken an interest in helping raise the food. Laundry detail hadn't even heard the word airplane all day. This wasn't the day he had feared at all.

Toby re-assured himself that these people would eventually realize the wonderful service the "Man" had provided for them. Those awful people that had taken them would surely have killed them all. He was certain of that. They gave him the chills every time he had to deal with them.

Bud and Mary Jo were both tired when they turned in for the night. They laid there in bed staring at the ceiling, their minds filled with too many different thoughts to sleep.

Bud almost let his wife in on Roy and his master plan, but thought better of it. Not yet, not until they had things in place.

She was holding up so well through all of this he couldn't risk pushing her over the edge worrying now. He rolled over and gave her a goodnight kiss and laid there trying his best to fall asleep. With their backs to each other and their eyes wide open, Bud thinking of his plan, and Mary Jo knowing he was keeping something from her. They laid for a time in silence, until pure exhaustion won out and they were both asleep.

Chapter 13

Halloway and his first group of men left at four hundred hours from Calico. He continued to fill them in on their mission along the way with everything he could so far. He knew his men had complete trust in him but he could sense a little surprise when he told them what Donny and Wanda thought was happening out there in the Nevada desert.

If it were anyone but Donnyboy he would have directed him to the nearest police station and probably nearest psychiatric hospital.

While the Colonel and his men continued their drive Donald awoke and he joined Wanda in the diner. She had already started preparing for the men's arrival. As usual she was outdoing herself. She was up around four a.m. herself making pies and getting a twenty-five pound turkey in one of the ovens.

The smell of the homemade custard and Dutch apple pies were driving Donald crazy. He was busy at one of the tables making copies of the map he had drawn. He couldn't risk going in and making copies in case some nosy well meaning neighbor saw them.

DESERT DECEPTION

The scratches on his arms and face had improved with the lotions he applied last night. His body was still a little sore from all the crawling he had done, and his encounter with the two bikers at the bar, but he could handle it. He found some aspirin in the bathroom and took two tablets first thing this morning.

Wanda asked if he wanted to eat now, or wait for the rest of the guys? As hungry as he was, he would wait. At least for awhile. Until all the wonderful smells coming from the kitchen drove him crazy.

A half-hour after the first squad of men left, the remaining five also started for Nevada. Whatever their Colonel's mission "Chevy" was, it was now underway. The rescue operation was now a reality. These men were pumped up. It was the first real mission two of the men had been on since joining Halloway's group. For the others it had been awhile since they were "live."

They all knew going in that this mission was covert. Halloway had gone so far as to say he would except all responsibility should things go wrong. These men didn't care about that, they had nothing but respect and total loyalty for this man. The unit's second in command, Jason, or J.P. as he was known, had been briefed the night before by the Colonel. He was busy filling in his group along the way.

The sun was just starting to peek out as they crossed the California-Nevada border. The contrast between the dark of night and brightness of the sun rising are so amazing in the vastness of the desert.

Halloway and his men were under an hour away when he called Donald. "Hey Donnyboy how's everything going your way? We're about there. Tell Wanda I'm ready for that home cooking she promised and I'm still thinking about marrying her."

Donald laughed and told his friend he'd have to fight for her.

Halloway continued, "My men are pumped and ready to help. You're going to really like this bunch Donny."

"I already do, just for helping us." Donald answered.

"Well we better be hanging up now. See ya soon buddy. I'll call back just before we arrive." His friend hung up.

Donald gave Wanda Halloway's message and she actually blushed. Donald thought how cute she looked standing there her hair pushed back from her face, flour wiped on her apron and red cheeks. She gave him a grin and went back to work.

The morning business was slow since she had opened, with only a few people having come in. Weekdays generally were slow, and today that was just fine with both of them.

Wanda started putting place settings up on two of the tables on the back side of the diner. She had promised them all a big breakfast when they arrived. She headed off into the kitchen to get prepared.

The phone rang again and Donald was surprised when he answered. It was Dave Hall wondering how things were going? He wanted to know if he could do anything to help out. He was pretty much going crazy wondering what was happening, and not being able to let on anything was up out here. Donald told him he appreciated the offer and not to worry, they were doing fine. He'd call him in a couple of days and fill him in completely.

Halloway called again to let them know both units were about fifteen minutes away. Wanda started frying up massive amounts of bacon and sausage. She brewed two more pots of coffee and placed some cut up melons and pitchers of orange juice out on the two tables. Her heart was racing and they weren't even here yet.

The two vans almost arrived at the same time. Halloway and his men were opening the door to the diner as the second van pulled into the parking lot. "Had a good tail wind Sir." Smirked the First Sergeant who had been driving the second van.

Donald greeted his buddy at the door as Wanda tried to usher them all inside.

Whitey, the First Sergeant who hollered from the second van, was the first to notice the tables set up in the back. "I'll be right here if anyone needs me. If this tastes half as good as it smells I'm in love." He threw his duffel bag on the ground near the door to Donald's room and sat down.

Halloway informed him that Wanda was already spoken for. He told the others to take a seat also. Donald was grabbing up their gear and throwing it in the backroom, out of sight in case any regular customers should come in. Wanda was busy asking everyone how they liked their eggs cooked and headed back into the kitchen.

When Donald returned the men were already helping themselves to coffee and juice. He cleared his throat to get their attention, "I can't tell you guys what having you here means to us. We got ourselves involved in a pile of shit that just keeps growing."

Every man's eyes were trained on him. "This place we're headed to is really bizarre guys, but let's eat and you can all relax a little before we go into details. Here are some quarters for the jukebox. I'm going to help our hostess, Wanda, get out the food." He slapped a few dollars worth of quarters on the counter and turned to the kitchen.

Halloway joined Wanda and Donald in the kitchen while his men fought over which songs to play. "Donny, did you get enough good information to enter this place or do you and I need to get a little more today?" He was taking a plate from Wanda as he spoke. With these guys, he knew to get his food first.

Donald answered as Wanda loaded up his hands. "I was hoping you might want to drive out there with me for a little re-con. I got a lot of details yesterday but they all involve the backside."

The two of them grabbed a seat at the counter. Donnyboy continued, "I really would feel better knowing what the front of this fortress was like. I don't know how close we can get but I'm sure between the two of us we'll see enough. It will give your guys a chance to go over the maps I drew from yesterday. Wanda would love having some company. She'll probably put all of them to work." Laughing, the two friends began to inhale their plates of food.

The rest of the men were grabbing up the sausage, bacon, eggs, hashbrowns, and cornbread as quickly as it came out of the kitchen. The sausage gravy was leaving by the pitcher.

Halloway stood to address his men. "Did I tell you this woman was the desert's best kept secret or what? Donny and I are going to leave in a bit to finish up some surveillance. You guys are to stay behind and look over some maps Donny made yesterday. You need to help this little lady clean up too, then maybe she'll feed us some more of her great cooking later." The men started cheering and thanking Wanda for the great breakfast. "Keep low key guys and do what she says. Wanda, you're in command now. Please fill these guys in on this whole situation; including your knowledge of the area. Men, you listen to this lady and follow her orders."

"Bill, stop embarrassing me in front of these men. Your men will be no problem. Get going you two." Wanda was shooing them out the door.

Halloway's men got a kick out of someone giving the Colonel orders for once. They knew better than to laugh out loud.

The Colonel grabbed up a small bag and headed out the front door.

Donald swallowed the last bite of cornbread as he headed out right behind Halloway. The two of them jumped into Wanda's Jeep and were off on their mission.

For a few minutes they were just old friends on a road trip listening to some great oldies. Donald found himself thinking of their time spent in Viet Nam. When he looked at his old friend he even washed away the years and saw the young "hell raising" Bill Halloway he had spent so many long hours with. Soon the mood returned to present day and the seriousness of this trip.

"Donny what kind of sick son of a bitch would keep people out here against their will? I mean look around. It isn't this bad for most people in jail." They have "rights" you know. Halloway was staring at the unchanging beige scenery out the Jeep's window.

"I haven't even began to think about why the place exists." Donald answered half to himself, and half to answer his friend's question.

Halloway turned facing Donald, "I spend a lot of time in the desert in Calico, but I can get away if I need to. I'm not stuck in a small space like you described. That's what prison is like. Three squares, a roof, somewhere to sleep. Most people don't come out the same as when they went in.."

"I know Bill. I've thought about what this is doing mentally to those people. We both know that most captive people shut down eventually. They either become consumed with anger, or a part of them dies inside. I just hope they've not started that process. I can still see some of the blank faces you and I liberated in Nam."

He turned and looked over at the Colonel. "What the heck do you want me to call you anyway. Do I call you Colonel, Bill or Halloway?

"You can call me anything you like. I'm just really glad we can call each other friend again. I didn't realize how much I missed a part of those days, but I did. I still see a lot of the faces too. Let's go kick some butt again!" Halloway was staring straight ahead as he spoke.

They were coming up to the road that would take them down past the entrance of this place. Or a least that's what they were hoping for.

Donald slowed the Jeep down, trying to keep the dust to a minimum. He didn't want to create any attention if he could help it.

Within a few minutes they had reached the two lane paved road that led to the driveway of the compound. They were coming off a short cut Wanda had told Donald about.

Halloway took out his binoculars and tried to see the front of the place. All he could see was a long driveway and alternate roads off it. They were going to have to chance stopping and getting a better look from the road.

Donald stopped the Jeep and raised the hood. He took out a water container to pretend they had overheated if they were noticed.

Halloway couldn't see anything but the road and maybe the glimmer of fencing off in the distance. He could see the large mesquite tree Donald said was partly hiding the largest building.

Donald reminded him of his view from Dave Hall's plane. The road had a circle in it with branches out into the desert. Weird like they planned on future roads for more development, or false starts for some reason. Donald thought he remembered three fake branches before the real continuing road to the property.

They both knew they couldn't chance another fly over if these people were being held against their will. Frustration filled both men.

The two of them went over the things Donald knew for certain. The camp, fortress, or what ever they called themselves had at least two guard towers. The person Donald observed assigned to the rear didn't seem professionally trained or much concerned about unwanted visitors.

It seemed the people being held here had somewhat free run of the place. Or at least they weren't confined to the barracks type buildings. This fact would work well for them once they got into this place. If they moved quickly and didn't have direct eye contact they could blend in for the few precious minutes they would need to overcome any resistance.

The two of them decided not to chance driving up the entrance road any further. Putting the person in charge on edge by being noticed could mean the difference between a clean mission and one with casualties. For now they're best choice was to drive to the location of Donald's re-con mission.

The soldiers and Wanda were having a great time back at the diner swapping stories. No one had come into the diner for over an hour. Wanda had some great stories about the old days in this part of the desert. She was filling the men in on the area they were going to and of course had to keep it interesting with some wild memories. Some of the men had some wild desert stories of their own and Wanda was laughing so hard her guts hurt.

Over all the laughter Wanda barely heard the phone ringing. She got up and ran for the extension in the hall by Donald's room.

By the time she answered the men were completely silent and ready for anything.

Wanda composed herself and answered, "Wanda's Diner. Wanda speaking."

"Hey Wanda, thought you might like to know some information I just received." It was Ben, Wanda's dear old friend. "Those guys who buy up all that propane and supplies placed a big order for early tomorrow morning. They were telling Jimmy, the store clerk, they were nearly finished with their own power supply and this might be the last large order they'll need. They're sending two trucks so they can get both propane and food supplies at the same time. Been so hot lately they're having someone meet them there before the place usually opens." The phone went silent for a minute, "Wanda you there?"

"I'm here Ben. I'm just still taking in everything you just told me. How the heck did you hear about all this?"

" I ran into Jimmy at the gas station today and he remembered I seemed interested in those folks. I couldn't wait to call and tell you." Ben sounded pleased with himself.

"I really appreciate your calling me, and like I promised before you'll be the first one I fill in on why I was so interested in this stuff. Thanks,Ben, you're a good friend. Got to get back to my customers now. See you in a few days." Wanda felt bad not confiding to Ben what was going on. She knew she could trust him with anything, but the fewer people involved in this the better for the kids. She prayed they were still okay.

When Wanda re-entered the room the men were all staring wide eyed at her. They had heard enough to know she had something to share with them.

"You guys are not going to believe the good fortune that just came our way." She continued to repeat Ben's call to them. As she spoke she could see all the faces in the room light up the more she filled them in.

"I don't know whether to call Donald and the Colonel or not. After his story about sneaking up on this place I don't want to draw attention to him at the wrong time." Everyone agreed it was better to wait.

Who knew they would be handed a possible Trojan Horse. The excitement level in the diner shot through the roof.

Jason told Whitey, the first sergeant nicknamed for his blond hair, to grab someone and go check out this store. Whitey asked Wanda where they were headed and how to get there. He and two other soldiers would take a look at this place. Everyone else waited for the Colonel and Donald to return. They were in their van and headed to check the place out within minutes.

The rest of the soldiers at the diner were playing out all kinds of scenarios for tomorrow. The men started putting all their equipment neatly together. A few soldiers helped Wanda with cleanup while others re-checked the equipment. The whole diner was filled with hope. It was nearing lunchtime, and the men needed to "blend in" more. They broke up into two smaller groups.

Donald had driven slowly down the dirt road. It didn't seem as far in to the first hill today. The two men got out and rounded the first hill. Donald filled Halloway in on what lay ahead. They stood talking and decided it was time to check in with base.

"Hey Wanda, it's Donald, are the boys behaving?"

"Donald get back here quickly. You and the Colonel won't believe what has happened here." Her voice was excited.

"Wanda you're scaring me now. Is everything okay? Did the police call? We're at the back of the camp and nothing's going on here. Tell me everything's okay!" Donald's voice was dead serious.

"Donald hurry back, its great news and the boys are checking things out right now! The police aren't involved but I would rather tell you two in person. I think we hit the jackpot Donald, come back here and I'll tell you everything. It's an answered prayer, I'll let you get started back, goodbye." The phone was silent.

Donald turned to Halloway who had heard the seriousness in Donny's voice and was feeling some of his own now. "Donny what the hell was all that about? What's going on?" Halloway was right in his face now.

"I really don't know. Wanda told us to hurry back that a prayer had been answered. She said some of your men are checking into it right now. Let's get the hell out of here buddy." The two of them sprinted to the Jeep. They were back on the main road in no time.

"What could have them so fired up back there? I haven't ever heard Wanda this excited. Man it would sure be nice to get a break in this mess."

The Eagles came back on the radio. Halloway cranked it up and to the beat of "life in the fast lane" as they were flying down the highway headed to the diner. They both kept their eyes open for a state trooper. That's all they needed now was to get pulled over.

As they passed another billboard pitching Senator Hudson's task force bill it brought the Colonel back his thoughts. He broke their silence, "I hope we can pull this off without a hitch. I've been so involved with Senator Hudson and his three goons lately over that task force he's forming. I really hope I can keep my unit's noses clean. He would shit if he knew what we were up to right now. I think that man is a little "off" having been raised up in the skinhead country of Idaho. Maybe that's why he's so adamant about fixing America. he's seen what these wackos can do. Anyway it's nice to have a break from all that bullshit."

As he turned to look out at the roadside he continued, "The man isn't all bad though. One of his best friends while growing up was killed in a shootout with the Feds a few years back. I guess the Senator took in his friend's young son and cares for him like he was his own. Never seen the kid; but I've heard he's never been in trouble with the law and he's supposed to be real polite. Must be off in a boarding school or something kept away from all the press he's been getting lately."

"Man I hope we pull this off for everyone's sake. Including the nutcase. Maybe you'll get an accommodation from him for ridding America of this place. Maybe he'll want the credit. Keep watching for state troopers." Donald stepped on the gas a little more.

At the Outpost food and supplies, Whitey was just pulling in front of the general store about the time Wanda was talking to Donald. He went in and walked to the back for some soda. He passed the door to the back room. It was two metal saloon style half doors. You could see over the tops into the loading dock. It wasn't very big so the two trucks would have to take turns backing up to be loaded.

If they were going to hit these trucks it would have to be at the same time unless the drivers both got out to help each other load.

While he was inside, the other Sergeant with him checked out the back of the dock area. There wasn't a lot of room to go unnoticed out there. Hopefully it would still be a little dark at 5:30, 6:00 in the morning. This was the east side of the building so luck was with them. There were the remnants of an old gas station, and a still in service garage right next to the store. The truck drivers could park one car or van next to the service garage un-noticed.

After walking around out behind the store he came and asked where the bathroom was so the clerk wouldn't be suspicious. Whitey paid for his soda and waited in the van. This seemed like it could go down really easy and that always scared him. Made him feel like he forgot to check something.

They would have to take the drivers hostage because there wasn't any good place to hide them for long. They needed all the time they could get if this place was as big an operation as Donald thought it was. The Sergeant got in and they headed back to Wanda's.

Halloway and Donny boy pulled in just as a family was walking into the diner for a late lunch. They were probably scared when the walk through the door; everyone stopped and looked at them expecting the Colonel and Donald instead. Wanda quickly made them feel welcome and was off getting their drink orders for them.

Again the door opened and in walked Donald. Both men took a seat at the counter anxious for the news. Jason took the initiative to get them alone. "Welcome back sir. Let me show you the work the men and I did out in the desert today. I have it out in the van. Would you two like to go over it now before you eat or after lunch?"

"We'd love to see it now. Come on Donald let's go look over their findings," Halloway said as he was standing and heading for the door. Wanda asked if they wanted their usual and both men nodded yes on the way out.

Once outside the diner Jason began to fill them in. Both men could not believe the gift they'd been handed. Today had seemed so hopeless on ideas for getting into the camp without being noticed and without a full on gunfight.

"Well, buddy, sounds like there's no turning back now. We just got handed a Trojan Horse and one last chance to use it." Donald was looking straight into Halloway's eyes as he spoke. "It's scary not knowing for sure that the kids are in there but you saw that place yourself. Something's going on there and it doesn't smell right at all."

Donald looked both at Jason and Halloway. "What you guys thinking? Is it a go or not? I want you to know man I'll still love ya if you change your mind. This isn't going to be an easy mission. We definitely will have to figure out as we go along who's the enemy and who are the friendlies. Both sides are going to be freaked out when we go in so I figure we'll get hit from everyone at first."

Whitey pulled into the parking lot just as Halloway and Jason were giving Donald the thumbs up. The three of them joined him on they're way back into the diner. They warned him about the family inside and would wait to talk over options once they had left. These men had one thing on their minds right now and that was filling the hole in their stomachs.

Wanda was just offering the family some of her pie for dessert as the men entered. They had to decline but promised to save room on their return trip. With that they were on their way out of the diner.

The minute they were gone the men were briefed on everything. Donald and Halloway described the camp; Wanda described the desert, and the store's layout by Whitey filled in the soldiers on everything. The diner was humming with excitement, everyone breaking into groups to get ready for the early morning mission. Donald looked around the diner and thought, God this feels good!

As the men went over their plans, they didn't even notice Wanda closing down the place early. She nearly had all the turkey and side dishes set up on the counter buffet style when Halloway and Whitey offered their help.

" I thought you guys would need to eat early and I don't think we'd be able to hide the fact something was going on here any longer if anyone else came in. I'll get this all set up for you and shut off the outside signs. Whitey you can pull the blinds shut over there and switch on the light at the end of the tables. I'm going to get out of here so you men can do your thing. There are three pies under the counter I saved for you." She was just setting up the last of the needed dishes on the counter as the room went quiet. The rest of the men had noticed the food and plates now.

"Wanda what's all this?" Donald was saying as he noticed the diner being closed down. She had already flipped over the open sign to closed. Now she was turning off the outside sign and neon sign in the window.

DESERT DECEPTION

"I was telling your friend Bill I didn't think we would go unnoticed any longer. I'm going to take off and leave you to your planning. What time do I need to be here to make some coffee and breakfast? be sure and close the window blinds for ." At that the men were all smiling. They could get real used to this type of treatment before a mission.

The Colonel had to go and blow it for them. "Wanda you show up at your regular time tomorrow. We know how to make coffee, and the breakfast part just doesn't happen before an early mission. We'll grab some toast or something. I need these guys to go back to Irwin with me. I don't think they will if you keep spoiling them. Thanks for everything!" The men were all yelling thanks as she was grabbing up her purse and jacket from behind the counter.

"Donald I trust you'll shut the place down. Lord knows you've had enough practice lately. You men take care and please stay safe. You're all like sons to me already and I couldn't bare to have you hurt." She gave them all a hug on her way out to Donald's car.

The men stopped to fill they're plates and went back to preparing for tomorrow. They would be turning in early tonight.

Chapter 14

The sun was just rising over Paradise when Mary Jo awoke. She hadn't slept well last night due to construction noises below the recreation hall. Even though the workers tried to be quiet, it seemed they had worked through the entire night. This was different than the occasional late night construction noises she had heard since arriving here.

She quietly got out of bed and dressed. She stepped outside just in time to see the first hints of bright orange and pink peek through the dark sky. Soon it was a full sky of pinks and oranges. This really is beautiful she thought. Standing there watching the sunrise, she noticed Trish coming out of her bungalow. Mary Jo made a noise to get her attention. Trish walked down and invited her on her early morning walk.

Mary Jo went in and wrote a note for Bud. She didn't want him freaking out if he woke up and she was gone.

"What's got you up so early?" whispered Trish. "I usually don't run into anyone except the hired help when I walk this early."

"I guess I just couldn't sleep. I had no idea you walked at the crack of dawn. Is it always this pretty?" Mary Jo noticed Tom straining to listen near his window as they passed. Man he really bugged her.

Trish had noticed him too, as she often did on her morning walks. She looked at Mary Jo and nodded, letting her know she'd seen the jerk too. "It's always pretty and I enjoy the quiet time to think. Not that it's ever really loud here in Paradise, but you know what I mean."

As they rounded the row of bungalows they exchanged words with the guard on duty. Mary Jo recognized him as one of the men they saw on their arrival here. He said it was nice to see she was adapting well. Adapting! More like surviving.

"Did you hear all the work going on late last night? It seemed like they never stopped until early this morning." Mary Jo made sure the little slime Tom wasn't around as she talked.

"Yeah I sure did hear them. Something's going on around here. We haven't seen much of Toby lately either. He's usually much more involved in the day to day stuff than he has been. I noticed on my walk yesterday morning, that most of the solar panels that were lying next to the other side of the rec. hall are gone. That must mean they've installed them already. I also noticed a second large truck is parked outside the compound. Must have brought in more construction supplies while we were all asleep.

When they finished their walk Bud was sitting in the doorway waiting. He too couldn't sleep anymore. The three of them went over to the rec. hall to get some early coffee and visit more, totally unaware of the rescue mission underway at Wanda's.

Trish talked more about her time in Vietnam. Her heart was in the right place. Nothing could have prepared her for the things she soon would face there.

She was still in her teens when she had joined the Red Cross as a Donut Dollie. They were supposed to help the men's moral with games and having someone from home to visit with. The little training she received before going over there really didn't cover anything she encountered very well.

Donut Dollies were not supposed to be in combat areas, but sometimes combat didn't pay attention to that rule. Many times the medics were so overburdened that the girls had to step in and help with the wounded.

Trish was in a particularly busy unit and learned quickly how to help out. Young boys were dying in front of her. Others were so messed up they wished they had died. Some stayed lost safely inside themselves. People left there, forever changed. Some both physically and mentally. The time spent in Viet Nam had made Trish interested in becoming a nurse. She really enjoyed helping people.

Bud and Mary Jo told her about they're meeting Donald and his few stories about Vietnam. Bud was convinced he wasn't part of their kidnapping.

Mary Jo couldn't bring herself to completely believe he was involved. "He had trusting eyes." But she still had some doubts. Bud interrupted "Whatever that means."

Trish would have enjoyed talking with Donald from what they shared with her. There's a kinship between people that spent any time there, an unspoken bond of some kind.

The rec. center was beginning to fill with some other early risers. Time to start watching their conversation topics and who was nearby listening.

"Morning, Tom, been in the garden yet this lovely morning?" Bud knew he hadn't been but liked yanking Tom's chain.

"Morning guys. I see you're all up early today. Where's your neighbors? I thought you two were always together now." Tom didn't wait for an answer. He was headed for some coffee and was doing a number on Bud also. Trish and Mary Jo smiled at each other. The little worm actually was being funny. Bud wasn't amused. Tom really bothered him.

Trish noticed Bud's mood and started talking about the changes she had seen around Paradise the last couple of days. She also mentioned the big difference Bud and Mary Jo's being here had caused in CC. "You two have done more for her recovery than anything Roy or I could have done. I think she's going to be okay now. There's still a ways to go for her; but she's out of the shell she escaped into after her baby's death. Maybe you were sent here for her. I know, I know, it sounds stupid but some things really do happen for a greater reason. Okay I'm done preaching, let's get out of here." Trish stood and started for the door.

The newlyweds followed closely behind Trish. Once outside Bud felt better about his little run in with Tom. He usually wouldn't let some little punk like Tom get to him, but in here this guy really bugged him. Rounding the corner Bud could see Roy coming out his bungalow door. He ran in front of the girls and joined his friend heading to the garden.

"Man, Roy, we've got to get this plan in action soon. Something's going on around here and I don't know how much longer I can pretend I'm starting to accept this place. I really don't want to lose my cool. This place brings out the worst and maybe some of the best in me." Bud went on to tell him about the morning exchange with Tom. He filled him in on Trish's latest observations also.

Roy put his hand on Bud's shoulder. "Hang on buddy we're so close to being ready to leave this place. Believe me I know how frustrating this situation can be. When CC went through everything, I just wanted to kill them all. I mean I was ready to wipe this place off the map."

Roy looked around to make sure they weren't being overheard. "If Trish hadn't step in and knocked some sense into me, I would be dead and CC would never have come back to reality. Maybe even a few other victims would have died with me. Let's work on this patch of dirt." Roy sat down and started checking the leaves making sure there weren't any bugs moving in.

As if on cue, everyone's best buddy Tom arrived in the garden. "Hey guys what's on the agenda today? The girls not interested in helping right now?" Tom settled in the row right next to the one they were working on.

Roy spoke without even looking Tom's way. "Well Tom you pretty much should be able to see what needs done by now. Just dig in. Who knows what the girls are up to? I think they might be finishing the tunnel they started last night out of this place." Tom didn't think that was funny but Bud did and he started laughing.

The girls had gone to get CC. It was about time she started getting out and walking with the two of them. Everyone they passed smiled and said hello to her. The guard they had seen earlier went out of his way to compliment CC on her looks.

Any place but here they might have actually liked the man. Not really, anyone who could work in a place like this would never be a friend on the outside.

The three men were totally involved in the culling of the garden and didn't notice Toby first walk up. "Morning men I see you're all doing a fine job getting this garden up and running."

Within one second Tom was on his feet reaching to shake Toby's hand. "Morning Sir, We sure are happy to see you out and about again. We haven't seen much of you lately, hope you've been feeling fine?" Bud and Roy were almost ready the throw up watching this pitiful exchange.

"I've been fine, Tom just a little busy lately. So many projects here are coming together at once, I really haven't had much spare time."

Toby looked right past the little weasel and addressed Bud. "Bud I could use your help again. How are you and your lovely wife finding your way here? If you two need any changes such as different clothes sizes or any special needs items please let me know. We really are not the enemies everyone first thinks we are. Can you come with me right now Bud?"

Worried about his wife he glanced down where the girls were walking and figured they'd be fine for awhile. "Sure Toby, lead the way."

" You two carry on and enjoy your gardening." Toby turned and walked off headed for the far fence and around the corner to his bungalow with Bud right beside.

Tom felt a little jealous and watched until Toby and Bud rounded the corner out of sight. "See he's really a nice guy. I think he does care about all of us no matter what the rest of you want to think." Man this guy was really pathetic was all Roy was thinking.

The girls wound up at Trish's for her special iced tea. They visited like a bunch of schoolgirls and it felt great. It was getting hot and the iced tea tasted exceptionally good right now. What Trish wouldn't give for an iced cold beer she thought as she held her cool glass against her forehead? The three of them nodded hello to Toby and Bud as they walked by. The smirk on her husband's face let her know everything was all right.

"I wonder what all the noise was last night?" asked CC after seeing Toby. "Maybe they're adding a new room or something. I heard hammering really late, even after Roy fell asleep."

Mary Jo and Trish told CC about the solar panels being off the ground and the completed work they saw done on their morning walk.

"I'd love to join you guys tomorrow morning if I could. It sounds like you really enjoyed this morning's sunrise. If it's okay I'll ask Roy if he would mind my joining you?" CC's face was filled with excitement. She was looking so much better with her shorter blonde hair combed and styled. She was wearing a little make-up this morning.

The girls were getting bored and headed for the rec. hall to watch a video. This was going to be a lazy, fun kind of day. It was beginning to get too hot to do much of anything else. Besides all of them were really enjoying each other's company. They finished their teas and left for the rec. hall.

When the ladies neared the vegetable garden Roy let out a loud wolf whistle. CC blushed, while Trish and Mary Jo just stuck their noses in the air.

"Dream on boys we're spoken for." Mary Jo yelled at the men.

CC stopped just long enough to ask Roy about walking with the girl's tomorrow morning. Roy thought it was a great idea as long as she didn't expect him to go with her. CC ran to catch up with Mary Jo and Trish.

As the girls entered the back viewing area someone had just started the old movie "Sabrina." This was one of Trish's favorites.

Sitting in the darkened room she could feel someone's hot breath on her neck, and Mary Jo turned expecting to see her husbands face. Instead it was Josh, and he kissed her cheek before she could pull away. "What the hell do you think you're doing? What is your problem? I have no feelings for you and I'm happily married." She was talking so loud everyone heard her.

"Josh just smiled at her. "You think I'm scared of your husband? I've whipped men twice his size. You think you don't want me now, but that'll change. You won't be able to help yourself. I see the way you look at me."

At this point Trish jumped in, "What the hell you think you're doing Josh? You don't have too many more chances here. Is that it, are you trying to get thrown out of here?"

Josh got up and left the building. Everyone went back to what they were doing after staring at Mary Jo for a minute.

She tried to watch the movie but the encounter with Josh kept running through her head. Her husband was not going to deal with this well at all!

Toby was back in his office going over last minute details with Ken and Mike about tomorrow's supply run. They would be replacing the two regular drivers just to make sure nothing was overlooked.

Toby was excited about the recent progress at the camp. They were actually coming in ahead of time on some of the major projects. He had Bud helping to install the solar panels and hook up one of the new generators. His mechanical skills were coming in very handy. They would finish up after tomorrow's delivery.

He dismissed the two of them and decided to fill the "Man" in on the wonderful progress they had made.

"Hello." answered the gravelly husky voice.

"Hello sir this is Toby. I couldn't wait to share some good news with you. We are ahead of schedule on our solar energy project and the remodeling of the lower food preparation area. The men will be leaving for our last large supply order tomorrow morning at 05:00 hours. When are you going to be able to see the great work that's been accomplished, here at Paradise? Any chance of a visit in the near future?" Toby was talking fast like an excited school kid.

"Well son, as you know I'm pretty busy lately. I'm very pleased to hear of the great progress there. You're doing a fine job. I'm hoping to have some free time next month after everything calms down a bit. Right now I'm too deeply involved in business matters to be able to slip away anywhere. How are new members adapting to Paradise?" The "Man" sounded truly pleased.

"There's still some resistance but they seem to be getting more acclimated every day. I think the two newest, the Millers, have been a help to the young lady who lost her baby in delivery. She seems to be talking more now and joining in on activities. I'll let you go. I know how busy you are with your new project. Take care sir, Goodbye." Toby was quite pleased with everything now.

Bud finished up the work Toby had asked him to help with, and headed back to his friend's place.

The two of them decided to call it a day and play a game of pool at the other end on the rec. hall from where the girls were. It had become too hot to stay out all day and who wanted to spend the whole day with Tom anyway. A lazy afternoon and evening was just what the doctor ordered.

The girls were finishing up watching "Sabrina" when the dinner bell sounded. All three of them wiped tears from their eyes as they got up to go.

As Mary Jo saw her husband at the other end of the room she ran into his arms.

"What's this all about babe? I was only gone an hour or so. Did you miss me that much?" Bud looked around the room and saw everyone had stopped in their tracks and were staring at the two of them.

"What's going on honey? I can tell something's very wrong."

She started to sob a little and told her husband everything. The stares, the stopping her on her way to Trish's, and the kiss.

Bud put his arms tightly around his wife and walked out of the room. Roy and the girls followed closely behind.

They immediately went into the dining hall but Josh wasn't there. It was okay; Bud would deal with him later when everyone else wasn't around. He gave his wife a kiss on the cheek and told her not to worry.

Everyone was eating dinner as usual when CC stood up and wanted to toast her new friends, Mary Jo and Bud. It made her husband feel good to see life coming back into his wife.

Something shifted Bud's thoughts to the Chevy. He suddenly was overwhelmed with sadness. That car was such a part of him, he hated to think of it being dumped and left to rust somewhere. When he got out of here, he would find the people responsible for this and make them pay. Thoughts of his car and what he had learned about Josh were really ticking him off.

His friend noticed the mood change and asked, "What's up, buddy?"

Bud let out a sigh, "I was just thinking about my Chevy I told you about. I really hate to think about her gutted and rusting somewhere. I know I could build another great car someday but she was special, real special. You and I have got to talk privately."

"Hey, guy, let's get out of here and leave the ladies alone." Roy could tell Bud needed to get his mind on something else. He was challenging him to another game of pool. Winner buys the drinks. They both wished that were true. Man an iced cold beer would go down nicely about now.

"Ladies, Bud and I have a pool game to get to so we'll be leaving you now. Come on over when you're ready to go home. See you." He grabbed Bud's arm and headed for the door.

Bud's mood change didn't go un-noticed by Mary Jo or Trish either. They both watched him as he left the building. Thank God Tom didn't get up and go after them. He was too busy kissing up to Toby who had joined them tonight at dinner.

A few games of pool and Bud had temporarily forgotten about the Chevy's fate. All he cared about now was kicking Josh's ass. And he cared a lot!

The girls showed up and the men were trying to show off for them, big time. If you didn't know better you would assume these people were out on the town having fun.

That feeling was short lived. Bud excused himself and asked Roy to make sure that his wife made it home safely. Mary Jo tried to follow but the look on her husband's face when he said "no" stopped her.

Bud sprinted over to Josh's door and threw it open. "You son of a bitch, keep away from my wife!" He was swinging at Josh as he spoke.

Josh raised his left forearm and blocked the first punch but couldn't block the second. They were going at it full force by the time the guards entered the room. Tom had run to tell them he heard fighting going on.

It took three guards to break the men apart. Both of them were bleeding from the nose. Bud's shirt was torn and Josh's tooth had been knocked loose. They were still hollering at one another.

Both men were taken in handcuffs to Toby's quarters. As they walked passed the rec. hall Bud saw his wife crying on the steps.

"Don't worry honey, I'll be all right. Stay with Roy tonight if I don't make it back home. I love you babe." He turned and walked with the guards.

"Well you two what started this brawl?" Toby was asking them.

"He's been hitting on my wife, and kissed her while I was off helping you today."

Bud turned to Josh; "This isn't over. You stay the hell away from her. She doesn't want anything to do with you."

Toby stood and walked over to the men, "Calm down both of you. I think some cool down time is needed. Ken would you take these two and lock them in the holding cells for the night? We'll figure out what needs to be done tomorrow to solve this problem. I don't want anymore trouble out of either of you tonight. Do you both understand me? None! Get them out of my sight!"

Ken grabbed Bud's handcuffs and Mike grabbed Josh's, off they went to the holding cells.

Once the guards had left the building the two men continued to taunt each other, only now they did it much quieter.

After a few minutes of silence Josh began to speak, "Hey Miller, you're a lot tougher than I thought you were. You landed a few good hits. I know your old lady's not interested. I just like stirring things up in here. They'll probably get rid of me for this one. I kind of don't care, if the alternative is spending the rest of my life here."

There was a pause before Josh continued, his tone became more serious, "and you need to be careful how much you help them get this place going. Right now their focused on building this shit hole. Once that's done they'll focus on their real plan; which is producing a new generation of people just like them. How long you think they're going to let people stay here who aren't contributing to the "Grand Plan." They didn't build this place to be a resort. I think your friend Trish has been safe so far because of her nursing skills, and I think the guards like her too. Anyway, I think on the outside we might actually have been friends."

Bud let out a "hmm." He was still breathing heavy from being so pumped up. He sat for a minute before answering trying to take in everything he just heard. "What the Hell are you doing stirring things up for me? I don't need this kind of attention. I'm still pissed off at you for hitting on my wife."

Bud got off his bed and walked closer so as not to be overheard, "Everything you just said makes sense, the sick bastards. I haven't given much thought to the future here. I've only been thinking about how we're going to get out of this damn place. Don't give up yet, Josh. I know this place changes people, it's already changing me. I'll lie off, but you better leave my wife alone, or I'll show you how much I've changed. She is off limits! We've got to work together."

Josh laughed, "I bet you would. I hope we can get past this and I can get your wife's forgiveness. Anyway I'll be backing off so don't worry. See you around, Miller." Josh's light switched off.

"See you around Josh. Don't worry about tomorrow. I think they're too busy with projects to do anything with you just yet. Goodnight." Bud's room went dark.

Bud lay there, staring at the ceiling, thinking about what Josh had said. This place was nothing more than a damn breeding camp. History re-visited, Hitler's perfect race.

Mary Jo grabbed some clothes to stay the night at Roy and CC's. She really didn't want to be around anyone but staying alone, in this place, wasn't an option. They all three talked briefly, but Roy could tell she didn't want to visit. She was too concerned about her husband.

Roy and CC got ready for bed and Roy turned off the light. Mary Jo threw a blanket on the sofa and lay down. She cried herself to sleep, hugging her pillow worrying about her husband.

Chapter 15

The men at Wanda's were up and dressed by 03:30 A.M. Donald had the men help with last nights clean up before turning in. He was making coffee and instructing them on what to pull out of the freezers and stock up for Wanda later. They even put place settings out at the counter and the tables.

There wasn't a lot of talking among the men, just mental preparation going on. The men knew their roles in the upcoming mission and now they were just eager to get started.

Donald was actually getting good at this coffee thing. The pots were being drained as soon as he got them on the counter.

Halloway gathered his men one last time to offer them an opportunity to sit this one out. He really hoped that if anything went wrong he would be able to take all the blame for their participation.

Kidnapping was a federal offense and he knew eventually that the FBI would be brought in. He hadn't come up with a real good story yet for why he and his men were involved. He was always good at thinking on his feet and hoped this time would be no exception.

No one in the unit even thought for a second about bailing out. These men were great at what they do. The only thing they were thinking was when are we going to get started?

Wanda had left her Jeep for the men knowing it would blend in more near the store. Everyone around here knew her car and wouldn't give it a second thought. Whitey was going to drive one of the vans holding the rest of the team. They would park along side the auto repair garage as if the van was left late last night for repairs this morning.

A few of the guys stepped out for their last smoke while the others used the restrooms. They started loading the gear into the van. They made sure they had duct tape and handcuffs for the soon to be prisoners. Last minute gun checks and extra ammo clips just in case they were needed. Silencers on their weapons in case they needed to fire.

They were lucky that the guards that came for the supplies wore khaki pants, or a least that's one of the things that Ben had told Wanda was weird. They weren't the casual types of khaki pant. These khaki pants seemed like some sort of uniform. Ben found it very odd they always wore them. Most young folks dress a lot lighter out here in the summer. Some hardly dressed at all.

The van was finally loaded. Medical supplies and water were put into the back of the Jeep. It was 04:00, time to roll out.

The Colonel rode with most of his squad in the van. Donald had three men with him. They were going to pull up first and make sure they weren't already at the loading dock.

As the men left the dim glow of the one light in the diner's parking lot, the desert's total blackness became apparent. The stars were so bright they lit up the sky creating a beautiful contrast.

The drive to the market only took them eighteen minutes. Donald pulled in slowly next to the repair shop. The three men with him had bent down in their seats. Once he was parked in a darker area between the shop and market the others were given the all clear.

Donald radioed the men in the van on the walkie-talkies they had set up. The van was soon pulling in on the other side of the Jeep. They tried to hide most of the van from the stores view, hoping not to involve Jimmy, the clerk. The hurry up and wait game was in motion now. Nothing to do but wait. Two of the men had gotten out of the van and positioned themselves behind the trash dumpster. It was located next to the loading dock.

One soldier, Jason, had himself in position across the street with binoculars to see what was going on in the store.

Once the trucks had arrived from the encampment Donald would enter the front of the store if it was open or enter the back. He needed to distract the clerk long enough for his team to overtake the driver. The two men next to the dumpster were there to stop any additional people should they be in the trucks. They all were hoping not to have to involve the clerk at all.

At about quarter to five the store clerk pulled up and parked in front of the building. He didn't even give the extra cars a second glance. He seemed more in a hurry to get opened before the trucks arrived. Just a few minutes after he entered the building half the interior lights were on. Now the lights over the loading dock were shining brightly.

Donald could hear his own heart beating. He wasn't scared. He was eager for the mission to begin. Within minutes he was getting his wish. Coming down the road was a cargo van and a larger delivery truck right behind it. The headlights were washing over the Jeep so the men, including Donald, stayed down as low as they could.

The cargo van pulled up to the dock first. This was exactly what the men had hoped for. It meant the driver of the van would be helping load the heavier things in the truck after he was done loading. If the larger truck loaded first it might have left for the camp.

The rolling door to the dock flew up and there stood the store clerk motioning the men inside. The larger truck parked off to the side and out came the driver to assist with the vans loading.

The men were all waiting to see if anyone else came out of the trucks. Good thing they did. A second man came out of the larger truck carrying a clipboard. They all were wearing khaki uniform pants.

Once inside the store Jimmy was looking over the order on the clipboard. He was motioning toward six stacks of product already loaded into boxes. As he and Ken, the guard from Paradise went over the invoice and checked off each stack it was rolled to the dock and loaded.

Mike the other guard and a younger man Robert were taking off the boxes. They were making shorter stacks to even out the weight and make sure the stacks wouldn't fall over in the van. As soon as there was just one stack left inside Mike walked to the back of the larger truck and rolled open the door. Inside the men could see three large propane tanks.

The propane filling station was out behind the store. Mike was backing the truck up as close as he could get safely. These tanks would be too heavy to lift on and off the trucks. This meant Halloway's men didn't have much more time. The clerk had come out back to begin filling the large tanks. While he continued with the propane the two other guards finished the loading of the van. When finished they went in and helped themselves to some of the free coffee put out for customers.

Once the tanks were full and the truck door rolled down the two men went back into the store. Mike walked over and poured himself a cup. So far so good the soldiers thought. Donald had not had to involve himself with the clerk.

The two men behind the dumpster had repositioned themselves. One of them had entered the cab of the larger truck and the other was waiting behind it.

Two other men had entered the back of the van and positioned themselves in the small isle between the stacks of boxes. Two others crouched down flat against the loading dock in front of the van.

From across the street Jason could see the men paying for the order, then approaching the back of the store. He radioed the rest of the men and let them know they were on their way out.

The three men from Paradise shook the clerk's hand and helped him pull down the rolling door. They heard a click from the inside and headed to their trucks. This time Ken and Robert headed down the steps leading to the van as Mike headed down the other side toward the truck.

Halloway's two men beside the loading dock struck simultaneously. Their hands were over the mouths and around the two guards before they knew what hit them. As they grabbed Robert and started to drag him behind the side of the van he managed to kick the side of the body.

DESERT DECEPTION

This made just enough noise to cause Mike to turn. He thought he heard muffled voices following the thump. The moment he turned to ask if everything was all right the man behind the truck lunged at him. The two of them fought until reinforcements had Mike bound and gagged.

This was just enough distraction for Robert, the younger guard to break free. He drew his gun and tried to fire. Whitey drew his gun and hit Robert in the hand, knocking his gun to the pavement.

The young guard let out a holler, which even caused Jimmy inside the store to pause and listen for a minute. Whitey had the wounded young man down with his hand over his mouth in seconds.

As Jason watched form across the street, Jimmy looked out the windows, shook his head and then started back to work.

Everyone was out of the van and Jeep within seconds. Whitey took the keys out of Ken's shirt pocket and jumped into the driver's seat of the van. Donald had helped overtake Mike and was throwing his keys to the man already positioned in the truck.

They put the three of them into the back of the army van and immediately bound their hands and feet.

Two of the men took Robert to the Jeep and cared for his wound He was then thrown in the back of the van also.

The truck and van pulled out away from the store the same direction they came from. The clerk inside hardly paid any attention to them as he started getting the store ready for business.

Jason ran back across the street and jumped into the back of the van with the prisoners. The Jeep and the Army van soon pulled out and followed the first two vehicles. About a mile up the road they had pulled to the side to re-group and get more information before driving to the compound.

The three prisoners were demanding to know what was going on. "I'm afraid you have mistaken us for someone else or just picked the wrong trucks to rob. We don't have anything of value in our trucks or any money on us." Ken was almost screaming at them showing how overwhelming this was for him. "You men have made a big mistake. We are only getting supplies for our community. We work for a very rich and important man who won't be happy if anything happens to us or his supplies."

Donald had entered the truck during Ken's plea for information. "You'll be happy to know we want nothing to do with your damn supplies or your money. What we do want is to get into that camp of yours un-noticed. You're going to give us information on how to do that. We need to know if we'll be stopping at any checkpoints on the way in or unlocking any gates ourselves. Once inside where do we drive? How many men will be at the other end?" Donald was looking directly at Ken the whole time he was talking.

Ken looked him in the eyes and said, "Go to hell!"

Donald grabbed Ken's face in his hand and turned it directly facing his own. "I've been to hell. I didn't like it much there but I learned a few good tricks while I visited. You see you little dip-shit you have two people I do care about in that camp, and three out here I don't give a damn about. One way or another I'm getting into that camp today. You can be around to hear about it or you can disappear from the face of the earth out here. I really don't care either way."

"You there," Donald was saying to Whitey trying not to use names, "Take the younger one into the Jeep. I think we need to convince this tough guy we mean business." As Whitey grabbed Robert tears started to spill out the sides of his eyes. He was almost all the way out of the van when Ken spoke again.

"You are wrong on your take of what we are doing out here. We are providing a safe, caring society free from people the likes of you. Leave the boy alone, I'll tell you what you want to know."

Donald and the drivers of the two vehicles led Ken from the truck.

While the three of them were interrogating Ken, Halloway was having a little talk of his own with Mike. "I see you're no fool by the way you have just been keeping still and watching what was going down around you. I know you have some sort of ranking at this camp because you were entrusted with this assignment. We really don't want a lot of unnecessary people hurt or killed. If what your friend said is true and you feel you're helping those people out there than you need to tell us everything so they won't become casualties. As I'm sure you have guessed we are professionals at these things. No matter what, we will enter that camp shortly. If you want to save your friends lives you need to start talking." Halloway was talking to him in a calm authoritative voice.

Mike started talking so fast he barely stopped to breathe, "Mister, we were only sent for supplies. You put way too much value on this trip. When we get back to camp we just drive in. The guard at the gate will hold it open for us. There are no secret passwords or codes. There will be two armed men as you enter camp. They are stationed in the towers on the East and West sides of Paradise. They may wave but other than that they aren't concerned with these trucks at all. We are just going to park next to the larger building once inside. We were planning on getting breakfast before the rest on the place and unloading after we ate. What are you going to do with us now?" He was staring into Halloway's eyes trying to see if his answer would be honest or not.

Halloway looked him straight back in the eyes and told him the three of them would remain in one of the vans under guard. They would be kept hostage and handed over to the authorities after this was over. "Tell me more about this Paradise? Who's in charge and where will he be when we get there?" Halloway knew time was running out and they needed to get on their way. He would keep Ken with him in the back of the larger truck.

Donald had just finished questioning Ken and the two of them; Donald and Halloway were comparing stories. Seems they got the same answers and now needed to get going and try to make up for lost time.

Donald took Ken's hooded jacket and put it on. Whitey put on Robert's and jumped into the delivery van beside him. Two other men were hidden between the supply stacks in the rear.

Halloway and three of his men climbed into the back of the propane truck keeping Ken with them. He was actually glad Jason was driving the truck. He was a crazy driver when it didn't matter and a great driver when it did. Besides that he was about the same build as Mike. From a distance he wouldn't stand out.

The rest of the men and the two prisoners would stay back in the van and jeep, driving in to camp only after the first group made it in safely.

The four vehicles started back down route 375 directly for camp. Time was catching up to them as they could see the sun starting to rise. They needed to step on it and take advantage of any darkness they could to sneak into camp less noticed.

Trish and Mary Jo both woke before sunrise for their morning walk. Leaving Trish's bungalow they noticed a different guard on duty at the tower. "Mike sick today? He's always here when we walk."

"No Ma'am, He's just running an errand he'll be back soon," answered the young guard.

The girls turned and started around the side of the buildings. Once out of the guard's sight Mary Jo broke down to her friend how worried she was about the fight last night.

Trish let her know usually after a cool off period nothing more happens. That might not be true for Josh this time because he's used up all his chances.

As Trish and Mary Jo rounded the rec. hall they noticed both of the trucks that had been brought into camp were gone. Mary Jo spoke first. "That must be where Mike has gone. He's picking up something for camp. Between the guards and Toby lately I get a bad feeling we're going to be in here a long time."

Trish answered. "Don't try to think that way because if we give up hope, they've won. Besides they don't know your husband and Roy the way we do" They both chucked at that.

Turning to walk down past the bungalows, they saw Tom heading for the garden. "For crying out loud it's still dark," remarked Mary Jo. "He must be sneaking around trying to hear something to go tell Toby."

As they past Tom they said hello and quickly headed for Trish's for some tea bags and cups so they could have early tea in the rec. hall this morning.

Donald's van stopped a little before the turn off to camp. He told the drivers of the other van and the Jeep to wait 10 minutes past the time they disappeared from view on the driveway. After that, they should enter the road and bear left at every opportunity to enter the camp.

Donald and Halloway started in. Whitey had his hood pulled up tight to cover his face completely. Jason was right behind with the men riding in the back of the truck with the propane.

As they approached the camp they saw it was bigger than it looked from the road and from the desert behind it.

The main building was a straight shot in from the fence. Off to the left of that they saw the buildings the men said were the camp leader and on site staff quarters. As they got closer they saw one of the men leaving his gun tower to come and open the front gate for them. He was waving them through and Donald returned his wave and nodded as he drove past the man. Jason followed waving and nodding also.

As they pulled in next to the recreation building and parked Donald jumped out immediately. He was headed in the direction of the hostage bungalows or as the guards had called them the "guest quarters."

Jason exited the truck cab and rolled up the back door three quarters of the way to allow the men inside to exit if they needed. He called the guard over who had opened the gate. "I could use your help over here for a minute. I'll help you with the gate in a second."

Inside the truck the men positioned themselves closer to the rear. They would try to capture this guard before anyone could become suspicious.

The guard came walking up to the back of the van. "What do you need me to do?" He asked Jason as he neared.

"Can you get up in the truck and help me lift off a few light things before Mike comes back?" Jason kept his head down and to the side.

Jason was lucky. The guard was jumping into the truck as he answered him.

Once his feet touched the truck bed he knew he was in big trouble. He tried to dive out the moment he caught sight of Halloway and his team. Jason was now right behind him. The guard tried to get one good punch in before his head hit the floor. He would have one bad headache in a few minutes. The men drug him to the front of the truck and bound and gagged him while Jason kept watch.

Whitey and Donald had been standing at the end of the row of bungalows watching to see if Jason needed any help

Donald couldn't wait any longer and stared down the row of prisoner's quarters. Jason and Whitey followed closely behind.

As Donald turned he noticed a figure bent in a garden area. He also noticed two females exiting a bungalow at the end of the row. It was starting to get brighter now. He was trying to keep his head down to keep from being discovered. He passed Tom and just nodded slightly. Whitey and Jason did the same as they passed him.

Mary Jo went back to Trish's bungalow to grab some honey they had forgotten. Trish was walking, nearing the garden area watching the exchange between the guards and Tom. Something wasn't right. She looked down at the guard's feet and noticed the familiar shiny black boots were missing. In their place were Army boots. Government issued Army boots.

Trish and Donald's eyes met. She froze for a moment as if asking are you here to help? Donald caught her looked and nodded while he held his index finger up to his lips.

At this time Tom noticed something wasn't right. He stood and asked the three of them if they were new to Paradise. When they just said huh ha he started to turn to run to Toby's quarters. He too had noticed the boot difference.

Trish nodded in Tom's direction. This caused Donald to turn and see him trying to get away just in time. Donald ran and grabbed the back of Tom's shirt. As he pulled Tom toward him he landed a punch to the side of Tom's head. That dropped him to the ground out cold.

Whitey and Jason quickly drug his limp body to the back of the garden. They tied his wrists and leaned him against the back wall in a sitting position, halfway hidden by garden supplies.

Mary Jo caught up to Trish just as Jason and Whitey were coming out of the garden area. As she looked over at them, Donald turned around and their eyes met.

"Oh my God, Donald, it's you! What are you doing here? What's going on?" Mary Jo was excited and talking loudly. Trish quickly ushered them back to her bungalow before anyone could hear Mary Jo. The three men just waved at the guard returning to the rear tower as they entered.

"Are you part of this Donald?" Mary Jo continued much quieter.

Donald winked, walked over and gave Mary Jo a big hug. "I am now. Wanda and I have been searching everywhere for you two. We'll talk later! We've got to get everyone up and out safely. Can you two help us? We have more men arriving any minute and I really don't want to have anyone hurt if possible. Mary Jo, where's Bud I need to speak to him? I promise we can catch up later." Donald was watching the guard in the tower through the window as he was talking. The man seemed uncomfortable with the situation.

DESERT DECEPTION

Jason picked up on the tension Donald was feeling. "Sir I'm going to get the Colonel and let him know what's going on. I need to let him know that friendlies are involved now."

Jason was out the door and heading for the truck. A second camp guard passed him with just a quick nod heading down the walkway going to Trish's place. He turned the corner and headed off to the leaders quarters.

As Jason passed the tower he told the guard he'd be back in a few minutes to relieve him. Jason glanced at Tom's body as he passed and felt safe leaving him where he was. He didn't want to cause the guards to become any more suspicious than they already were.

He went to the back of the truck and whispered, "Colonel you need to come with me. We have found the people we were looking for and civilians are now involved. Donald is meeting with them right now and we have one unfriendly captured and need to keep him that way."

Halloway and his men exited the rear of the truck. The Colonel made sure to keep his hood tight over his face. His large build was enough to cause someone to recognize he was someone different. They didn't need his black face alerting anyone here he didn't belong.

When the four men rounded the corner they met Donald and the girls. Donald told Halloway about Tom in the garden and two of the men lifted him upright and were walking with him between them. Mary Jo was opening the door to her bungalow with the men right behind her.

"My husband and another man were locked up last night in two holding cells beside the larger building. I don't know if all the guards here have keys to the holding cells. The two regular guards with keys aren't here now."

Donald had a big smile as she finished talking. Both he and Jason pulled the large key rings they had taken from the captive guards out of their pockets. "Would these be the keys you're talking about?"

"Oh my God lets go get him. I'll show you where they're being held!" Mary Jo was at the door as they stopped her.

"Slow down! We have to still blend in around here. Let's all just walk calmly." Donald opened the door and followed the two women.

Once inside the building the men quickly went and unlocked the cell holding Bud. Mary Jo ran in first. As the rest of them entered, Bud let out a loud "What the Hell?"

Mary Jo ran over and told him to be quiet. Donald entered the room. Bud couldn't believe his eyes. "Oh my God is it really you?" Donald gave him a slap on the shoulder and with a grin started explaining what they needed to do. First they needed to make sure Tom was properly tied up and gagged. No problem there, Bud had wanted to do that since he met the guy. In fact maybe he needed knocking out again.

Two of the men needed to head out to the two guard towers. Control of the towers was essential as the rest of the unit entered camp. The guard down by Trish's place was already acting antsy and they didn't need him calling in more help.

What they didn't realize is he already had asked the other camp guard to relieve him for a few minutes. He had told him about all of them entering Trish's bungalow. It was very rare at Paradise that any guards entered guest quarters. The original guard was now crouching down at the end of the bungalows next to the wheelbarrows. He needed to get into the empty end bungalow and plan his next step.

As Jason approached the guard, he called out, "Mike needs you to help unload the van before everyone's up and about. I'll take over your guard post for now. You better get a move on so he won't get upset. We already have had a few problems with some of the guests as you probably have noticed."

Jason kept his head down a little as he spoke so the guard wouldn't see his face.

The replacement guard was coming down the steps as he was talking to Jason. "I wondered why you guys were spending so much time inside that bungalow. The other guards were getting upset about it too. Did that troublemaker husband of hers try to start something again? I knew he was faking adjusting to this place."

Just as the guard turned to face Jason he realized this guy didn't belong here. He tried to pull his pistol but could only use it to get a few good hits in. Jason kicked the pistol out of the guards hand was put him in a chokehold. He quickly dragged him off kicking and trying to scream. Jason dragged him into Trish's place.

A few of the men down by Bud's ran down to help tie up and gag him. Jason wiped a smear of blood from his lip where the guard had connected on one of his punches.

Meanwhile Trish was trying to quietly move people into the rec. room. She made her way along the walkway trying to be as quiet as possible. "Folks we need to all go into the rec. room for a very important meeting. Please, go now. You'll have time to finish whatever you're doing before breakfast. It's very important to get over there now."

Seeing the guards running down the walkway to Trish's scared most of those who witnessed it. Of course everyone was confused, but most of them headed over to the rec. room anyway.

One of the men held at the camp saw Jason knock out the tower guard and started to run over to them. Trish stopped him in his tracks. "Trust me, Ron, when I tell you everything is alright. You know I wouldn't do anything to harm any of you here. Whatever you saw just now you need to keep to yourself and get your family into the rec. hall. Please don't ask questions just trust me on this, it's all okay." He put his hand on her shoulder, looked into her eyes and headed back the other way.

Mary Jo was inside the recreation building and was asking everyone to have a seat. "Please don't worry. We just need to have everyone here for the meeting. It won't take long and you can get back to whatever you were doing."

Trish was knocking on Roy and CC's door. Lucky for all of them Roy answered. "Roy you need to get CC over to the rec. hall and leave her with Mary Jo. Come right back here to Bud's bungalow. We are getting out of here. Don't freak out at anything or anyone you see. Hurry and you'll be filled in completely."

"Hi Trish," CC was saying as she came out of the bathroom, "Are you here for our early morning walk?"

Trish smiled, "Not this morning, CC. You need to go with Roy to see Mary Jo over at the rec. hall. See you in a few minutes."

Trish left Roy and CC's to let the three other single women know what was happening. All but one answered their door and quickly headed to the rec. hall.

Outside the window of the last bungalow, Trish called quietly to Susan, the last single female. She got no response but was pretty sure she was heard.

While this was going on one of the guards was heading from Toby's quarters to the front tower. He was lured from his post and taken at gunpoint to Bud's quarters. This happened none too soon as the men saw dust rising off the road into Paradise. At the gate stood Whitey smiling and ushering in the rest of the rescue force.

All this commotion wasn't unnoticed. One of the mess workers had watched the people filtering into the rec. hall. It was strange to see so many people going into the building this early. When he looked up at the front tower on his way to the rec. hall he noticed it was unmanned. That was reason enough to apprize Toby of the situation.

He walking faster and faster anxious to reach Toby's quarters, trying not to draw any attention to himself. One of Halloway's men noticed him just as he entered the building. He signaled to the others and two of them ran over behind him and entered the building themselves. The door the man had entered was just ahead on the left. They could hear raised voices coming from inside the room.

"Sir, I'm telling you something is going on. The guests are all gathering in the rec. hall and the front tower was unmanned. I have a bad feeling about this," The cook said frantically.

"Calm down. I'm sure there is a good explanation for the guard stepping away from his post temporarily. I sent Ken and Mike out very early this morning to pick up a rather large shipment and the tower guard may be giving them a hand. As for the people gathering in the rec. hall, we'll just go and see what they're up to. You know we're short handed while three of our staff is off helping our benefactor. Don't be overly concerned. I'm sure there's an explanation for everything."

In the back of his mind Toby wondered if he shouldn't call for reinforcements. Why hadn't Ken or Mike come by to let him know they were back? Why hadn't they dropped off the invoices?

"You go ahead and I'll be right out. I just need to finish getting ready and I'll join you so we can check this out. Thank you for your concerns, and keeping me informed. As I said I'm sure it's nothing." Toby walked him to the door and closed it right behind him.

The young worker felt a little better but still had an uneasy feeling in his gut. As soon as the door closed two of Halloway's men jumped the young man before he made it two feet out the door. He managed to get out a muffled "Toby, look out," and kick the wall making a loud thud before he was subdued.

As he closed the door Toby was thinking of calling the "Man" and letting him decide how he needed to proceed. He heard the word "Toby" before he heard a loud bang outside the door. Toby ran over to a secret entrance in the office wall, which led to an escape tunnel. He reached to close the door behind him just as the office door flew open.

The secret door shut just as Halloway's men reached the paneling covering the emergency exit. The men began pushing on the wall all around the area until it popped open again.

Once they entered it was pitch black and it took a minute for their eyes to adjust. The escape hatch lowered to a crawl space almost four feet in. After Jason got on his hands and knees. He saw feet disappearing in the tunnel ahead of him.

"Go tell the others to surround this building in case this exits on the outside. I'll keep pushing forward from here." He began crawling into the tunnel.

As Jason made the first turn he heard the all too familiar click of a gun being cocked. "Phew" Was the sound the bullet made as it just missed his head.

Jason paused and got on the walkie-talkie to the others, "He's armed and I'm taking fire down here. Sir, do you want me to return fire or give him leeway?"

"Protect yourself if you need to. If he fires again, you are to return fire. Men, ready your weapons." The Colonel had hoped it wouldn't be necessary for them to use their weapons but he wasn't going to let his men be sitting ducks either.

"Phew, went another bullet down the tunnel. This time Jason returned fire. He heard a muffled "aah." He knew he had wounded Toby. He just didn't know how badly.

Toby had been hit in the right calf. He managed to make it to an exit door in one of the other rooms in his barracks. He pulled himself up, through the opening, in great pain. Toby made it to the desk in the center of the room and had just picked up the phone trying to warn his partners and mentor.

One of Halloway's men was pointing a pistol directly at his head. He ordered him, "Put the phone down and move back two steps, Sir I will not repeat it again!" The Sargent cocked his weapon and stared into Toby's eyes.

Toby slowly sat the phone back into the cradle. "I don't know what this is about. Who are you people? What's going on here?" The blood was running down his pant leg and forming a pool on the floor.

"Put your hands on top of your head and turn around slowly." The Sargent's stare did not waver as he spoke.

As Toby did what he was told, a second soldier entered the room and came up behind him. He reached up one at a time and brought Toby's hands down behind his back and slapped on a pair of handcuffs. "There is no need for any of this." Toby was saying as the handcuffs went on. "We are all civilized adults here. Whatever you're after can be discussed without all this."

"You need to take a seat, and remain quiet until we have secured the building. Sargent wrap this around the prisoners leg to stop the bleeding." He threw him a piece of rope still in his pocket from the store earlier.

The two remaining soldiers went down the hall, opening every door and clearing each room, until they were satisfied the quarters were empty except for Toby and the cook.

Toby had just sat down when the office door swung open and Colonel Halloway entered. He walked directly over to where Toby was seated. Turning, addressing his soldiers, "Good work men."

He pulled up a chair and sat across from his prisoner. "You must be Toby. Let me begin by saying I don't take kindly to people shooting at my men. I have heard a lot about you and your camp. You and I are going to have a little chat and I recommend you hold nothing back. I really don't take kindly to liars!"

Halloway paused for effect and pointed to Toby's bleeding calf. "I'll get someone to take care of your leg wound after we talk."

Staring into Toby's face he continued, "According to any records we are not even here, so we can't be held accountable for anything that happens. Do you get my drift?"

Toby looked into the black colonel's eyes and lowered his head, then nodded yes. His leg was throbbing now and he wasn't in much of a fighting mood.

"Let's begin with who you work for. I need to know how you get in touch with each other and when you're expecting your next contact?" Halloway didn't have time to beat around the bush. He would be contacting his friend, Willy Dee, with the F.B I. soon. Once they were involved it would be impossible for him to get any more answers the rough way.

As the questioning continued in the office, Whitey had joined Mary Jo in the recreation hall. He filled her in on what was happening.

Ron joined Mary Jo and Whitey up front, once he got his family situated in the front row. From his brief interaction with Trish, he knew something big was up.

Beside them sat a bewildered CC looking at her friend, Mary Jo.

There were fourteen of the camp's prisoners in the room. With Bud, Roy and Trish off helping Donald this was a good turnout. Only a few prisoners stayed away probably fearful of getting involved.

Whitey asked Mary Jo and Ron to look around the room and see if anyone there would pose a problem to this rescue operation. Both she and Ron gave the room a quick glance.

One of the kitchen workers had taken a seat at the rear, next to the door. He had his head down a little trying to blend into the crowd.

Whitey motioned to his buddies standing at the entrance and the person was isolated and removed to Toby's quarters and now posed no problem.

"Ladies and gentlemen, please remain calm as we explain what is happening here." "We," he motioned to the other soldiers by the door and himself, "are not associated with this encampment. We are here as a rescue mission and need your cooperation to make sure everyone makes it out of here safely. Mary Jo will speak to all of you. Please listen and do as she says. We have a few areas to still mop up around this place and can perform this much safer if you are all protected in here."

Everyone started talking at once excitedly. They were asking who sent them? When will they be leaving? Some were wondering if this was a ploy by their captors.

Mary Jo and Ron were assuring everyone this was for real. "We were as surprised as you are, but Bud and I personally know one of our rescuers. We really are getting out of here! Please do as they say. These men are professionals and will do everything to keep us all safe." Again the chattering among them started up.

Whitey left to meet up with Donald and Bud.

Bud went back and let Josh out of the holding cell. He needed his help keeping everyone in the rec. hall out of harms way. Josh couldn't believe what he was hearing. He knew something was going on when they came and got Bud, but a rescue operation wasn't his first thought. Josh went to the rec. hall and covered the back half of the room.

Now Bud was busy knocking on all the bungalow doors telling people who had not gone to the rec. hall to stay inside. If he didn't get an answer he just went to the windows and in a slightly raised voice asked everyone to stay indoors. Bud figured about four or so people chose not to leave their quarters.

After Bud left, the tower guard who had been hiding in the end unit quickly made his way down to Roy and CC's bungalow. Once safely inside he exchanged his khaki uniform for some of Roy's clothing. Now he would blend in with the others and could find out what was happening here.

As he rounded the corner of the rec. hall he saw the soldiers outside of Toby's quarters. This could only mean the camp commander had been taken hostage. Now he would need to find a way to escape. He saw two of the men bring Tom into the rec. hall and leave without him.

The tower guard made his way in, head down, while Mary Jo was talking to the crowd. He passed the front speakers and saw Tom sitting off to the side, out of sight from most of them. He took the seat next to Tom, and when he was recognized held his finger up to his lips to quiet him. The guard put his head down and said, "I'll need your help to try and fix this." Tom nodded, and they began whispering to one another.

Tom had been holding ice on his face where he had been punched earlier. He asked Mary Jo if she would be kind enough to get him more, knowing she couldn't help but get him some.

She looked at Tom and actually felt sorry for the guy. "Sure Tom, I'll be right back with some more ice." She walked over to the small beverage area by the card table.

When Mary Jo returned and knelt down to hand the ice to Tom she felt a hard object poke in her ribs.

"You better not scream or let anyone know there's something wrong." The guard was telling her. His gun was under a jacket he had picked up. "You and I are going to take a little walk out to the vehicles parked beside here. If you so much as look funny at anyone I will kill you. Do you understand?" Trembling, she nodded yes.

Both knees felt like Jell-O and her palms were soaking wet. She managed to get off one evil look to Tom before she turned headed for the door. He just put his head down.

Ron looked over and asked if she was okay. She looked pale and he was worried.

She gathered all the strength she could and answered; "I'm fine Ron. I just need to go check on some things. Please keep everyone calm while I'm gone."

The two of the made it down the steps and over to the side of the van without incident.

One of Halloway's men came around the front of the van and startled the guard enough to pull back his arm a little and expose his gun.

"How you two doing? Need any help with anything?" The soldier was buying time.

As he shoved the gun barrel tighter against Mary Jo's ribs the camp guard answered, "We're just taking a little breather, you know with all that's going on around here."

The soldier continued past them pulling his weapon out of its holster as he did. He gave a friendly nod to the camp guard in passing. He turned around behind him grabbing the arm that held the gun while putting his own weapon against the guard's temple. "Drop your weapon! Ma'am, step away now."

Mary Jo jumped so hard she almost lost her footing. The guard dropped his gun onto the ground. "Now kick it over toward the lady." The soldier was commanding him.

As the gun slid near her Mary Jo reached down and picked it up. Another soldier positioned outside of Toby's barracks realized what was going on and ran over to assist. Mary Jo handed him the gun and ran back inside the rec. hall hoping to find Bud inside. She was shaking uncontrollably.

Donald, Whitey, and Bud were headed to the mess hall. They knew they would encounter working staff in there. Bud was going to walk in ahead of the other two. His plan was to act surprised that he was the first to arrive this morning.

It was nearing time for the breakfast bell so they needed to hurry. Whitey and Donald still had on the camp guard's jackets. They would enter a minute or two after him with their heads down slightly. Their hands were in their pockets holding the guns they might need.

They needed to give him time to see where the guards and cooks were positioned in the room. As Bud entered he noticed only one cook and one guard. This was the cook he didn't like at all. The one who always told him, "I'm watching you, don't think you're fooling anyone here."

"Well, well, did your cooking already scare everyone away this morning or am I just that early?" Bud was exceptionally cocky this morning. Probably because he knew today he would get away with it. He felt so good right now. Donald and his army buddies had brought the life back in him.

"You're sure full of yourself this morning aren't you?" The nasty cook replied. Bud smiled.

"Well now, let's see how full of yourself you'll be now that we're not alone? Welcome, gentlemen. This little smart aleck was just wondering where everyone was."

The two men nodded and looked at Bud to find out where all the staff was located. Bud just nodded his head to the right and they saw the one other guard standing at the end of the food line.

The guard was getting nervous watching the interaction between them and not hearing anything from his two co-workers. He put his hand onto the pistol in his pocket.

Donald started walking over to the guard and halfway there asked, "How's the coffee was this morning?" He got within five feet before pulling his gun and aiming it directly at the young man's head.

Without hesitation he steadied his right wrist in his left hand, "You need to put your hands on top of your head one at a time slowly. Bud will walk over to you, then and only then, you will bring them down behind you one at a time. Do you understand?"

The guard looked like a deer in headlights, afraid to move as he nodded, yes.

Whitey had pulled his gun at the same time and was aiming at the cook. She was so dumbfounded and couldn't even move if she wanted to.

Donald threw a pair of handcuffs to Bud. The guard started to bring his hand up out of his pocket holding the gun but looked into Donald's eyes and thought better of it. He let the weapon drop into his pocket.

Bud came up behind the young guard and put his left wrist into one cuff. He had a little trouble opening the other cuff but soon had it in place. The guard wasn't going anywhere.

Bud made his way over to his "favorite" cook and Whitey threw him another pair of cuffs. These he put on just a little tighter than the last pair. "You know you might be right about me feeling full of myself. How are you feeling right now?" Bud took her shoulder and was leading her to the door.

As he neared the exit Bud heard a muffled sound. When he turned he saw Alice, the only nice camp worker standing at the door to the kitchen. She had apparently been in back, getting more supplies when they had entered.

Whitey cocked his gun and aimed right at Alice. He stopped waiting to see her reaction. She stood there sobbing.

Bud yelled, "Stop! She won't be any problem I'm sure. Alice, come with us peacefully please."

Alice's voice was cracking, "Okay Bud, just tell him not to shoot me." Her legs were wobbling as she walked over to them.

"Whitey I'm sure we can trust her to not try anything stupid. She can walk with me." Bud motioned Alice in front of the rest of them.

Donald led the guard out first. The prisoners were all taken to Toby's building. They were brought in to the Colonel.

Halloway had his prisoners removed to the front of the building. He excused everyone but Donald and Bud. "I'm going to bring in the FBI now, and we all need to have the same story. I want you two in here so you hear exactly what I tell them." Halloway walked over to the line Toby always left free for calls from the "Man" it had some kind of scrambler attached to it.

"Federal Bureau of Investigation. How may I direct your call?" The switchboard operator asked.

Halloway cleared his throat and said, "May I speak with Director William Dee, head of Western regional, please."

"May I ask who's calling and what this pertains to?" She was already ringing Agent Dee.

This is Colonel Bill Halloway. Please tell him it is urgent that I speak with him." Halloway knew his old friend would except a call from him. He wanted to make sure he knew this call was business.

"One moment Sir. I'll connect you. Please stay on the line."

"Halloway old buddy! What's up? The operator made it sound important." Willy Dee, as Halloway called him, headed operations for the western states. He was based in the Los Angeles, California office.

Sometimes he would send a few of his men over for special training with the Colonel in Calico. They had worked together and been friends for about five or six years.

"Willy is it safe to talk? I have a situation I need to keep as few people as possible involved. I need the Army to think I've been working with you on something."

"Go ahead man you've got my full attention. We are on a secure line and I'm here alone. What's up?" Willy was curious to hear what he had to say.

As Halloway filled in the agent, he became more and more interested. "I can have a crew up there in a little over an hour. Is there a place where we can land safely?" Willy Dee was already paging his assistant to get hold of some of his best men.

"Colonel Halloway does this have anything to do with a missing young couple from Idaho? We just became involved in an interstate hunt for them. Their families and some local police suspect foul play in their disappearance."

Halloway let out a sigh of relief. This was the out he needed for his squad's involvement.

"Yes, Willy, it sure does involve them. As we speak they are both okay. I will fill you in when you get here. Please keep this under your hat. All those involved are not accounted for. This operation must include some pretty big players."

Halloway paused and turned to Donald. "Just a second I'll check for where the best place to land a plane is. I just happen to have someone with that information right here with me."

Covering the receiver with his hand Halloway asked Donald, "Can your friend who lent you his plane be trusted to keep quiet and show the FBI how to get to this place? Does he have a big enough runway for one of their planes to land?"

"Yes to both questions. He has kept our whole operation a secret. Mr. Hall would help in any way possible. I'll give your friend, Agent Dee, directions and call Mr. Hall right now."

Halloway introduced Donald and handed the phone to him. "Hi, this is Donald are you ready for those directions?"

Willy Dee answered, "I'm ready, fill me in on where we need to go and who I need to contact. Sounds like you boys have been busy up there. Can't wait to meet you in person. I'm going to give you a phone number I want you to give to your friend. Have him call me if it's a go and I'll get any other information I need directly from him. Great work, guys. See you soon." He gave Donald the number and hung up.

"Men, we are in luck. It seems the family has filed a missing person's report for Bud and Mary Jo. Since it involves kidnapping the FBI are already involved, and will gladly accept credit for their recovery." He pushed back his chair and continued, "We need to lock all of the staff from here in one location. Are we sure we have everyone out of commission?"

Bud answered first. "I know the two other guards are still down in Trish's bungalow. Someone moved Tom, the one idiot whom actually liked being here, over to the rec. hall with the others. If it's possible I'd like to stop him from an escape attempt, if you get my drift."

Bud was looking at Halloway hoping to get the go ahead for beating the crap out of Tom. When it didn't come he continued, "My good friend Roy is helping watch those three. As for the mess hall crew they are all taken care of and being held in this building."

Donald was still smiling from Bud's comment about Tom. "You would be proud of the way this guy handled himself today. I think we have everyone accounted for. We still need to move the original three out of the van and free up their guard."

"In case you haven't figured it out, Bud, Halloway and I are old Vietnam buddies. We've saved each others ass's more than once." Donald continued, "I'm not sure you two have even been formally introduced." The two men shook hands.

Trish had left her bungalow and headed for the rec. hall. She knew this would all be especially hard on CC. She arrived there right after the latest rescue update.

She made her way through the few people standing and put her arm around her friend. "Are you okay CC? Roy is busy helping out to make sure everyone will be all right. He asked me to be here with you in his place. Do you understand what's happening here?"

"Trish I'm really scared! Last time anyone talked about leaving this place we lost our son and Roy nearly died. I couldn't face losing Roy." CC was ready to break into tears.

"CC this is totally different. We are going to go free, back to our normal lives. I don't know how normal they'll be after going through this but we'll be rid of this place." Trish just held her and rocked her in her arms for a minute. She needed to have Mary Jo take over so she could find out more about what was happening in the rest of the camp.

When Trish reached Mary Jo she saw how upset she was. She calmed her friend down while one of the men tied up Tom again.

Trish headed over to the door of Toby's barracks and knocked.

Jason answered and remembered her from earlier. "Come on in. Thanks for your help earlier. Let me get your friend Bud and Donald out here to fill you in on things." Jason disappeared into Toby's office.

"Sorry to bother you, Sir." Jason turned and faced Bud. "Bud, that cute brunette friend of yours is down the hall. Do you want to fill her in on what's happening or should I?"

Donald spoke before Bud had a chance to answer, hoping he meant Trish, "I think we both better fill her in. You started to mention earlier that she spent some time in Nam. She doesn't look old enough to have been there." Donald paused and looked at his buddy. "Don't get any ideas, Halloway, I saw her first."

Trish walked into Toby's office. "Bud, you need to go see Mary Jo. She needs you now."

"What happened Trish, is she alright?" Bud was getting very nervous.

"She's fine now but she was involved in an attempted escape by one of the guards. She was taken at gunpoint. He scared her pretty bad." I think she'll feel better the minute she sees your face.

Bud ran for the rec. hall. Along the way he passed Halloway's men escorting the out of uniform guard. "This the son of a bitch that threatened my wife?"

"Yes Sir it is." Answered one of the men.

Bud dove at the handcuffed man beating him savagely. "No one hurts my wife! No one!"

DESERT DECEPTION

The guards pulled him off after a few seconds. Hell, he deserved everything he was getting.

Bud calmed himself down a little and ran to Mary Jo.

She was sitting up at the front row by CC and Ron. She told Bud what had happened including Tom's part in the attempted escape plan.

Tom was still sitting all smug off to the side.

Bud walked right up to him and hit him so hard in the jaw he flew off his seat to the ground. Tom was yelling for help but no one seemed to be able to hear him at first.

Bud picked him up and hit him again. "You little bastard I hated you before you put my wife in danger now I could kill you with my bare hands." Bud was in a rage.

Another man from the camp pulled Bud off telling him Tom wasn't worth going to prison for. He was right. Mary Jo pulled him away from the whimpering bleeding excuse for a man.

Back at Toby's office Trish was talking to Donald. "Well Bud, sure knows the right people. None of my friends could have pulled this off." Trish was smiling looking at Donald.

Trish offered him her hand, "Nice to formally meet you Donald, I'm Trish. I hear we both have time spent in Viet Nam in common. When were you there?"

Donald still had her hand in his, "I, or I should say we," He was pointing over to his friend Halloway, "were there on and off from 1964 to early 1969. When were you in country?"

Trish looked Halloway's way and gave a little nod. "I was there from mid 1970 to 1971. I was serving with the Red Cross. I was a Donut Dolly. I was mostly in the Lai Khe village area. A lot of good people were there with me. I even got to meet General Westmoreland. That was exciting!"

"I'll be damned." Donald said, "We were there briefly in December '67. Got to see the Bob Hope Christmas show. Now that was a trip. For awhile you forgot all about where you were and just enjoyed a great show."

Donald turned toward his old friend and smiled. "Remember that Halloway? We were acting like a bunch of idiots. Hell, Halloway, I remember you rushing up on stage and getting your butt thrown off of there. What a blast that was."

"I do remember that indeed. I even vaguely remember the recreation building there. If I remember right it was a pretty good size building. Trish, nice to be formally introduced. Thanks for your help in this operation. From what I've been told you kept a lot of people safe through your actions. Now I know where you got those skills."

Halloway got up and headed right for the door. "You two will have to excuse me. I have to meet with my men and come up with a new action plan now that the camp in secure. See you both in awhile."

All of the sudden Donald noticed the phone in Toby's office. He thought of Wanda back at the diner. She was probably going crazy wondering what was going on.

"Excuse me I have to make a quick call." Donald was lifting the receiver.

"Please go ahead I'll give you some privacy." Trish started for the door.

"You really don't have to leave this won't take long. I just need to fill Wanda in. She's the sweetest lady you'll ever meet and I know she must be worrying herself sick."

Chapter 16

Wanda had arrived at the diner about fifteen minutes after the men had left. She had not been able to sleep and finally gave up trying. She thought she'd make it in time to see the boys off but she was too late. They had even done a good job setting her up for the day.

Being a weekday, business had been pretty slow. Ben had come by in the morning for breakfast. She knew he really came to make sure she was all right and look around to see what she was hiding from him.

He noticed her car was missing. She told him Donald borrowed it so he could have air conditioning on his route today. Another little white lie, she hated lying to her friend.

About nine, right after Ben finished his breakfast and left, the phone rang. It was the sheriff's office looking for Donald. They told her the Miller's family had reported them missing. Now they needed to have Donald come back in for more questioning.

At the diner the lunch rush consisted of only seven people. Wanda had way too much time on her hands to worry about how things were going. She figured things must have started okay or she would have heard from the store owner by now.

A few minutes after the last two lunch customers walked out the door, the phone rang. It startled her so much that she practically jumped a foot in the air.

"Wanda's Diner, may I help you?" She answered.

"Wanda, we did it!" Donald was so happy to be able to give her the good news he was almost yelling. "We found Mary Jo and Bud. Everyone is okay and we'll be back there soon."

Wanda couldn't believe her ears. "Donald, I am so relieved. Are they there with you right now? Can I talk to them right now? Thank the Lord you're all okay."

Wanda was so excited she almost forgot the earlier call. "Oh the Sheriff's office called earlier and wondered what you were up to. They wanted to speak with you again because Bud's family filed a missing person's report. I told them you were busy making deliveries and I would have you call them. I don't know how that will effect you friends involvement."

"Don't worry Wanda we have that covered now. Don't you worry anymore about anything. Just relax now and I'll fill you in on everything later. Bud and Mary Jo aren't here right now, but I promise you'll get to see them soon. I hate to do this to you but there might be a lot of people there for dinner. Sorry! I've got to go help the guys. See you later, Wanda. Bye." Donald knew that would keep her busy until they returned.

Wanda hung up the phone and immediately started for the freezer to get something out for dinner. She was so happy. She thought only about those two kids walking back in here. She decided on a thick beef stew and some homemade cornbread. She could make a big batch and feed everyone.

Back at the camp Donald hung up the phone and turned facing Trish. She had a pleased look on her face and smiled.

"You really care for that woman don't you, Donald?" Trish asked.

"She's like my Mom. There's not a mean bone in her body and her heart is huge. You'll get to meet her and see for yourself later. Or at least I hope you'll come back to the diner with us."

Donald realized he was assuming she would want to. She might want to get as far away from this desert as she could and he wouldn't blame her if she did. "I'm sorry I wasn't thinking. You probably want to get back home as soon as possible. It would be great if you could meet Wanda before you do."

"I would love to meet her. In fact I can't wait to meet her. Thank you for the invitation. I need to get back over to the rec. hall and check on some friends. I'll see you later. I really enjoyed our conversation. Thanks." Trish was out the door before Donald could respond.

The men had moved all the camp workers into the two holding cells that Bud and Mary Jo had been held in their first night in Paradise.

Bud got a feeling of great satisfaction seeing Toby, Mike and Ken on the other side of the safety glass. He couldn't keep himself from saying, "You men settle in. We'll talk more later." All three just shot him a dirty look.

Bud headed for the rec. hall to meet up with his wife, Roy and CC. He needed to be with Mary Jo right now. He needed to hold his wife in his arms.

As Bud entered the room Mary Jo ran to him. They held each other tightly.

"Bud do you believe this? I'm happy and sad and everything at once."

"What do you mean you're sad? This is great! I'm so ready to get out of this hellhole I can hardly wait for the FBI. Once we're done talking with them I want to get the hell out of here." Bud was still holding her tightly.

"Bud don't get me wrong I can't wait to put this place behind us. I'm sad because in spite of everything else, we've made some good friends here and I'm going to miss them. She looked over at CC and Roy. They are so happy right now. I really want to stay in touch and help CC recover more. Helping her kept keep me from going crazy."

"Mary Jo, nobody is going to forget the friendships we've made here. We all have something very different from other people in common. How many people have you met that were kidnapped before? Just as I thought, none." Bud caught Roy looking his way and nodded. He would miss Roy a lot himself.

Trish came in the door and walked right up to Bud and Mary Jo.

"You guys got any room for me in that hug?" Trish wiggled her way in. "This is exactly what I needed."

Jason was up in front asking everyone to please take a seat and listen for a few minutes.

"We have a few minutes before the FBI will be arriving. They will want to talk with everyone so please be patient. We know you are all more than ready to get the heck out of here. Please take care when you do leave this place. You have all been through more than I think you realize. It's going to take some time to adjust back to your regular lives. Please give yourselves that time. Thank you."

Trish stopped Jason on his way out of the room. "Thanks for everything, including your understanding of what's happened here. Do you know if we will be leaving with the FBI, or with you guys? My vote, if it matters, is with you guys."

"I don't know just yet. I will find out, and let you know soon. You're welcome, Ma'am. Thanks for your help also." Jason headed back to Toby's barracks and the rest of his men.

"Excuse me, you two. I need to get a hug from Roy and CC also." Trish slid away from Mary Jo and Bud.

CC was so excited to see her good friend she ran straight for her as she approached.

"Can you believe it, Trish? It's over, we're getting out of here. We get to see our families again. We'll get to do whatever we want. Roy's going to take me shopping and out to dinner. Isn't that great?" CC was more excited than Trish had ever seen her. Maybe a part of her had to shut down in here to survive this place.

Trish gave CC a huge hug. " I can't wait to pick out my own clothes and decide what I want to eat again either CC. You and Roy will have to give me your address because I really want to visit after we're out of here."

CC's face changed a little. "Trish I hadn't thought about not being neighbors anymore. I really don't want to lose you as my friend." Some of her new found confidence was gone.

"You won't ever lose me. You're stuck with me for life now. We just won't see each other as often." Trish smiled as Roy walked over.

"Well girl we did it! We really will be leaving this place. I wondered if it would ever happen for sure. Damn I can't believe it. We're really leaving here." The smile on Roe's face was priceless.

Donald asked Bud and Mary Jo if they would get everyone together in the recreation building. They needed to make sure everyone was accounted for. Some of the people who had not wanted to leave their bungalows had already come over after Trish had gone down the isle asking everyone to join them.

They knock loudly on doors this time around. There was no way that anyone was not getting the message they were free.

Donald rejoined his buddy Halloway just as Agent Willie Dee was calling back. The agent asked to speak with Donald. "Well, I hear we have you to thank for all this coming to a happy end. Your friend Mr. Hall has been a great help and we are preparing to drive there within minutes. Great job on finding those kids. I look forward to meeting you soon."

Donald felt great but there was one thing he thought would make this all a little better. He asked the Agent for one favor. "Agent Dee, there is one favor I would love to be able to have done. I would never have known there was anything wrong if it hadn't been for an absolutely cherry '57 Chevy that Bud restored. It was taken by the local Sheriff's office and impounded. Is there any way we could have that delivered to Wanda's diner and parked in the rear? I haven't told Bud and Mary Jo that it was saved yet and I think they could use a good surprise right now."

"I don't see any reason that couldn't happen immediately. I'll call the local Sheriff and have it done right away. That's a great idea. Wish I could see their faces. See you shortly. Tell that friend of yours I look forward to seeing him as always. Thanks again." The phone went quiet.

He was grinning from ear to ear as Donald called Wanda. He let her know about the surprise he was setting up.

"I think that's perfect. I can't wait to see those kids for myself. I don't think they have any idea how much a part of our lives they've become." Wanda paused a minute. "Donald, do you think I can let my old friend Ben in on everything now? He has been such a help, and he knows I've been keeping something from him."

"I think that would be fine, I really would like to thank him personally for making our job here so much easier. Bud and Mary Jo would want to thank him for all his help too. Go ahead and ask him to be there when we all arrive. Got to go Wanda, see you soon."

He left the office and went looking for the Colonel. Donald wanted to spend a little more time with his good friend before everyone else was around. He found him down the hall asking one of his men to relieve a guard watching Toby.

"Hey, buddy, got a minute?" Donald called out.

"Always got a minute for you, Donneyboy." Halloway answered.

"I wanted to thank you and your unit again for everything. You guys really went out on a limb for me. I don't know anyone else that would have done that. I didn't realize until today how much I've missed having you around. I really don't know what I would have done without your help." That was a scary thought.

He continued, "You're the best friend anyone could ever have. I haven't felt this good for a long, long time. Damn I still can't believe we pulled this off."

Halloway gave Donald a friendly hug. "Donny, you're one of the best friends I've ever had. Don't ever think just because I haven't talked to you for awhile that would ever change. This was just as rewarding for my men and I as it was for you. I'm glad it's coming to a good end. As far as losing touch, that isn't going to happen. Especially since you turned me on to Wanda's cooking. We might have to train out this way every so often now." Halloway was rubbing his belly as he spoke.

The soldier stationed in the front tower was the first to see the approaching vans, carrying the FBI Director Willie Dee and his men. He hollered down to Whitey to open the front gate.

Halloway and Donald were informed of the men's arrival and went out to greet them as they drove in.

Agent Willie Dee jumped out, and walked over to Halloway extending his hand to the Colonel. "What the hell kind of place was this? I can't believe someplace this large went unnoticed this long."

The Director turned to the Colonel and continued, "I was thinking on the way here about some studies done on rats being in kept in places like this. They provided all the food and water they wanted. Eventually when the space got too tight the rats resorted to cannibalism. Just how long did they think this could go on before the space became too limiting here?"

He turned toward Donald and again reached out to shake hands. " Sorry didn't mean to be rude, I'm Agent Dee are you Donald?"

"Yes sir I am. I don't know what would make anyone think this is Paradise. You're right about this not remaining unnoticed for much longer. I don't think they figured the human spirit being so strong in their plans for a safe and isolated society. I'm glad to meet you and I'm ready to assist you if need me." Donald gave him a firm handshake.

"My men will take over the prisoners if you two will point us in the right direction." Agent Dee was motioning for his agents as he spoke. " I want to get you and your men, Colonel, together so I can get an idea of how this takeover of the camp went down. If I'm going to keep you out of this publicly I need to have my facts straight."

The other agents headed off to relieve Halloway's men after getting directions on where the camp personnel were being held.

Halloway sent Jason to gather the entire unit and meet up in Toby's office. This would be the first time since entering camp they would all be together.

After everyone was accounted for Halloway introduced Agent Dee. "Some of you have met Agent Dee before at base camp. He will keep our involvement here a secret. I'm not sure this would sit well with everyone back home even though it turned out all right. He wants to get a picture of what's gone down here today for his report. Please fill him in, starting with the take down at the market this morning. Make sure the wounded prisoners are attended to first."

By the time they finished Agent Dee had a stack of notes in front of him. He was impressed with the skill and professionalism the soldiers had shown. He had tried for years to talk Halloway into checking out a job at Quantico, but he always turned him down. It was time to meet the rest of the people now.

Agent Dee, Donald, and the Colonel headed for the rec. hall. The rest of the men waited in the office.

As the men entered, the room went quiet. Donald walked to the front and grabbed Bud and Mary Jo. "Agent Dee, I would like to introduce you to the couple missing from Idaho. This is Bud and his wife Mary Jo."

"Nice to meet you two. You certainly had a lot of people looking for you. You're family and friends really care about you. I am going to need to get a statement from you both and will need you to come to L.A. for a line up soon. That trip can wait a little so you can get together with you're friends and family first."

Bud shook his hand first. "It is nice to be meeting the FBI. We'll do what ever you need to help put these animals behind bars."

The Agent walked to the front of the room and addressed the people. "My name is Agent "Spencer," his alias, I am with the FBI and we will be getting you all out of here soon." With that the room got very noisy for a minute. "Please bare with us for a little longer. We need statements from all of you and need contact information. Agents will be interrogating you shortly and we should have you all on your way within a few hours." That line brought cheers.

Donald told Bud and Mary Jo they would be riding back with him and Halloway's men. Wanda would never forgive him if she didn't get to see with her own eyes that they were okay.

Trish was standing right next to Mary Jo so Donald invited her to come with them, also. He was pleased when she accepted his offer again.

Mary Jo shot them both a smile. She was picking up on a little chemistry here.

Agent Dee interviewed Bud and Mary Jo personally. They were the reason for the FBI's involvement and he wanted them to be able to get out of this place as soon as they could.

Their story was incredible, first the group of thieves, then this person, the MAN, buying them. It all sounded outrageous, but it was all true. This case was anything but over.

Willie Dee would have to keep this investigation top secret. Only his immediate team would be filled in. This had to involve some major players. With the three missing camp guards unaccounted for he knew it wouldn't be long before the head honcho knew his camp was through.

After they were interviewed Bud and Mary Jo went to find Roy and CC. They exchanged addresses and phone numbers. Mary Jo and CC were crying as they said their good-byes. Roy and Bud were close to shedding a tear themselves. They promised to get together in Idaho soon.

Trish made the rounds and said her good-byes also. She had been here longer and had become close to so many it was hard to leave some of the people.

CC really was going to miss her the most. She was like a real older sister to her. It was hard for Trish to leave with CC standing there, crying.

Halloway and his men got the vans and Jeep ready for departing while the agents finished interrogating Trish.

Donald, Trish, Bud and Mary Jo all got into Wanda's Jeep. As they turned and started out of the camp both girls had tears in their eyes.

CC and Roy stood waving until the Jeep was out of sight.

Trish spoke first, "I can't believe we're out of there." She turned and kept watching as the camp got farther and farther away.

Bud added "I knew we would get out; I just had no idea it would be with Donald.

As they drove back to the diner, Donald filled them in on all the help he had received from Mr. Hall and Ben.

Bud told him they had seen his plane but thought it was just a person learning to fly.

It was amazing to learn that buying supplies played such a big part in their being found. The camp was so close to not needing those big supply orders any more they may have never been noticed. That thought sent a chill up Trish's spine.

Donald looked in the rear view mirror and saw a sad look come over Bud's face as he gazed at the passing desert. He knew he was probably thinking about his Chevy. He felt bad not having told Bud his car was waiting for him, but he really wanted to surprise them. When Bud asked how Donald knew they were missing he told him it was a long story. He would tell them later.

Trish and Donald talked most of the way to Wanda's. They had so much in common. Both loved traveling, they had been kris crossing the states looking for something to catch their eyes or hearts.

With all the conversation it seemed to take half as much time to get back to the diner.

As they neared Wanda's everyone, even Trish grew more excited. Turning into the lot they saw the big sign She had hung across the front window. In bold letters it read WELCOME BACK!

The Jeep hadn't even come to a stop by the time Wanda was next to it.

As Mary Jo got out she was locked in one of the biggest hugs of her life. Both women were crying. Wanda looked over at Bud and said. "You come over here and get in on this. You're not getting off that easy." Bud joined the embrace and felt loved.

"Well who's this?" Wanda was asking as she gave Donald a welcome back kiss on the cheek of his own. She was looking directly at Trish as she spoke.

Mary Jo answered first. "This is Trish. She is a great friend and also is the reason we didn't go crazy in that God forsaken place."

Wanda walked over threw her arms around Trish too. "God bless you for keeping these two safe. I hope you'll be able to stay and celebrate with us tonight?" She motioned toward the diner, "Let's get inside I'm sure you want a cold drink or something to eat."

All of them realized they hadn't eaten all day. With all the excitement food wasn't a priority. Just inside the door the smell of the stew was more than anyone could resist.

Halloway and his men pulled in just as the four of them sat down. "I suggest you get a bowl fast. You haven't seen those guys around Wanda's cooking. Grab anything you'll want now because it will be gone soon." Donald was grabbing his bowl as he talked.

"Umm, Umm, Umm, What little slice of Heaven am I smelling?" Halloway had barely entered the room and he was hooked.

He walked over and put his arm around Wanda's shoulder. "This woman here is spoken for." His men were all coming in right behind him. "You hear me men. Don't even try to win her from me." Wanda turned six shades redder.

Trish was watching this entire interaction, and for the first time in a long while felt really happy. She wondered if Bud and Mary Jo really knew how fortunate they were, that they had these people come into their lives.

"Hey Bud and Mary Jo, could you two help me bring in some more supplies for Wanda?" Donald winked at Trish as he said this. "If you would help me carry them we could make one trip.

"Sure we'd love too. We owe you guys so much for saving us it's the least we could do." The two of them were on their feet following Donald to the back door of the diner.

As they passed through the door Bud thought he would pass out. His heart was pounding so hard from excitement. He ran to the Chevy the minute he caught sight of her. His wife was one step behind.

"How on earth were you able to save her?" Bud was crying now. "I thought for sure she was chopped up for parts or buried out there in the desert somewhere. This is too much!"

Trish caught her first glimpse of the car she had heard so much about at camp. It was as beautiful as they had said. She couldn't help but cry seeing the two of them so happy. She had cried more today than she had in years. These people truly touched her heart.

"I think you should know, buddy, that this car is how I knew you were in trouble. Because you made her so beautiful the original thieves couldn't trash it." Donald was standing next to the Chevy talking to Bud, who had slid behind the wheel. "I wanted to tell you at the camp, but the look just now on your face was worth the wait.

Mary Jo got into the back seat and pulled the seat up. "Look, Bud, they missed it!" She was retrieving a money purse from under the bench seat. In it was $500.00 they had set aside in case of an emergency.

"Served the bastards right they missed it!" Bud was saying.

Everyone but Bud and his wife went back inside. They needed a little more time with the car that saved them.

As they were walking back in the diner Trish said, "I can't believe we were saved by this car. That's just too much. We all hoped someone in our families would show up on a white horse to save us. Instead it's an acquaintance turned good friend, with this old classic Chevy. Like I said that's just too much."

After Bud and Mary Jo returned inside Donald filled them in on the whole story. Over his shoulder stood Ben Johnson listening to every word. He had arrived while they all were out back looking at the Chevy.

"I want you all to meet someone who is also responsible for your freedom." Wanda introduced Ben to the four of them.

Bud got up and shook his hand. He thanked him so much for scouting out the area for strange things going on. "I don't have any idea how we'll ever repay all of you here," he was saying loudly. "I guess free auto repair if you're ever broken down in Indian Wells or any part of Idaho is a start." Everyone got a laugh out of the offer.

The phone was ringing and Wanda ran to answer it. It was Agent Dee asking for Halloway. "Just want to let you know everyone is safely out of there. I left a few of my men behind in case the three missing guards or the ringleader show up. What a can of worms this is. I just hope we catch the big fish. I'll be in touch soon to get any additional information I need. See ya buddy, goodbye."

"Everyone listen up." Halloway waited until the room was quiet. "That was the FBI letting us know everyone is out and on their way home." The men let out a cheer. "Let's not celebrate too much. There are still some missing bad guys out there. Including the Man behind the camp's existence. A few agents have stayed behind hoping someone will show up or lead them to him. Anyway this nightmare is over for everyone held there. Wanda you got any beer hidden here?"

"I didn't even think to get something like that, sorry. There is the store down the road. Beer sounds like a great idea."

Donald jumped up; "I'll get the beers and be right back. Want to come Trish?"

"Yeah I'd love to. I kinda like being able to decide where I want to go and when. I could get real used to this." On the way to the door she shot Mary Jo a thumbs up. Seems she and Donald were hitting it off after all.

Wanda pulled Bud aside and told him he could use the phone in the hall. He and his wife needed to let their folks know they were okay.

He couldn't believe how good it felt the minute he heard his mom's voice. "Son, I'm so glad you two are okay. That woman, Wanda, called us earlier to let us know you were alive. I guess she made the police there give her the home phone number. We can't wait until you are home again safely." Bud let his mom know it would be a day or two but they were definitely ready to come home.

"I love you son, please be careful on your way back. I don't think any of us could take anymore bad news. MJ's mom is right here and wants to talk with her."

Bud handed the phone to Mary Jo. "Hello, MJ, are you there?" her mother was saying loud into the phone.

"Yes, momma, I'm here. You have no idea how good it is to hear your voice." Mary Jo was sobbing now. "Momma you are not going to believe us when we tell you everything that's happened. Thank the Lord above we met some good people on this trip too; or we wouldn't be having this conversation. I can't wait to see all of you again. We have to go, Momma, but we'll see you in a couple days. Give our love to everyone and tell them all not to worry. Bud and I are fine. Bye bye Momma."

Just as she hung up Donald and Trish returned with the beers. Even though she hardly ever drank Mary Jo couldn't wait to join the rest of them and drink one. The pop of the ice cold can and the thick foaming liquid going down her throat was wonderful. This was the best beer she ever tasted. She clicked her can with Trish's and took another long gulp.

Halloway's men had one can each for their victory celebration. The sound of pull tops popping and ahs filled the diner.

It made Wanda a little melancholy as she looked around the room. She was going to miss all these people being around.

Her old friend picked right up on her mood. "Hey, you'll still have me around. I promise I'm not going anywhere." Ben was saying as he put his arm around her shoulder and gave her a squeeze.

Wanda gave Ben a squeeze back. "I guess we're stuck with each other, Ben. Two old desert rats here for the long haul. I better get some more food out for everyone."

She went and got another huge pot of stew and more cornbread from the oven.

Ben wasn't the only one to notice her slight mood change. Donald crossed the room and put his arm around her. "I promise I'll keep in better touch with you. I never realized until this trip just how much you mean to me. Somebody's got to protect you from Halloway. I think he's half serious about marrying you." That brought a smile back to her face.

Everyone shared stories concerning this whole fiasco. It was funny how both sides were aware of the other without knowing who it was. Donald told Bud how he had noticed the men with the wheelbarrow. They laughed when Bud told them all, it was he and Roy.

The Colonel and his men needed to get going. They were already a day later than anticipated and needed to be back on base tonight. Saying goodbye was hard on the old friends. Each had awakened a part of them thought to be long gone.

Halloway walked over and put his arm on Donnyboy's shoulder, "I'll see you next week sometime in LA I'm sure. We have some unfinished business with Willie. I can't tell you how good it was to be on a mission together again. Hell at times I felt like I was in my twenties again. Trish, I hope to see you again also. See you all later." Halloway was out the door with his men.

With all the gear and men gone, the diner felt strange. One night together celebrating their freedom and soon everyone would be returning to his, or her, normal lives. Donald dreaded the thought.

Chapter 17

Willie Dee called Wanda's early the next morning. It seems they would need Bud and Mary Jo in for a lineup sooner than they thought. One of the brothers was going to court on a different charge in three days. He would be transferred out of the area. They needed to do this before that trial started.

After getting back in L.A. Agent Dee had done some checking up on Rick and Lou's backgrounds, only to find out they often stayed with a younger brother, and his wife and baby. The three of them sounded very much like the three people the Millers had first stopped to help.

The agent sent some men over with a bench warrant to have them brought in for lineups of their own. they needed to get everyone together at once for lineups.

Mr. Hall offered one of his Cessnas for them to use for the trip. The four of them had gone to thank him personally for his help in their rescue.

Donald, Trish, Bud and Mary Jo would be in LA tomorrow. A van would meet them at Burbank airport and bring them directly to FBI headquarters.

They all needed to turn in early and try to get a good night's sleep. Wanda had given the four of them the use of her home and she had been staying at the diner. She was happy to see how well Donald and Trish seemed to be getting along. They had become pretty much inseparable.

Trish really had nowhere to get back to. She did want to see her family again and tell them all about her experience. She was avoiding the lecture on keeping in touch so people would know when you were in trouble. Right now she didn't care. It turned out that she and Donald had so much more in common than just Viet Nam. She really was starting to like this guy.

The four of them got up at 6:00 a.m. to head for Mr.Hall's.

Everyone loved the ride because Bud insisted on driving the Chevy. This was the first time Mr. Hall had seen this famous car, and he was pretty impressed.

They didn't have much time to spend visiting. Donald did his plane check and gassed the Cessna up. Mr. Hall promised he'd take good care of the Chevy. They boarded the plane and off they went climbing high over the desert. Donald circled and dipped to say so long.

Ed moved the car immediately into the barn. He wasn't taking any chances.

It was really different, flying over the desert. You noticed the changes more in the landscape than when you just drove the highways. The shadows from the hills painted pictures in grays and blacks. The new adobe style homes mixed in with the tin shacks. It seemed like no time had passed before they were over more populated areas.

As they neared Los Angeles the skies became much more crowded. Passing by Ontario Airport they saw three planes staggered waiting to get permission to land.

They were hustled right into a landing pattern at Burbank airport. Donald assumed Agent Dee had something to do with this. One pass and they were cleared to land.

All the air traffic up there was scaring Mary Jo a little. She was new to this flying thing and would be happy when her feet felt solid ground again.

Just as promised there was a FBI van to pick them up almost the minute they stopped taxiing. It was nice to just get ushered past all the regular stops most people had to make. This must be how the rich and famous feel when they travel.

Whipping in and out of L.A. freeway traffic was a new experience also. All of them wondered how anyone could do this on a daily basis.

When they exited the freeway they saw a set of buildings that must be the headquarters. Good thing they sent a van because a person could get lost here. The driver stopped in front of the second building and the agent riding in the right front seat got out and led them inside.

Once inside they walked past cubicle after cubicle. At the end of the hall they were led into Director Dee's office. His secretary just nodded as they walked by with the other agent.

Agent Dee stood as they entered and motioned for them to have a seat. "I'm so sorry to have to delay your homecomings. As I said on the phone we are under the gun on this one. Rick will be going to Atlanta tomorrow on other charges and I didn't know when I would be able to get him back here. Thanks for coming on such short notice."

The four of them sat down facing his desk. I'll be taking Bud and Mary Jo downstairs after all the suspects are in their prospective line-ups. I have some people I want you to look at. They might be the young couple that first tricked you into stopping.

He told Donald and Trish they could wait in the lobby, or be in the room with them. "Would you like to watch the t.v. in the break room down the hall? It's up to you. You're welcome to join us if you like." The secretary buzzed and let him know they were ready downstairs.

Donald and Trish wanted to stay with their friends. Both for support and because this was interesting.

As they entered the dimly lit room Mary Jo could feel the sweat pooling in her palms. She had no idea this would make her so nervous. She took one of the water glasses off a tray and took a sip.

A lawyer representing one of the suspects was also in the small room. After everyone was situated the room went dark. On the other side of the glass the lights came on. A line of people came and stood under numbers painted on the back wall.

After the suspects walked in they had them all turn at once and face the darkened room. Almost immediately Bud and Mary Jo picked out Rick and Lou. Yes they were sure about the two men being involved. they were the men in the diner that day. The agents had all the men say a few words. Number five and number one were definitely involved. They would never forget those voices.

As Rick and Lou stared in at the darkened room Mary Jo felt a shiver run down her spine. She swore Lou was looking directly into her eyes.

After saying they would swear in a court of law that these were two of the men involved, the people in the line up were asked to leave the room. After they were gone the lights came on briefly.

"Are you ready for a few more line-ups or do you need a break?" Agent Dee was asking them.

Mary Jo grabbed a drink of water and held onto Bud's hand.

They were ready to see more suspects. The same lawyer remained in the room.

Once again the lights went out and this time young women walked in and turned to face them. As Cindy turned Mary Jo felt so much anger toward her. The fear she felt when Lou looked their way wasn't present now only hatred filled her. The nerve of Cindy, using an innocent baby like she did. If the wall weren't between them Mary Jo would take care of this one herself.

Once again they both swore they would testify in a court of law that Cindy was involved. As Cindy was asked to step forward a second time she tried to play the tough, street smart broad. She looked straight into the dark glass facing her as if challenging anyone on the other side.

Again the room was emptied.

Trish saw the change in Mary Jo. "Are you okay? That girl really got to you didn't she?"

"Yes she did, Trish. She actually enjoyed using her baby to lure us. That's so pathetic and cruel. I look forward to facing her in court." She took another drink and faced the window again.

"One more batch of people and I can get you out of here. Are you ready?" The agent paused for a minute to answer a question the lawyer had asked him privately.

The room went dark again and the door to the other room opened once more. This time around a line of younger men entered. Number two was John, Cindy's husband. As he turned and faced the glass he knew it was all over. When asked to step forward his head dropped down.

"That's him, number two, the one who took us to the house." Bud and Mary Jo both said at the same time.

This family business was now officially closed. Mary Jo couldn't help thinking about the baby. What a mess to be born into.

"Agent Dee what's going to happen to the baby?" She asked.

"We'll try to find a decent family member to take him in. If one can't be found he'll be placed in the foster child program. From there he'll become available for adoption if his mom and dad can't get their act together. These people never think about the lives they're ruining when they have young children "

"That is so sad," was all Mary Jo could say. This had drained them more than they thought it would. Especially worrying about the baby. After signing some paperwork they were free to go. The same agents would return them to the airport. And now they should be left alone until this case went to court.

Leaving the FBI building Bud thought he caught a glimpse of Toby being led down a hallway. He was slowly favoring his wounded leg.

On the way to the van Trish told Bud she had seen him too."I thought I saw Toby in the hallway. I hope they lock him up forever. That guy is not all there. Let's get the hell out of this place."

They enjoyed lunch at the airport. It was kind of fun seeing all the different people in the terminals. They all couldn't wait to leave all the congestion of LA. streets.

Back in the cessna they were ready for take off and to leave this case and L.A behind them. Donald started the engines and headed for the taxi lane.They were cleared for take off as soon as they hit the runway.

The sky got clearer and clearer the farther they flew out of the Los Angeles airspace. There were actually some beautiful spots in the mountains behind the freeways. You could see areas with water in them and some beautiful homes tucked in the mountains. Much of the return trip was quiet. Everyone seemed to be reliving their ordeal in their own way, silently. Seeing most of those responsible already in custody helped ease some of their anger and frustration.

Bud was worried when they finally landed back at Mr. Hall's. He didn't see the Chevy where he left it. He freaked out a little, until he caught sight of her paint in the barn. That car was more loved and protected than most people's children were.

This would be the last night they spent here in the desert with their new friends. Tomorrow the newlyweds would sleep in their own bed back in Indian Wells Idaho.

Trish was going to hang out with Donald on his route until they both decided what they were going to do next. Whatever it was they both wanted it to be together for now. First a little detour to Las Vegas sounded good to both of them. It was nice to have another wanderlust to be with. Anything was possible.

DESERT DECEPTION

While they were busy planning their futures, Agent Dee was still trying to wrap up this case. No one had offered any information about the MAN.

He couldn't get a lead on who Joe was either. Mary Jo and Bud never saw his face. They didn't know if they would recognize his voice from the van if they heard it. They thought they would but couldn't be sure.

Back at FBI headquarters they had indeed seen Toby. He was being brought up to the Director's office.

Toby had not given the FBI any information. All he kept saying was they were providing a safe and caring society for a select few. They had not done anything wrong. When asked who this MAN was he denied knowing anyone by that name.

This would be round four in the questioning of Toby. He was taken to the lounge area in the center of the cubicles. Behind Toby, on the wall was a large television. As the Director was questioning him, once again, his men came running into the room.

"Sir, You have to see this. It's Senator Hudson. The crazy bastard's going to introduce his new crime task force plan to the public. The thing hasn't even passed yet and he's proceeding like it has." All the agents gathered under the T.V.

Toby just kept facing the agents, his back to the television. His expression was only a blank stare. He kept his eyes on the glass reflection of the televison behind him..

As they turned up the volume the Senator with his three bodyguards walked up to the microphones. "Ladies and Gentlemen we have become a society run by gangs, thugs, and drug pushers. We are no longer living in the paradise America once was." the familiar rough husky voice began.

Toby's ears perked up. He looked at the images reflecting on the glass walls of the room. A large confident smile filled his face. If he needed to be sacrificed for the cause, so be it. He had nothing to say to these men.

The End

Or is it?

Printed in the United States
48626LVS00005B/18